GOOD MORNING, LOVE

Ashley M. Coleman

SIMON & SCHUSTER PAPERBACKS

New York London Toronto Sydney New Delhi

Simon & Schuster Paperbacks
An Imprint of Simon & Schuster, Inc.
1230 Avenue of the Americas
New York, NY 10020

First Simon & Schuster trade paperback edition June 2022

SIMON & SCHUSTER PAPERBACKS and colophon are
registered trademarks of Simon & Schuster, Inc.

For information about special discounts for bulk purchases,
please contact Simon & Schuster Special Sales at 1-866-506-1949
or business@simonandschuster.com.

The Simon & Schuster Speakers Bureau can bring authors to your live event.
For more information or to book an event,
contact the Simon & Schuster Speakers Bureau at 1-866-248-3049
or visit our website at www.simonspeakers.com.

Interior design by Ruth Lee-Mui

Manufactured in the United States of America

1   3   5   7   9   10   8   6   4   2

Library of Congress Cataloging-in-Publication Data has been applied for.

ISBN 978-1-9821-6862-9
ISBN 978-1-9821-6864-3 (ebook)

GOOD MORNING, LOVE

TRACK |

There's nothing like a high-energy concert to get the blood flowing. The bass is vibrating through my chest. The lights move back and forth from the stage to the crowd, blinding me on the two and the four. When the beat drops, my body instinctively finds the rhythm, my head nodding to the sound of the heavy 808 drum machine. Tau Anderson runs to the front of the stage yelling "Hands up" and the crowd obeys, under his spell.

The piercing screams of thousands of devoted female fans bounce off the arena walls and into my overly stimulated ears. There's a good chance I might be flashed as women clad in fashionably risqué outfits jump around. It's not like I don't get it. I get it. Tau has it all, he's talented, rich, and undeniably attractive. It's hard to pinpoint his best feature. His smile is nice, he has the impeccable magazine-cover body and smoldering eyes that can turn any no into a yes, but the whole far outweighs the parts in his case. From what I'd heard, he was a hot mess, like any other young guy coming up on fame and fortune.

I follow closely behind my boss, Dawn, as the usher lights our path to our seats at the Barclays Center. Looking up toward the cheap seats the people all look like colorful dots. The rows of black chairs infinite. Flanked by the largest screens I'd ever seen, the stage commands the massive space. I shouldn't be surprised when we make our way down the stairs to the floor; being with Dawn always meant access. There's a small area for VIPs right before the pit, the liveliest area in any venue, where fans crowd close together at center stage. Standing room only. It seems all of Brooklyn is in attendance. We make it as the show is in full swing. Tau starts his new single "Pop That."

We're so close, I scan the stage and recognize Malik. We played some sets together a few years ago before I was confident enough to get onstage by myself and try out some of the songs I'd written. I attempt a slight wave though I'm certain his vision is impaired by the stage lights. I'm happy for him. He has it made as a guitar player in Tau's band. At the same time, I can't help but wonder if, and when, I'll ever get my own moment in the sun.

The drummer hits a tight fill and Tau runs back out from the side of the stage with explosive energy in his fitted destroyed denim and high-top Balenciagas. His hair is a sea of generous dark waves against his tawny brown complexion and the diamonds in his chains lay and sparkle against his shirt like the signs along the Las Vegas Strip. Being front and center at a concert has its perks. He's a vision of young money, a mix of Black excellence and street prowess. Tau wipes his face with a gray face cloth. I can't help but roll my eyes as he makes a big dramatic show of throwing his sweat rag into the crowd. Predictably, the women bump and pull and grab, wrestling around until one triumphant warrior emerges from the melee. He winks and pulls up his shirt revealing abs that aren't made but crafted. The winner jumps up and down waving the cloth fanatically in surrender of all her common sense.

After the high energy of "Pop That," he looks over the crowd and announces he's slowing it down. As he looks out into the audience, he's the picture of sex appeal. I twirl my nameplate chain as he stands at the center of the stage placing the mic on the stand to sing. The lights come down all around the arena and a sea of cell phone flashlights illuminate the space.

His soft falsetto is angelic as he goes into "Think About Me," his breakout single from the *Black Light* album. Hearing it again now takes me back, six years ago, when I was still interning at a small studio called Matrax during college. The first time I heard the single I made everyone shut up, grabbed my guitar, and charted it out so I could sing it myself. The writing, his voice, the arrangement, it had to have been one of those moments in the studio when everyone knew they had something, something special.

The stage goes dark as the crowd erupts. Just as the applause settles down a low rumble of chants begins. Like an avalanche picking up more snow as it tumbles down a mountain, more and more people join in demanding an encore. Dawn and I make our way out of our row and walk toward the left side of the elevated stage to meet a production assistant who'll take us to meet him. A blonde with a tight ponytail dressed all in black with an earpiece and a walkie attached to her hip waves us over. We follow her through the doorway where players would normally come out for a game. The hallway is lined with people, including press and an array of photographers. I recognize a few celebs, Swizz Beatz, Busta Rhymes, Bryson Tiller, and the actor Rome Flynn. I give them the slight nod to let them know *I see you, but I'm not pressed,* as we continue past other doors with names posted on them. When we finally arrive at Tau's, we run into Frankie K sitting outside atop one of the equipment cases. He's the nephew of Zippy Bell, a huge R&B artist from back in the day. He recognizes my boss, and she remembers no one. I whisper "That's Frankie K" as we approach him.

"Frankie!" She smiles with her arms open wide, pulling him into an embrace by the shoulders before she offers air kisses on both sides of his face. "Great to see you!"

"You too, Ms. Garter!"

"Oh, please don't make me feel old. I'm already competing with all these beautiful young women dressed to the nines to see Tau. It's Dawn," she laughs, placing her hand on her chest. Whenever she did that, I was reminded of Regine from *Living Single* when she would make the same gesture while reciting her famous line "I'm amused and I have these!"

She introduces me to Frankie, who looks me up and down as if I'm the next object he intends to conquer. He has a reputation for pushing his limits with women eager to get into the business. It takes everything in me not to roll my eyes.

"Hel-low," he slithers. I shake his hand and quickly move to Dawn's side.

"Well, I have some business to get to. Good to see you, Frankie. Tell your uncle I said hello, will you?"

"Fa sho."

Right before we head inside, Dawn launches into her routine speech about not staying backstage for too long.

"It's nice that they invite you backstage and all, but we don't want to somehow be confused with the members of their orgy. We get in, seal the deal, and make a swift exit."

"I'm pretty sure they go to hotels for that type of thing, Dawn."

"If you say so," she says with a shrug. "I'm sure you've heard about this one's reputation."

"We'll be fine."

The blonde pulls open the door to Tau's dressing room; inside there's at least fifteen people standing around in the large common area. A few of them are members of the band. I spot another charting R&B artist, Chad White, and of course, the girls. I call them "MAC Makeup Girls." The ones who wear impossible high heels, never with a hair out of place, and have minimum income requirements for dates. I imagine there is a member of the crew who rounds up a few of them from the crowd after each show. A tall man with dark skin and the shoulders of a linebacker gives one of the cronies in the room the "business first" eye. He ushers the girls out a side door along with Chad White.

Blondie informs us Tau will be out in a second then disappears back out the door, talking into her earpiece. I look around, eventually spotting Malik in the sea of faces. He walks up to me as soon as he catches my eye.

"Carli, it's been a minute." A warm smile creeps onto his lips.

I can't help but smile back at him. "I know, Malik. You sounded amazing up there!"

"Aw man, listen. I'm just out here tryna get it. You still writin'?"

There it was, the question that never failed to stab me in the chest. As if I'd give up. I wasn't charting on *Billboard* yet, but I hadn't hung it up and decided to be, well, a quitter. Juggling my dream of writing music and paying my New York City rent was indeed a balancing act.

"Of course!" I muster with enthusiasm to hide my annoyance.

"Dope. You know what, Drew did tell me that! I subbed on a gig for Chad White the other day and he asked about you."

Drew was a name I hadn't heard in some time. But then again the small circle of musicians I came up with are all connected in some way. Well, the good ones. Smiling, and half listening to Malik, it's not lost on me that Drew seemed to still know what I was up to.

The energy shifts suddenly. It takes a few seconds for me to realize Tau has walked in from whatever bat cave is behind the double doors. Everyone stands up straighter, the volume of the scattered conversations dips, eyes shift in his direction. He's changed quickly into joggers, a pair of Penny Hardaway sneakers, and a fresh V-neck. Floating through the space, he exchanges handshakes and hugs with his crew as if to say *Job well done*. Frankie, who slithered his way in, takes it upon himself to let Tau know we're in the room. As if being a creep wasn't enough, Frankie also has the annoying habit of rubbing his hands together Birdman-style as he speaks. And then it clicks—Frankie must be on Tau's team.

"Hi, Tau, I'm—"

"Dawn Garter," he finishes for her, elongating the *a* in his slight southern drawl. "I know who you are. One of the most powerful women who can help lil' ole artists like me get these partnerships that pay us for a lifetime. Gotta know the moneymen. I mean, women. Respectfully." The small lines near his eyes deepen as he smiles.

"Well, hey, I am not mad at that. And I wouldn't say 'little old artist' at all. That crowd was pretty impressive." She nods and touches his shoulder gently with a freshly manicured hand.

Tau is one of Dawn's newest clients at her creative agency Garter Media and one of the biggest R&B stars out right now. And Dawn is, well, perfect. She always knows the right things to say, a trait that makes people fall in love with her. Not only was she incredibly intelligent, not to mention quick, she dressed better than the stars she represented. Everyone at Garter worked hard for her approval. There was nothing more terrifying than failing to meet Dawn's expectations. Sometimes I thought working for her might be easier if I actually disliked her, but it was impossible not to admire Dawn after rubbing shoulders with her daily.

"And this is Carlisa Henton! She is my right hand and will be working alongside us for these next few months. I wanted you two to meet. She'll be corresponding with you as well."

"Carli." I reach for a handshake but he pulls me in for a hug. He smells surprisingly fresh for a man that danced around a stage for forty-five minutes. I think of my best friend, Talia, who would say "Some men look like their balls don't stink," and I can't help but smirk. In his embrace, he gives me the quickest forehead kiss. I recoil, inwardly appalled by his overfamiliarity. Tau Anderson is clearly beyond the stratosphere of normalcy and suspended in the alternate universe that is fame.

He's also a lot taller than I'd imagined. If I had to guess, he was about five eleven or six foot. Which is nice because you could wear heels and still not be taller than him. I banish the intrusive thought from my mind, tuning out as he and Dawn do some more flirting and business talk. But I can't help but notice his eyes never seem to leave my direction for long. The thumping from Usher's set gives the floor a subtle vibration that reminds me I'm kind of sad to be missing him. This was his *GOAT* tour and he definitely checks that box in my book.

Dawn starts chatting with Frankie, who has expertly slipped next to her and Tau. I slide away to the other side of the room. He introduces Dawn to a few of the randoms who are maybe more important than they look. I can tell Tau's attention is waning. I'm not surprised when he gives Dawn a final hug and moves away from their circle. He turns and heads in my direction even though the exit is a straight shot from where he was standing. I look away, suddenly nervous as Tau moves closer to my corner. He seems to go out of his way to brush past me, and before he completely steps out of my path he whispers, "You're gorgeous," low enough for only me to hear.

Watching Tau slip out the door we came in through breaks my daze. It's clear no one saw what just happened. I spot Dawn moving around to work the room.

To kill some time, I scroll through my phone and check a few emails and texts.

Are you making the studio tonight? A text from Dylan.

Can't. Got pulled out to a work thing.

It doesn't take long before my phone buzzes again. **Damn, hit me when you get in.**

Which reminds me—Usher's show is still happening. I venture out, hoping to get a good view. Dawn wasn't going to wrap up anytime soon and I have been in love with Usher for at least half my life.

Making my way back down the nondescript corridor, I position myself in the darkness of the corner near the stage. The spotlight illuminates Usher's body as he embodies the greats like James Brown and Michael Jackson. Although now in his late thirties, he is considered an elder statesman of R&B. But he hasn't lost a step. He looks just as great as Tau out there, who is roughly ten years his junior. Twirling my curls and lost in "Confessions," I feel another hand in my hair.

"Carli, right?" The soft male voice is coming from behind me. I whip my head around. "I like your hair." It was Tau.

"Oh thanks," I stammer, completely taken aback. My hair is an untamed mane with thick, tight ringlets. It's taken some time, but I've grown to love my carefree fro. In normal circumstances I would flip shit about someone touching my hair uninvited but I'm technically at work, and he is Tau Anderson. However, this is the second boundary he crossed in less than thirty minutes of meeting him. It's dawning on me that Tau might just be an entitled jerk.

Before he can say anything else, a short guy with a face full of worry walks over and motions to him. A few seconds later Dawn appears from the shadows of backstage and I gather myself to head out. I guess the business meeting in the dressing room was adjourned. Before I move to follow her, I feel a hand on my arm.

"Hey," Tau says discreetly. "So what y'all bout to do after this?"

It takes me a second too long to find words. "Oh, uhm, heading home. The boss is heading out, so I'm heading out." I point awkwardly to the exit.

"That's unfortunate." He cocks his head to the side, showing off his gorgeous dimples.

I manage to utter a hurried "It was great meeting you," as I walk toward the backstage exit. The mid-August air was sticky outside those doors. Dawn is still in my view, but she's way ahead of me and I don't want to be too far behind her. It wasn't listed in my job description, but Dawn expected me to be as close as her shadow.

"How can I call you?" I hear Tau yell behind me.

"I'm sure we'll be in touch." Shaking my head, I start a little jog to catch up with Dawn. *Did he really ask about calling me?*

Dawn drives me to my apartment in her Mercedes E-Class. We

ride in silence. We've been together all day, which isn't far from the norm, and we're all talked out. Anita Baker's sultry voice emanates smoothly from the Burmester sound system. The jazzy chords of her voice remind me of those of a horn player. I nestle into the peanut butter leather seat and attempt not to drift off. This car could be one of my love languages and one day I was going to buy one for myself.

Like most of the young ladies in the crowd tonight, I enjoyed a good beat and didn't mind looking at Tau Anderson, but what actually piqued my interest was toiling in my apartment in hopes of writing a song twenty thousand people would sing word for word. Lately, I had been pulling all-nighters with Dawn way past normal work hours. The busy summer season was coming to a close. I hated that I was missing the session with Dylan and our producer, Red, tonight, but when I'm on official Garter business, songwriting takes a back seat.

We pull up slowly to the walk-up Talia and I share in Crown Heights as my neighbors mill about in the darkness of the night. It's easily past midnight. I exit the car as Dawn double parks. I hop up the stairs and she waits for me to open my front door. I flick the front light, so she knows that I'm good.

When I enter our third-floor apartment, Talia is curled up in the fetal position on the couch with the TV on mute, her laptop open, and her phone playing Elevation Worship music on the arm of the chair.

"Talia!" She jolts upright with the dazed look of a toddler.

"I'm up, I'm up." Her sandy-brown hair is all over her head and the pillow made an imprint on her skin. "How'd it go?"

"It was dope. You know Dawn, she's such a bawse. And the show was lit, the biddies were all out."

"Ugh, I wish I could have been there instead of drooling on myself." She reaches for her phone from the arm of our thrifted couch to catch up on missed text messages and pause her praise.

"And I'm not sure if Tau Anderson asked for my number or not."

I flop on the couch next to her.

"What? You were supposed to lead with thaaaat!" she yells as she reaches out to hit me. Her eyes are the size of marbles.

"Girl, I have no time to entertain that. I'm not even sure if it was real. I mean, there were all those girls there with the *good* push-up bras." I pull my nameplate chain to my mouth and watch as Talia gets up and folds the quilt that her mom had handsewn. We will never be short on quilts. Her mom made us a new one every holiday season.

"But *you* got his attention. Get out of here with that holier-than-thou BS. You know he's fine."

I roll my eyes before making my way to the kitchen. Opening the refrigerator, I hope something good will appear and settle on the Green Machine smoothie I never got to earlier. It was officially the weekend, thankfully. I didn't need to think about Tau Anderson anymore. To-night's concert would probably be the last time I saw him in person. If there was one thing my dad drilled into my head, it was to never fall for a musician. He would know.

"When are you coming to visit? It's been forever," my mom whines with the remnants of her Spanish accent.

My mother, Natalia Guerra, an Afro-Colombian woman who passed on her deep rich skin tone and big hair, grew up between the towns of San Basilio de Palenque and Cartagena. She came to the States with my grandparents when she was ten. All my grandparents spoke at home was Spanish, so she learned English from watching TV and through ESOL programs at school. She practiced and practiced until the accent was barely noticeable. She quickly realized Americans linked accents to a lack of intelligence and never wanted people to assume she was unprofessional because of it. But her accent still comes out from time to time. Especially when she whines.

"Mami, I don't really have the time or money to go back and forth. But I promise you, I'll be home for Thanksgiving." I roll over on my bed, facing my vision board, which is a smattering of inspirational quotes and pictures of the body I wanted to have, but didn't work out to get.

"I thought Thanksgiving was with your father this year?"

"No, Mami, this year is Christmas. You're getting old."

"I forget. But I am not getting old. Like fine wine, *mija*. Aging like fine wine."

"Of course," I concede.

"Just be sure that you are nah so focused on that career that you are nah thinking of starting a family of your own, Carlisa!"

"A family?" I scrunch my face looking up at the ceiling. That was one thing not on the board. Hell, I was still having smoothies for dinner. I toss one leg out of the covers of my bed. "Mami, I am not there at all. But I love ya! Talk soon!"

"But—"

"Bye, Mami!" I always had to make a swift exit when she started talking that family stuff. Her failed marriage somehow made her think nuptials, broken or not, was what I wanted for my life. For some reason marriage was seen as the pinnacle of all achievements. I saw it play out in real time on the internet. A post about a great career milestone got about fifteen likes. Marriage and baby announcement posts guaranteed hundreds of likes. Right now, my job and my music are my man and I'm good with that.

Before I can get a full scroll out on Instagram, a text pops up from Dylan.

Working with just Red is like working with the warden. Please tell me you're making the session today.

Absolutely.

Bet! Don't let it go to your head or nothin' but I kind of missed you.

Smh, hater! Anyway, I have something for you.

I finish with an eye-roll emoji then pull myself out of bed and take a quick assessment in the full-length mirror opposite my rumpled covers. I could certainly go without the stretch marks on my butt. But my mother's hips, well, they did me good since most girls were paying for them these days. I grab a T-shirt to pull over my camisole and make my way out to the kitchen. Talia is already up cooking breakfast. There were advantages to having this girl around.

"Morning!" I smile through crusty eyes as I sit on the stool at our breakfast bar. The clock on the microwave reads 8:15. Across from me, Talia proceeds to Milly Rock with the spatula in hand.

"Why are you so happy?"

"It's a new day, mamacita! Why not?"

Sometimes I think her optimism is genetic. Her parents, her sister, and brother are literally like the freaking Obamas or something. The complete opposite of my child-of-divorce reality, but having Talia around always feels like home. Her family has practically adopted me in the seven years we've been living together.

Talia was right. I was heading to the studio today and having that to look forward to always gave me a boost of energy.

"That smells good."

"Omelets."

Talia is seamless in the kitchen. She cooks with grace and precision. Her thin arms move swiftly from the counter to the stove. Adding ingredients, going over to the fridge for something she forgot. She packs in the final additions and waits to flip her masterpiece. "So you're working with Dylan and Red?"

"Yup yup."

"Cool. Red is so badass and Dylan, well, I don't know how you can focus." Talia throws the omelet on the plate and slides it my way. "There's some OJ in the fridge, but check the date," she giggles, pouring the rest of the eggs into the pan to start the process all over again.

"Please don't hype Dylan up. All he has to do is sing a note and the women are fawning," I say before opening the fridge. "Expired, womp womp." We look at each other and burst out laughing. "Water it is."

"When will we feel like real adults?" Talia says with a sigh as she finishes making her breakfast and slides it onto the counter. Leaning in, she takes a bite and savors the taste, even letting out an audible sigh of pleasure. She makes everything she eats look irresistible.

"Who knows, girl? I think about my parents and how they were already married by the time they were my age. The world is just different, I guess."

"I don't want to rush, but dammit if my parents don't make it look so easy."

"Well, yeah, your parents are basically the Obamas."

She scrunches up her freckled face and flicks a loose tomato from her omelet at me that I dodge. I contemplate the sentiment and realize it's something I've thought about a lot too. "Having it all together" and what that even meant.

"We're okay."

She nods. "Yeah, we're okay."

There was something daunting about the vast space of your mid-twenties. Everyone gave the same cookie-cutter advice, *take your time, everything will work out*, but time was tricky, it had a way of sneaking up on you.

We let the silence settle between us as we finish our omelets. With our bellies full, we rock, paper, scissors to see who gets first dibs on the shower. Talia feigns heartbreak when I win and heads to her room. I scurry to the bathroom, excited to get to the studio and see what Dylan did with the last song we worked on.

The Bronx was not on the list of places I wanted to travel coming from Crown Heights. Especially at 10 a.m. on a Saturday. I was always left debating over the hour-long MTA trek or the costly rideshare. Today, I check my bank account balance and walk down to the Utica Avenue train stop. I decide to save my splurges for the weekdays, so I forge my way on two buses after the train, which is always a delight. Walking up to Walnut Avenue makes me leery I might stumble upon a dead body like one of those *Law & Order* shows.

Red's placed a few songs with some up-and-coming signed artists. She used the money to grab a small spot to record on a regular basis. There's a ten-minute walk between my stop and the studio. As usual, the trash cans on the street corners are overflowing, stray cats protect their territory, and a stench of piss mixed with day-old liquor wafts in the air. The building housing the studio has steps resembling a fire escape. If you didn't know any better, you might think it was abandoned. As it should. Studio equipment is outrageously expensive. Looking abandoned is strategic in a neighborhood as sketchy as this one.

I enter the code to call up to the studio, the loud buzzer sounds and the door clicks. With no elevator, I start toward the fourth floor. When I finally reach it, I'm out of breath as I spot Red waiting for me at the door. For a split second I think she must have heard me noisily stomping up the steps but then I remember I called up. Maybe I should act on that vision board and do a sit-up or something.

"Hollywood!" Red gestures me into the small room.

I plop down in one of the black office chairs that sit in front of her small mixing board. To the right is her recording booth. The back wall is covered with a large mural. Hues of gold, orange, and green meld into one another. Red has a pretty decent setup. Guitars are placed just so on the wall. Adjacent to her board is her Kronos keyboard. The room's dimly lit, outside of the LEDs illuminating the console, even during the daytime due to blackout shades hanging from the windows. It was difficult to gauge how much time had actually passed when you were in Red's studio.

"What's up with you?" I pluck the lava lamp that sits on top of the board.

"Slavin'. As per usual. I got pulled into a new project. A group that just got signed." She sits down next to me, fixing her fire-engine-red ponytail before taking a bite of her breakfast burrito. She pops open the lid to an orange juice. My eyes move down to Red's feet. She has on the Jordan 3 Retros in blue. While I admire nice sneakers, Chucks are easy. Growing up, I was obsessed with the R&B artist Bianca. She had a sultry flair that made the tomboy vibe sexy. During one album cycle, she rocked red Chucks with everything. Dresses, on the red carpet, in videos—I guess it stuck with me. A small act of rebellion against the pressures of femininity.

"What time is Dylan getting here?" I was still bummed about missing the session last night. Being in the studio makes me feel that much closer to getting my name out there as a writer.

My phone vibrates, interrupting my daydreaming.

Carli, apologies for the weekend text, but some important updates for this week.

Weekends were not off-limits. I appreciated the pleasantry, but why the pretense? One weekend I had to leave my girl's twenty-fifth birthday party to handle a crisis with an artist who was pulled over with a gun in the car. The brands we'd partnered him with were seconds from canceling contracts and Dawn needed all hands on deck. Typical rapper problems. The work never stopped, and Dawn did not play about her clients. Foolishness or not, she made sure we knew how to spin things in their favor.

Tau is coming to the office on Monday, so make sure you're ready.

I read the text a few times before it sinks in. What in the whole hell was happening?

"That bad?" Her eyes don't move from the TV mounted above the board. An episode of *Chewing Gum* is on. I guess Red can sense my anxiety.

"Long story short, I have no idea whether Tau Anderson was trying to get at me last night and now I have a meeting with him Monday morning." I spin around in the chair until I get a little dizzy.

Red nods. "Oh yeah, how was the show?" Red seems high all the time, but I've never seen her smoke. She's in a constant state of chill that I won't even try to emulate. So many people in this industry have a myriad of vices and yet somehow, I found two solid collaborators in Red and Dylan.

"It was lit. He did some of the new stuff, which was cool. But it was when he threw it back to the *Black Light* album that the nostalgia hit, and I felt like I was back in Webster Hall when barely anyone knew who he was. Man, those were some of my fave records of his. They inspired a lot of the stuff I was writing then."

"Those records were ill, for sure." Red picks up her phone and starts to get up from her chair. "Well, business is business, right? Wouldn't be the first time you had to work with someone with their eye on you. I think men see me and automatically think I like women," she says, smirking.

Red has a rough exterior, but she's been married about five years, so she isn't for the BS.

"Yeah, and we see how that panned out," I say, shaking my head.

Red sits back down to finish her breakfast. Dylan is on straight industry time. It's so ridiculous how late artists can be.

After Dylan performed at the Music Matters showcase, he received great reviews, so we buckled down to work on an EP to follow up his single "Someone Like You." The goal was to get one of the records placed on a show like HBO's *Insecure*. Tons of new artists were being discovered that way.

"I thought this fool was texting to say he was here. He said he'll be another minute." Red answers a buzz and two minutes later Dylan bursts into the studio. His eyebrows are high and his jacket is a bit disheveled.

"I had to run some errands but I'm here. Perfect timing, right?" He grins while laying his book bag down on the floor near the third chair.

"Look, you're not a star yet," Red snaps.

"Oh, but I do shine bright, beloved!" Red is not for his games, but Dylan doesn't care. These two keep me thoroughly entertained.

"Boy!" Red rolls her eyes. "Look, we've wasted enough time. You've lived with this latest record, how you feel about it?" She sits down and leans back in her chair with her legs crossed, revealing argyle socks that match her blue-and-white sneakers.

"Oh, it's money. I've been working on some harmony parts that I think you'll like, too." Dylan rubs his hands along his faded black jeans. He's thin, with a hoop earring in his left ear and deep coils that look like they're reaching for the sun.

"Well, get in the booth, let's go!" Red rubs her hands together and turns her chair toward the board. I roll my chair up next to hers and pull up the recording software on the computer.

"Just like that, huh? You don't call, you don't write, you make me feel so cheap." Walking back over to the door, he turns the lights down lower. Reaching into his book bag, he pulls out a small diffuser in which he mixes frankincense and myrrh with the delicate touch of a chemist. He grabs the lighter next to a small row of candles near the window and lights each of them and places them back down. "You can't just skip the foreplay," he says with a laugh.

He starts walking to the small booth in the corner. Red bends her neck to the side and squints one eye.

"Maaaan, get in the booth."

Dylan was right. His harmonies have us floating. I sit back and listen as Dylan works out the bridge they never finished. Something feels slightly off and I try to put my finger on it.

"You hear that?" I turn to Red.

"Nah, sounds good to me."

"No, no, there's something." I close my eyes and let the vibrations of Dylan's voice settle into my spirit after he finishes singing.

"What's up? I liked that take," Dylan says.

"Carli's in here meditating or whatever she does when she's about to tell you something's off," Red says into the talkback mic.

"D, you're flat when you hit 'love' on the F. Like you're just a little below the note."

"Damn, you caught that, huh?" Dylan's voice comes through the speakers.

"So you heard it too?"

"Yeah, but you know, I liked the rest of the take."

"Womp, womp. We do excellence over here."

"Yeah, yeah, whatever."

Dylan does it again, this time with perfect pitch. Red and I look up as he emerges from the booth satisfied with himself.

He grabs his phone from the chair. "So, how was the dude Tau's show last night? You never hit me when you got in."

"I know, my fault. You know how it is moving around with Dawn. I was beat street by the time I got in."

"This one over here about to be Mrs. Anderson and whatnot," Red says nonchalantly as she reaches down to wipe some dust from her shoe.

"Oh, for real?" Dylan shifts his stance and looks at me.

"Ahhhhhh, you clownin', Red! That's definitely not the case."

"Oh, I'm sure he tried it. Yo, I had a homegirl get tangled up with him a year or so back. Did not end well, he had her looking crazy." Dylan pulls out his laptop. "I know we're wrapping but I need to send a few files right quick."

"Oh yeah, all good. I'm cleaning up this session and I'll bounce down what we have for now," Red says as she turns back to face the computer.

"So, what were you saying, Dylan?" My curiosity usually got the better of me.

"Well, she thought it was way more than it was. He was in town for the night, you know what I mean?" He pounds away at the keys on his laptop.

"Got it. Some girls don't get it. Make sure you don't do 'em like that when you're plastered all over TV screens."

"Imma be out here, getting all the girls that fronted when I got hurt and couldn't play ball anymore." He pauses, lost in his thoughts. "It's a crazy lifestyle, you gotta make sure you don't get caught up first though."

Dylan and I say our goodbyes to Red and head back up Walnut Avenue toward the park.

"So, what you getting into now?" He looks over as we dodge a gang of kids chasing one another down the block.

"Talia is going to be at the library late doing research, so there's nothing for me to do when I get home but write."

"Well, that's not the worst thing. That work ethic is why you will be one of the greats."

"Dylan." I push his arm, embarrassed by the compliment.

"You have no clue how amazing you are. One day, grasshopper." He tousles my hair and I swat his hand away.

We walk carefully, watching for broken glass and dog poop. The intense August sun ducks between a few sparse clouds and the warm wind tickles my face. My phone buzzes softly in the back pocket of my jeans.

Sorry I couldn't make it last month. I'm in Monaco. A text from my dad. They were so random and sporadic. Often apologies.

I don't reply. I let out an audible sigh before turning it on DND and tossing it into my bag. When we enter the park, it seems every pair in sight is a couple. They're holding hands, stealing glances indicative of new love. A redhead with a long braid and freckles is deep in conversation with the man to her right, oblivious to the cyclist trying to get around her. She's practically mesmerized.

"You okay?" Dylan asks after a beat. We take a seat at one of the stone benches along the pathway to rest our legs.

"I'm all right," I answer, my mind elsewhere. "You ever look at people and wonder what their story is? Who may be waiting for them, or where they're going?"

"And random-ass thoughts like that are why you will be an exceptional writer one day." He laughs and I join in. When the laughter fades, Dylan has a rare somber expression.

"What?"

"Oh, nothing. It's just been super dope to see your growth over the last two years."

We'd both come such a long way. I remember the first time Red introduced us. Dylan's whole vibe screamed creative. He came in talking about being influenced by artists like Phil Collins, Prince, and Eric

Clapton. Folks certainly in my top ten. Then he opened his mouth to
sing. I knew he would be a special artist in his own right.

"Wait, didn't you say you had something for me?"

"Right." I reach in my bag and pull out a black-and-gold box. "It's
the self-care line we finalized last week with Jhené Aiko."

"You love me. You really love me." He gives me a tight hug and
plants an exaggerated kiss on my cheek that I make a show of rubbing
off.

"You're gonna make me late." Talia puts her shoe on while hopping down the stairs at the same time. I pull the apartment door closed with my earrings still in hand.

"I'm out, I'm out!" I make sure to lock both locks and rush down the stairs behind her.

I'm not really the church type, but Talia is, so one day I decided to check it out after her constant begging. Her church was different from what I was used to. Occasionally, my mom felt compelled to drag us to church. The thought of the itchy stockings my mom would shove my legs into makes me shiver. At Talia's church you can wear whatever you want, the pastor is super young and trendy, and Dylan and a few other musicians I know play there. What more could you ask for? We typically did brunch after where the mimosas were endless and the smack talking was plentiful. No shade to God but that was kind of my favorite part.

I hit a quick jog to catch up with Talia. Her midi skirt sways back and forth in the wind under her cropped denim jacket. Her hair is pulled up into a tight bun and she hustles to get to the subway station close to our place.

"Every Sunday, B!" She puts one finger in the air while bouncing down the steps.

"Gah, I know! I was up late yesterday, I couldn't sleep."

We bustle through the turnstile in time to catch the 4 train. Service is at Gramercy Theatre, so we have to switch over to another train before arriving at our destination. Sundays were bearable in comparison to the nightmare of commuting during the week. The MTA was trash lately and we were all forced to grin and bear it.

We emerge intact as we hurry into the theater. The greeters are still kind to the latecomers. A total one-eighty from the ushers dressed in white from my hometown of Severn.

Talia motions to the left side of the auditorium where she asked her friend Fred to save us seats. Once we spot them, we shimmy across their row, ducking down and giving the head nod and hands-up to excuse ourselves for interrupting people's worship. The lights are bright, and five singers stand across the stage with their hands pointed to the sky. Dylan has his hat pulled low with a bass strapped across his chest.

Talia places her things down on the seat and we both exchange hugs with Fred and his girlfriend, Mari. Fred and Talia are in law school together and by way of hanging out to study, she also got super tight with Mari. They were both hella smart people but also just fun to be around and easy to talk to. I got introduced to them through church and our Sunday brunch festivities. It was crazy to see how effortless they were together. Fred, the law student, and Mari, the yoga instructor with her own studio. I wasn't privy to too many healthy relationships, so it was always nice to see. I was batting zero, clearly worrying my mother about whether or not she'd ever have grandchildren. I was her lone hope as the only child.

The curvy redhead belts a worship song from the stage, encouraging the rest of us to lift our voices as the music stops and only the kick drum booms. I love finding the harmony notes as the rest of the crowd sings in unison.

Talia's hands are clasped in front of her with her head tilted down. She's deep in thought. Law school was tough, but I admired how she knew exactly what she wanted and wouldn't let anything deter her from it. I loved that about her now, although that determination was off-putting when we first met. In the only class we shared, Talia was set on proving our professor wrong about W. E. B. Du Bois's take in *The Philadelphia Negro*. All I could remember thinking was, *Who is this girl?* But as fate would have it, we met back up through a Facebook post when I was looking for off-campus housing after my freshman year. There weren't a lot of options, but it turned out to be one of the best decisions of my life. I moved to New York literally with like a dollar and a dream and of course without my mom's blessing at first.

"Dios mio, mija, por qué? Nueva York está muy lejos y no tenemos familia ahí. ¿Quién va a cuidarte?" Occasionally, she broke out the Spanish when she was upset or extremely happy. For so long it was just the two of us. I couldn't promise that I would be back in Maryland anytime soon, but I had to follow my dream and everything told me New York was the place to do it.

The pastor preached a soul-stirring message about being sure to invite God into all aspects of our lives. I could appreciate that. I know there is a God up there, but sometimes I could get stuck in my own way, trying to "make it all happen." I'm sure he's had a good laugh or two on my account. I worked hard, but I wasn't opposed to sending up a few prayers about getting my songwriting off the ground. The work at Garter Media sustained me for sure, but I had a much bigger plan, a dream. Before this was all over I had to know what it was like to have people all across the world singing my songs.

Service ends and people from diverse backgrounds and ethnicities spill out of the theater onto the sidewalk. Dylan walks out with his large bass in tow. We stand waiting for Talia, Fred, and Mari as they chat with a few folks from their life group. They were small gatherings with people from church where they could get to know one another more intimately. I tried to make them, but my hours were nuts. Talia even hosted a few at our apartment. I think she's working on her sainthood or something.

"So, are we hitting our usual spot?" Mari asks as we beat the pavement away from the theater and jumbled chatter.

"I think so. Marv's is so chill and they don't try to kick us out. I know Agnes Café has better food but it's always mobbed," Talia explains.

"As long as there are mimosas!" I hit a twirl.

"We know, Carli, we know! Such a lush." Talia swings her bag in my direction.

"Whatever!" Turning to Dylan, I pat him on the back. "You killed praise and worship as usual."

"You know, I do what I can." He smiles and tips his hat to me like a cowboy from an old Western.

We make it to Marv's right before the big rush, so we're able to snag a booth. The décor is trendy yet industrial. The waiters are dressed in skinny jeans and T-shirts, adding to the laid-back vibe. Over the years I realized New York could be so random. The person next to you could just as easily be a retail sales associate or a VP at a label.

"All I am saying is, it seems impossible to be faithful when you have that many women that want to tear your clothes off. Baby, I am sorry, but God didn't make me a movie star or a musician for a reason." Mari rolls her eyes.

"That's ridiculous. You don't get a pass cause you're famous." Talia picks at the fruit left on her plate. "Most of those idiots were the cornballs in high school and then they get popular and finally get the attention they were starved for before."

"Whoa, easy, Tally! I played ball in high school and was pretty popular. I got into music once I got injured," Dylan interjects. "Fame only magnifies who you already are."

Fred loved The Tea Instagram page, and their latest post went into the details of Logan Lindley's cheating scandal. A tape surfaced showing the comedian leaving a club with a young hot thing who was not his wife, who happens to be pregnant with twins. His affair was the latest news dominating the Twitter trending timeline.

The waiter approaches the table to clear the empty dishes. He's tall with smooth brown skin and his white apron splashed with food is telling of today's busy shift. "I'm saying, my man," Fred starts while glancing up at the waiter.

"Ahhhhhh," Talia yells out. "Don't bring this poor man into your shenanigans." The waiter shakes his head with a laugh. "Well, Carli, you're so quiet, wouldn't you expect a partner to be faithful to you regardless how much money they had?"

"How did I get pulled into this?" I was purposely trying to mind my business. I can't tell you how many relationship conversations I've gotten pulled into with this group. And what did I know? Dating was the last thing on my agenda.

"There are a lot more important topics in the world. I mean, the political climate right now is bleak. Did you see what happened in Virginia?" I know my attempt to change the subject is futile.

"That is too stressful to think about right now, Carli," Mari says while shaking her head.

"Look, I wouldn't date an entertainer. I know them too well. And I don't trust them as far as I can throw them." I was starting to sound a lot like Barbara, my mom's best friend who was constantly warning against the trickery of men. "Should a woman expect her man to be faithful? Sure." I grab one of the extra beverage napkins from the table and write *faithful* on it before stuffing it into the small notebook in my bag.

"Well, tell us how you really feel," Dylan says playfully.

I give him a sheepish look. "I'm sorry, you know it's not like that. I wasn't referring to you when I said that. You're different."

Dylan nods and gives me a smile, but I can tell he feels called out.

Honestly, I hadn't had much luck with regular guys either. There was Damon, who my mom tried to hook me up with a year ago. He was the son of a lawyer at the firm where she works and she could barely contain herself over the possibility of me settling down with a guy with a *real* job. Things started off well and he didn't come with the usual issues I ran into with guys in the industry, but he had dreams of some doting housewife. Hard stop. Had to end that quick.

"Y'all are so unrealistic. But whatever, man. Most of these women are in it for the lifestyle. They don't care what their man does. His wife ain't going nowhere. It's gonna be a few awkward months and dassit." Fred nods like he is satisfied with being the only one who agrees with his point.

This could go on forever. The mimosas have my bladder working overtime. I scoot my chair back from the table and head to the restroom while checking for new notifications on my phone.

Tau Anderson is following you.

I push open the door to the restroom and stop to fix my mane in the mirror. I wipe the corners of my mouth where my lipstick smeared and open Twitter. A red notification is in my DMs.

Making me work. I like that. See you Monday.

TRACK 5

The persistent beep of my alarm clock wakes me and I squint to see. Seven a.m. I can sense someone moving quickly in the corner of my room. It's Talia, of course, rifling through my closet as always.

"Uhmmm . . ." I murmur through the taste of last night's dinner in my mouth.

"Oh, hey love, sorry, I wanted to borrow your chambray one-piece." She smiles with one eye closed.

Talia is taller than me by multiple inches, but somehow she still finds her way into my closet when she is searching for "chill" clothes. The counter to her girly, fashion-week style, I own a mean stockpile of denim and tees.

"Would you have asked if I hadn't woken up?" I prop myself up on my elbows and shake my hair out.

"Probably not. But I love you and today is the big day! You get to breathe the same air as Tau Anderson again!" She finally finds it in the mound of clothes that have accumulated on my closet floor.

"I really hate you."

"But you love me! Gotta go before I'm late for my class!" She hustles out of the room, closing the door behind her.

My meeting is at eleven, so I get to take my time getting into the office. I reach over to my nightstand and pull out my aqua-colored journal with START SOMETHING NEW threaded across the cover. I shamelessly love this journal. My mom bought it for me the last time I was home. There's something about the way the ink moves across the pages.

I find scribbling my morning thoughts therapeutic. I am able to examine my feelings of doubt and uncertainty without any judgment. I knew my friends were tired of hearing about how much I wanted to write songs full-time, so I whine and complain within the confines of my journal.

After purging my thoughts, I reach for my laptop. I open my review of accounts on the prowl for influencers and partnerships that might be a good match with Tau's brand. There are tons of notes scribbled from our initial onboarding where his team discussed what they were looking for as well. Ace of Spades is pretty much the new Cristal, and they wanted a new face for their expensive limited edition Champagne release. That would be my lead. It was sophisticated yet representative of young, new money.

I'd done enough slumming on the train this weekend so splurging on a rideshare felt right. Nothing like being fresh and ready as opposed to sweaty and frustrated dealing with the MTA.

Garter Media is in a twenty-floor brick office building on Sixth Avenue in Midtown. The hustle and bustle makes me feel as though I'm a part of the select few who have business to attend to on this side of town. Over the last few years, I'd gotten a lot more comfortable in the city than when I first started and felt like a little girl playing dress-up. The imposter syndrome was mostly at bay these days.

I take my turn in the revolving door and show my work ID to the security guard who flashes his crooked smile as I head upstairs to the twentieth floor. When I push open one of the glass doors to our suite there are interns scattered about and what looks like a fresh delivery of flowers.

"Hey, Siena!" I smile as I breeze past the reception desk.

"Do you know who's coming to the office today?" She sits under a huge sign with the GM logo and flicks her long wand-curled hair with blond tips.

"Oh, of course. I'm working on the project," I say over my shoulder as I head into Dawn's corner office. The view is sick. The cascading green landscape of Bryant Park down below is surrounded by massive glass and steel skyscrapers. Bright umbrellas from the Bryant Park Grill disrupt the gray shadows cast from the clouds above. Her desk is massive with a distressed wood finish. Everything has a rustic element with touches of glam. I slide in as she finishes up with one of the senior account managers and gives some interns their marching orders. I'm swallowed by her gray sofa with furry pillows and pull my laptop out of my bag.

"Morning, Carli, so what do you have for me?" She takes a long sip from her extra-large coffee cup. I'm not even sure of the size above venti but that's what she always has.

"Well . . . I was thinking three words, Ace of . . . Spades."

Although I'm confident, and have worked with Dawn long enough to know what she likes, I still feel nervous presenting ideas to her. She could be stern to the tenth degree. And she usually was. There was little to no room for error, and I'd done my best to rise to the challenge.

She rears back in her chair and brings her delicate index finger and thumb to her chin. Taking a half spin in her expensive ergonomic chair, she stops and gasps.

"Yes, and we can talk to Merlin's Yachts about doing a shoot. Real sexy. We can even use a few of the sports players on our client list and make it a great party."

"Yup." I relax my shoulders a little. "Also, there is a new app called Highline that I think may definitely be of interest. It pretty much gives the rundown of all the high-end lounges, hotels, and eateries in each city. Great for a touring musician without having to rely on their handlers so much. It also includes a gaming section where they can garner points for even more exclusive VIP experiences and gifts."

"Absolutely." Her eyes light up. "Don't use the word *handlers*, of course." She shakes her head back and forth.

"Of course not." I look up at the clock. About fifteen minutes before they were expected. But then again, musicians. I rarely expected them to be on time.

"Great, Carli!" she says, folding her hands together in her lap. "I have to say, it's been some time since I've worked with a young person as on it as you are. I want to really dig in with you, teach you what I know about this business. I think you have some great potential." She reaches for her Gucci frames to finish up her notes on her laptop.

"Oh wow, Dawn, that means a lot." I rock a little to get up from the low Chesterfield couch. "I'll go ahead and make sure everything is the way you like it in the conference room. I'm grateful for the opportunity."

"No, you earned the opportunity. Lesson number one: You do not get what you deserve, you get what you negotiate. Always remember, you are not here by happenstance, but because you bust your tuchus to get here." She leans in a little closer over her desk and whispers, "Especially us." She brushes her brown hand. "*Nothing* is given to us."

"Right." I straighten up and head toward the door.

"Great! I'll have you talk about Ace of Spades and the app, and I'll introduce the two other potential collaborations."

"Sounds like a plan."

I dart over to the conference room. Peonies, her favorite flower, were the delivery this morning. They're slightly off-center so I move the vase a little to the left as one of the interns looks on. Sadly, I refer to her as "Bangs" when she's not around but I think her name is Macy. I should do better with remembering their names.

"Precision is the name of the game," I say, winking at her.

"Right, okay," she says before scurrying out of the conference room.

Siena also got a hold of Tau's road manager and had his favorite drink, Nantucket Nectars Red Plum, and Doritos on a small table in the corner. Sure, it was still fairly early for Doritos, but you could never be too sure. There were also a few bright blue Saratoga water bottles in the center of the table. I glance down at my watch. Eleven. Why is my heart beating so fast?

As if on cue, the large man with the square jaw I saw backstage the other night is the first to enter through the suite doors. Siena is up from behind the reception desk, and I notice her skirt is a little shorter than usual. I guess we all broke out the good clothes today. Creepy Frankie K from backstage follows after the muscle man, and then there's Tau. It's as if his entrance is in slow motion as we all look on, interns and staff alike. He stops everyone in their tracks as they move to one side or the other to make a space for him and his team. His white shirt is unbuttoned to mid-chest with a gold Cuban link chain shining in the recessed lighting. His camel-colored pants are fitted, and his hair is smooth and well moisturized. He pulls down his shades and winks in my direction as Siena ushers them into the conference room.

My eyes roll hard as I position myself behind the group as they head in.

Dawn comes in offering up cheek kisses and pleasantries as she claims her spot at the head of the table. I sit down right next to her and the intern whose name may be Lacy. She's focused on setting up the laptop to project.

"Dawn, this is an amazing place," Tau says with a smile.

"Thank you, I'm glad you could make it. It's not often we have our VIPs in the flesh and not over the conference line." She spreads out her printed notes across the white oak conference table.

"I'm in New York for a few, about a month. Before heading back to LA in September to finish the tour and my new album. So, I said, why not? You have a great place." He stares directly at me. Dawn's eyes follow his.

"Well, thank you," she says. "You remember Carli from the other night?"

"She's unforgettable."

"Good to see you again," I say, ignoring his comment. "So let's get started, shall we?" I stand up and shake hands with Frankie and Mark—the chiseled, quiet guy who can probably kill with his bare hands if he has to—his security. Tau's big-picture manager Joel was on video chat from LA. "The gang's all here and we have some very exciting opportunities I think you'll like." I cue the intern to pull up the first slide. "This right here is an app that is going to change the way you travel . . ."

Forty-five minutes later, we have them nodding profusely and smiling about the potential of getting Tau in front of newer and bigger audiences. Expansion is the name of the game in music these days. No one is selling as many albums, so it is all about endorsements and partnerships to maintain the lifestyle musicians are used to living.

"Well, I'm impressed," Tau says, standing up from the table. "That's it for me, right? Maybe Carli can show me around the rest of the office while y'all handle the details?" He flashes his dimples like he knows they're a superpower.

"Wait, what?"

"Ahh yes, that sounds good. Carli?" Dawn darts her eyes toward the door.

"Of course!" I try to sound upbeat. Meanwhile, I can feel goose bumps rising on my skin. I'd been around my share of famous people before, but he was making me nervous. We walk out of the conference room under the watchful eye of Siena at the reception desk. I look down, out the glass windows of the office, and see a small crowd forming outside the building. "You really want to see the office? Really?" I ask.

"I mean, contractual talk is not necessarily my favorite thing. I'd rather some good conversation with better company."

I put on my most professional tone. "A tour it is, then."

We take a couple of steps down the long hallway away from the conference room. "This is what we call the stacks. We have a ton of archived magazines with great press and coverage from some of our deals for clients. We do some smaller team meetings here," I explain.

"I promise you don't have to act stiff with me." He puts his hand across his chest for emphasis. "You don't have to impress me like you do your boss."

I try not to notice the flexing pec peeking from under his shirt.

"I'm not," I stammer. His comment strikes a nerve. "I have to be frank here, Mr. Anderson. With all due respect, our relationship is strictly professional, and I'd like to keep it that way, so I would save your charm for the crowd that's forming downstairs."

He laughs. "Mr. Anderson? Oh, that's cute."

"I'm serious." Continuing down the small narrow hallway, I usher him into the lounge. A trip to Indonesia left Dawn inspired to re-model the area with colorful tapestry and low tables. Blown-up photos of Dawn with the who's who of music and entertainment adorn the walls in ornate gold frames. He plops down onto a pile of floor pillows stacked in the corner and brings his legs to his chest.

I stand near the door, waiting for him to move. I check behind me to make sure that no one else is privy to this exchange.

"I know you're serious." He's still smiling, which ignites a small fire of rage in my chest. "You're giving me very serious vibes with that face you're making. I'm just trying to figure out why."

"Well, that concludes the tour. Hope you enjoyed and I look forward to making these deals come to life for you. Great to see you again." I start to back out of the door and he jumps up and grabs my arm lightly.

"I didn't even see your office," he says, grinning. "Look, I'm here for a month to do some press, close a few business deals, and a little recording for the new album. But I'll have some free time on my hands. I'd love to be able to call you. Get to know you a little better."

"You cannot be that delusional, can you?" A bewildered laugh escapes my lips. "Regarding your account here, you can email me or call my office line." I pull a card from my notebook and hand it to him. Reaching for the card, he chuckles and weaves it through his fingers. As he passes me, he reaches for my hair and twirls one of my curls like he did the other night. A habitual boundary crosser it seems.

"I love your hair." He walks slowly back toward the conference room. I can feel my neck heating. Following behind him I walk in and shake hands once more with Frankie and Mark, who gives me what I think is a quick side-eye. What was his problem?

"This has been amazing, gentlemen," Dawn says. "Tau, thank you for being an active participant in your future. That doesn't happen too often and will take you far." She grabs his shoulder and kisses his cheek.

"Oh yeah, I'm involved. Spent a lot of my career just wanting to sing, but I quickly learned there's a lot more to it than that." He hugs Dawn and offers me a glance.

Siena hops up as she sees the group about to exit. They make their way out the conference room and I hang behind. She masterfully inserts herself right next to Tau and starts talking. I can only pick up a few words from inside the conference room. Through the glass I see her pull the Regine pose. Tau throws his head back and laughs, gently touching her arm.

As he trails out the door, Siena lingers, watching him walk away and biting her lip. I shake my head. *Some girls don't get it*. I think of Dylan's friend he mentioned over the weekend. *I* was that naive girl once.

"Carli, come see me in about fifteen after I catch up on some emails," Dawn says, interrupting my thoughts.

"Of course!" I gather my things and head to my small office that I share with Ryan, the other junior account manager. He greets me seemingly in high spirits as I check and see what's happening in my in-box. Ryan could have stepped out of a Sperry commercial. He has tanned, freckled skin, and his dirty blond hair holds loose curls. He struck me as the type to have grown up vacationing in Martha's Vineyard and who has socially liberal but fiscally conservative parents. We got along all right, but it was clear we came from two different planets. I shoot off a few responses before checking my watch to ensure I'm back to Dawn in fifteen.

Sending off one last reply, I glance at the clock and head back to her office. I knock although the door is open.

"Yes, yes, come in, superstar." Dawn smiles and pulls off her glasses. "Sit, sit."

I walk over and plop down, attentive.

"Great job in there. We are going to be able to lock up a few deals. Merlin is ecstatic about us using one of his yachts. I chatted with him after our meeting. We'll be shooting within two weeks, fingers crossed, in Miami." She bites the arm of her glasses, mulling over her next thought.

"Lesson number two," she starts. "Reputation is everything. I'm pretty sure Tau finds you, well, attractive. I know that it can seem enticing, but honey, those types of guys are only out for one thing. And I always want to make sure that personal business doesn't interfere with the business we do here. There's a strict no-fraternizing policy I hope you haven't forgotten about."

I center myself and respond quickly, "Oh, for sure, Dawn. I didn't even notice. My head is in the game, believe me. He's only another client to me."

I was being lectured about a guy I wasn't even interested in or giving the time of day. He was physically attractive, yes, but not at all someone I would let jeopardize my livelihood. As of now, songwriting didn't pay the bills. Yet, anyway. Clearly Tau had other thoughts.

"Of course." She gets distracted by an email. "Good work today as always. I'd like you to come with me to a meeting tomorrow. Ten, if you're available, and we can continue our lessons."

I appreciated her pretending I could be unavailable. "Sounds like a plan," I say in my best cheery voice before making my exit. When I get back into the safe space of my own office, I lean my head back and slowly exhale. *What the hell was that?* Somehow, I felt like I was in trouble because Tau Anderson thought my life was some kind of game. My phone buzzes, revealing another red notification in my Twitter DMs.

I'm here for a month. Let's not keep wasting time.

The arrogance.

I slam my phone facedown on the desk so I can attempt to concentrate. I blink a few times to help my eyes focus before Ryan catches my attention. He stands, gathering his phone and wallet from his desk. "A few of us are going to grab lunch, you coming?"

"Nah, I'm good. I want to get a jump on our afternoon meeting."

"Oh, but of course." He gives me a polite smile before disappearing out the door. I peek out of our office, which is diagonal to the suite doors, to see Ryan, Siena, and one of the senior managers heading toward the elevator. Last week I'd passed on happy hour. With the amount of extra time I spent with Dawn, I just didn't have an interest in spending even more time with coworkers who couldn't really help me get where I was trying to go.

When I look back up, the intern is standing there. "Is there anything else I can do before I head out?"

"Oh, no, thanks, Lacy," I say, taking a stab at her name.

"It's Gracie, but okay, Carli, thanks. See you tomorrow." She musters up a smile and my throat dries right up.

The final elements of the pitch deck come together for me right before the lunch crew returns. I was in charge of compiling all the notes while Ryan was up to present. So, I spend my break dragging and dropping text and photos in PowerPoint while slurping down some pho I ordered from the Vietnamese spot around the corner. I finish

with enough time to squeeze out a couple lyrics that have been swirling in my head all day. I grab my notebook and scrawl the few lines
quickly before my time is up. *Wish I could run, run away / never look back
/ on what we had / oh foolish love / look what you've done to me / made me so
ugly inside.*

Late afternoon, we filter into the conference room to a lot more
white faces than our previous meeting with Tau. We shake hands and
exchange pleasantries as Intern Number Two loads the presentation. I
don't even try to guess but make a mental note to ask Siena his name
later. Ryan takes his place beside the screen and begins our pitch. As he
gets to the revenue projections, the nuts and bolts, he starts to stumble.
Dawn's eyes shoot over to me. We went over these, but somehow he
was still lost in the sauce.

"As you can see here, wait, I had the numbers here just a second
ago," he says as he shuffles through his papers. The presentation had the
graphs, but there was more to explain about what they actually meant.

"Ryan, Ryan," Dawn interjects. "Please. Maybe that long lunch
has you feeling a little sluggish." She shakes her head. "Carli, can you
please?" She turns to me.

"Oh, yes, so as you can see here, with influencer marketing, your
company has the ability to increase revenue by at least forty percent in
the next quarter." I switch places with Ryan at the front of the room
and finish out the pitch. Ryan takes his seat as deflated as a kickball
losing air. I feel a little bad that Dawn called him out in front of the
clients like that, but I'd learned not to take lunches before these types of
meetings. The ones where the numbers were the most important part.

"It wasn't that bad," I try to assure Ryan when we get back to our
office.

"You know as well as I do that's a demerit," he says with a grimace
of pain. "I just got my notes a little mixed up." He rubs his hands across
his desk as if it can offer him some solace.

She totally kept score. I knew it and he knew it too.

The day drags on. I make my way to the train to head home to Brooklyn the minute Dawn gives me the green light.

Dylan's voice fills my headphones as I listen to the record we cut over the weekend. I shoot him a text with a few notes for our next session. I can't believe how well my pitches went today. It was exciting to be working with someone like Tau, but his confidence felt dangerous. And more so, I would prefer to be writing with him as opposed to shooting a campaign. But like always, I had to juggle professionalism and possible networking opportunities for my songwriting when it came to our music clients. And now there was this other element of being pursued on social media by a star. That part was new.

"So, what are you going to write back?" Talia holds the phone toward me. I stretch out across the ruffled comforter that covers her bed.

"I've been working on the whole 'I'm ignoring you' thing."

"That doesn't seem to be working! I mean, what's the big deal, Carli? What if he's actually a solid dude?" She moves her ridiculously large books she was reviewing before I barged in with my crisis.

"The big deal is, my boss literally gave me a talk about guys like him and warned me about my reputation. And I'm feeling pretty confident he's a jerk."

"That's rough. I know you're always trying to show up for Dawn, and working at Garter might lead to songwriting connections, but hey, this is your life, son!" she says, exaggerating her New Yorkness. She pushes my hair out of my face like my mom used to do when I was younger.

"It's not the end goal but you know, it's how I'm sustaining my life right now. Most of the other up-and-coming musicians are out here trying to find two nickels to rub together." I pause. "I don't even know him. Sure, he's attractive, but it's like bro, I'm working. Give me a break. And guys like that aren't into girls like me, Talia. I'm not a MAC Makeup Girl."

"Maybe that's not what he's into. You're gorgeous without even trying." She rolls her eyes and hits me with a heart-shaped throw pillow. "The man is stalking your Twitter!"

"You're not too shabby yourself, skinny-minny," I say, laughing. "The bottom line is, right now I need my job and I need to finish working on Dylan's project because that could actually be a good look for me. So, I ain't thinking about Tau Anderson. Besides, you know musicians are trash."

"I hear you, believe me. But I don't want us to be two single biddies in this Brooklyn walk-up foreva. All we're missing are the cats."

"Dumb!" I can't help but cackle. "I'm out." Being serious with Talia only lasts a minute. I tap the doorjamb as I head to my bedroom.

I close the door and sit down in my faux leather desk chair. He was pretty diligent finding me on Twitter. I open the app and click on my DMs.

My boss thinks you like me. Very discreet. I need my job.

Maybe that was too harsh. I wasn't sure, but I wanted things to return to normal so I could focus on other things besides dodging advances from Tau freaking Anderson.

I do like you.

Tau's response pops up before I even have the chance to scroll through my timeline.

Shit.

TRACK 6

The morning air is crisp from the overnight rain. I walk to meet Dawn down in the Flatiron District for our meeting with Blair Liv, RCA's head of marketing. Blair is working with a few artists he wanted to pair with Dawn, and as her newfound protégée I'm tagging along for the ride.

It's cool to be learning the ropes, I guess. But I always imagined myself sans Dawn, sitting across those huge desks with these big-time music executives and playing my songs while everyone nodded along. I was a step away from everyone I needed to know for my songwriting career to take off, but I was on the wrong side. Dawn's list of who was who in the industry could change things for me in an instant. That truth sat right beside me at every meeting.

As I make my way into the lobby, Dawn waves. She's wearing black track pants with a red stripe down the side that match her red Nike Huaraches.

"Right on time," she approves.

We stop at security to show our IDs and receive visitors' badges before heading up to RCA's floor. Blair is waiting for us at reception and greets us both with big hugs before ushering us into his huge corner office with floor-to-ceiling windows overlooking the city. A framed copy of *Time* magazine hangs over his desk with the only president worth acknowledging on the cover. Clearly Obama had scrawled his signature across the top.

After pleasantries and settling in, Dawn and I sit across from Blair with headshots sprawled on his desk. With each one he gives a spiel about their music and branding. Most with facial tattoos and grillz make Dawn shake her head profusely before she lands on a cute, young, fresh face with bone-straight hair and cheekbones from the ancestral gods.

"Aminah," Blair says as his eyes light up. "She's amazing, can play piano, guitar, and she writes. We'll see how much of her own stuff gets on her debut project, but I'm not mad at it."

"Perfect."

"You mean Lil Trap doesn't do it for you?" Blair says with a grin.

"Blair, I have not gotten this far by working with just anybody."

"Ha! You haven't changed a bit, Dawn." His eyes have a familiarity that makes me wonder if he and Dawn were ever a thing. Blair's voice has a smooth tone as buttery as his skin. Tall, with a full beard that gave me all the Philly rapper vibes, he was fine, as far as older men go.

"So what do you do at Garter?" He turns his attention to me.

"I'm a junior account manager."

"She's a star, Blair, I'm telling you. She knocked a meeting out of the park with Tau Anderson recently. I'll see what she can cook up with little Miss Aminah as well."

"Oh wow, okay, nice! Tau stopped by yesterday. I met him as a young kid when his team first started shopping him around. Too bad we passed on him. His A&R, Omar, got lucky." He shakes his head. "Are you an artist yourself? Do you sing?"

I'm lost for words. I do my best to keep my business and creative sides separate, but I want to yell, "Yes! Can I write with Aminah? Can you put Dylan's song on your Generation Next playlist?" But I have to be reasonable. Dawn doesn't even know I write, let alone sing. Most often she did the talking, so even though we spent a lot of time together, I don't think she knew a lot about me outside of work.

"In the shower," I laugh, and they join in.

"Fair enough, I thought I may have recognized you from somewhere," he says as he begins collecting the headshots from the table. "I'll connect you with the rest of Aminah's team, Dawn, and we can go from there. I'm excited to see what you come up with."

"Delightful." She puts her hand out and Blair takes it to help her up from her seat. "It's always a pleasure." She bats her mascara-lined eyelashes.

I loved how some women could throw on the charm and boy did I feel like she was laying it on thick with Blair. I was only charming by accident, rarely on cue.

He starts to walk us out and stops.

"Oh hey, I forgot, Aminah is actually in town for a bit. She has a show tonight if you're free?" His hand lingers on hers.

Dawn pulls out her phone and fiddles around to get to her calendar.

"I can stop by. Carli, are you available?" She turns to me.

"Of course."

"Good, one sec, let me make a stop before we leave," Dawn says, waving at Blair as she heads toward the restroom.

"Well, I'm looking forward to this collaboration. I'll see you tonight," Blair says before turning to head back to his office.

"Blair." I hear it tumble out of my mouth before I have time to think. Shit. *Am I really doing this?* We were alone and in this tiny window of opportunity, I could tell him how much I would love to write for one of his artists. The pace of my heartbeat quickens, and my palms collect sweat. My hands find themselves clasped together as he waits anxiously for the rest of it. "It was really great to meet you."

"You too, Carli." He shakes my clammy hand and disappears back behind the glass doors of his office. Dawn walks out and we make our way back past the cubicles, music blaring from one of the conference rooms. Through the glass windows, a few staff members sit nodding along as a thin kid with massive locs sings along to the song blasting from the speakers, his musical fate in their hands. I pull out my phone to tell Talia I need a rain check on our movie night. It looked like it was going to be a long one. But that wasn't anything new.

Dawn and I grab lunch before heading back to the office to knock out some work. The plan is to head out a little early so Dawn can make a stop before the show. It feels like a blur once we get settled at the office. The day is packed with meetings. Around six, we send our last proposals then make our way to SoHo in lovely New York City traffic.

We pull up outside the Louis Vuitton store and park in a loading zone. Dawn's picking up something she ordered. The sales reps know her by name. I wander around the store in awe of the price tags. I cannot even imagine shopping somewhere like this. My prized purchase to date was a Gucci belt from a sample sale that Talia dragged me to. It smells expensive in this store. My eyes land on a small, checkered fanny pack. I reach for it, fingering the leather. It's definitely a lot more luxurious than the bags I get from Ross Dress for Less.

"We'll take this too." I hear Dawn's voice and look up. The sales associate is walking toward me quickly but instead of kindly escorting me out, she grabs the bag before heading to the back. In a few seconds she reappears with a small box containing a fresh pouch and my head spins.

"Oh Dawn, I . . ." I stammer.

"Carli, please, it's on me," she says with a wink.

I cannot believe my boss is buying me a Louis Vuitton fanny pack. Moments like this made me think I had to be nuts not to appreciate this job.

Dawn laughs more with the tall, lanky cashier who looks fresh off a runway. As she hands over her black Amex, he bags everything up and turns to Dawn. "Would you like me to carry this to your car?" Waving her hand, Dawn shakes her head, grabbing her large bag and handing me my own. "Thanks, sweetie, but we can handle a couple of bags." We plop the bags into the trunk of Dawn's Benz before hopping in to head over to Aminah's show.

"Thank you so much, Dawn, I really didn't expect that," I start after she takes off.

"Carli, you've been doing great, it's my pleasure."

"This was just very kind."

"You're welcome."

We find a small lot to park near S.O.B.'s on Varick. It looks packed from the line forming outside the building. Dawn saunters her way past onlookers to the door where she's on Blair's list. We walk inside and make our way downstairs to the artist area. She smiles and hugs nearly everyone she sees. Some folks I recognize, some I don't. I'm try-ing to keep my eyes open after the long day we've had. Somehow this chick was thirty years my senior, but it didn't seem like Dawn missed a step. Maybe I needed to get into the ridiculously sized coffee game.

"Aminah, meet Dawn and Carli." Blair beams, encircling us all in his arms. "They're going to be helping you go next level."

"Nice to meet you." Aminah nods and shakes our hands with both of hers. Her tiny waist is accentuated with a high skirt and a cropped top. Her makeup is a natural yet flawless soft glam look that translates effortlessness but takes a considerable amount of skill to pull off. She's noodling on her guitar and going over a few parts of the show with the rest of the band.

"Well, we know you need to get ready, but we're looking forward to the set," Dawn interjects into the awkward silence.

"I'm sorry. This part has been killing me all night." She shakes her head and plays the chord progression again.

"Try the major seventh." I don't mean to blurt out the suggestion, it's just so obvious in my head.

Aminah looks up with wonder from her guitar. The rest of her bandmates nod with enthusiasm. She begins to strum the song with my chord suggestion. She stops and stares at me in amazement.

"Yes!" She pauses. "Thank you, sweet pea. What was your name again?"

"Carli." I smile uneasily to the stares of Blair and Dawn. "Okay, we'll leave you to it!" I say as I head for the steps.

We walk up to the main floor, which is filling in. The whole place is tinted red from the uplighting, and the infamous S.O.B.'s logo is static on the screen onstage. The large pillars are adorned with posters of Aminah with a similar two-piece but it's a tan faux leather. The VIP area is toward the back but I'm eying the bar. I figure the only way I'm going to survive is probably with some whiskey.

"I'm gonna grab a drink. Would you like anything?" I ask Dawn.

"I'll do a Dewar's on the rocks," she says, reaching for her card.

Free designer bags, drinks, and VIP experiences, maybe I should quit this whole dream thing and just be happy with what I have, I think as I walk over to the bar. The music is thumping, and I nod my head and swing my hips from side to side while I wait for the bartender to return from oblivion. When she finally gets back to me, I place the order for Dawn and I.

"I'm starting to think you may be stalking me." A slight country drawl in my ear makes me turn around. "Ey, Ms. Henton, right?" Tau smiles as he leans in and brushes his lips on my cheek.

"Uh, hey . . ." I hesitate, thinking of the last DM he sent me.

"I think I'm starting to like New York."

"Look, I saw your message . . ."

"Yo boy!" I'm interrupted as Blair reappears. He walks up, giving Tau a handshake and hug. "My man. I'm so glad you made it out. I thought you were giving me the Hollywood 'I'll make it.'"

"Aw man, never that. If I say it, Imma do it," Tau replies.

"Carli! You good?" Blair asks. "We have a tab. I hope you're not paying for drinks. Or is this guy buying you drinks?" He pats Tau play-fully on the shoulder.

"Oh, I didn't know." My eyes widen.

"My darling, these are on me! Give her whatever card back, please! These two beautiful people are good all night," he yells over the music, and the bartender returns with the scotch and my Jameson and ginger ale while motioning for Tau to give her his order.

"Thanks!"

"All good," Blair says and smiles as he spots Dawn in the VIP and heads her way, shuffling through the various bodies standing and wait-ing for the show to begin.

"Blair buying you drinks, huh?"

"I was just at a meeting with him and Dawn this morning."

"Nah, nah, I'm just saying Blair's good peoples. If he likes you, that's a good thing. He's been my man since way back."

The young lady returns with two shots of D'ussé and I watch as Tau's eyes scan the room. He motions one of the shots toward his se-curity guard, Mark, who looks at him with a blank stare. He laughs and downs both, shooting the empty glasses back over to the bartender before dropping a fifty down as a tip.

"I'm going to head over," I say, motioning to the VIP area.

"Me too." We follow Mark's lead through the dark club. "I guess this may be like a first date, huh?"

"Not at all." I roll my eyes as Dawn waves Tau over and the DJ an-nounces that Aminah will be coming on in five minutes.

The place is crawling with execs from Sony, and I wish I knew how to maneuver talking Garter business and somehow mentioning my own music. The pain of missing my opportunity to talk to Blair is still fresh.

I decide to distract myself by watching Tau effortlessly work the room. He takes photos with some of the folks he knows and some he clearly doesn't. He's generous with his time, attentive. But he seems to know exactly where I am in the room even when his focus is elsewhere.

Our orbits collide when we end up side by side near the stage. As I try to wander away, he grabs hold of my wrist, gently signaling for me to stick close. I should pull away, but his touch sends a warm jolt through my body. Instead, I join in the conversation with a rep from one of the streaming platforms as Tau's fingers sway back and forth at his side discreetly finding mine. Tau introduces me as a part of his team at Garter before thanking the rep for always giving his music top billing on the playlists they curate.

The lights dim and a single spotlight illuminates Aminah, who's center stage. She's holding on to the mic with two hands and belts out her first note, which has perfect pitch. The band picks up her cue. Scanning the crowd, she repeats the same note as she goes into her first record, which I think I've heard somewhere before.

"Dope, right?" Tau asks. He's close enough for me to hear him over the music.

"Definitely," I say, nodding.

"I'm hoping we can get on a record together."

"That would be different."

"Yeah, I'm working on some different things while I'm here."

He takes a sip of his third drink and moves in closer. Everyone's attention is on the stage. For a second, it's like he's a normal guy and I have to remind myself he's Tau Anderson.

Aminah is killing it. Her voice is different from what's out there. It's bluesy, a nice contrast to her contemporary lyrics and look. And damn, she can really play the guitar. I love singers who are also players. My dad was always adamant about me learning an instrument and not solely singing. I spent long nights studying, perfecting new chords so I could impress him. Envy creeps up as I watch how free Aminah is onstage. I try to imagine her singing one of my songs.

Tau leans in and whispers in my ear, "So, what are you getting into after this?"

"There's always an after with you."

"Long days, longer nights, you know? I like to move around. There's always somewhere to pull up."

"Heading home," I say, rocking to the midtempo Aminah plays.

"Oh, word?" he says with shock in his dark brown eyes.

"It's been a long day."

"Well, where are you? Maybe we can take a ride and I can drop you off."

"Not a chance," I say without thinking. I look over at Dawn. She's about six feet to the right of us with various bodies in between. She's nodding along at Blair, touching his forearm when she talks, but she keeps stealing glances in my direction. "I came with my boss; I'm leaving with my boss."

"You really going to play this game, huh?"

"I don't play games, Tau. But it was good seeing you." I pat him on the shoulder and head over to Dawn.

"Ha!" he laughs and swirls the brown liquid in his glass.

We stay for a couple more songs before saying our goodbyes and Tau waves, looking out over the top of his glass. I can feel his stare penetrating my back. I turn around hoping to catch his eye, but Tau's focus is on a MAC Makeup Girl in a tight dress who has found her way into the open space beside him. Figures. The warm breeze on the other side of the doors brings me back from whatever fantasy Tau Anderson was selling.

I'm not quite sure how I lose Talia in the small aisles of this grocery store, but she's nowhere to be found between the rows of cereal boxes and cans of Glory's soul food. Peeking down each one, I look for her bold tribal-printed cardigan and messy bun. We're grabbing night-in essentials to ensure our movie-watching experience is up to par. Thankfully, her meeting was canceled for the evening, so she was able to squeeze me into her schedule.

As I stand in the middle of the narrow aisle trying to decide whether I want homestyle popcorn or lightly buttered, an older woman with sturdy legs bumps me with her wide hips and then looks at me with disdain as if I had bumped into her.

"Wah do this feisty girl?" I hear her say in a thick Jamaican accent as she approaches the counter. Rolling my eyes, I pull the Pop Secret homestyle popcorn off the shelf and continue on my hunt for Talia.

"How is it you always disappear in here?" I finally spot her picking out mangoes in the back corner. "I was about to have to tell this auntie about herself."

"Ma'am, we are about the only non-Jamaicans in this neighbor-hood, you don't want beef unless it's in a patty."

I shake my head as we put our things on the counter. I pull a ten out of my new fanny pack to cover my end of the bill.

"Pretty gals, whatagwan? Seventeen." The store owner smiles, the light reflecting off his shiny silver cap.

"Thank you!" Talia smiles as she grabs the bags.

The cars buzz down Utica Avenue as we pass the vague storefronts of "Checks Cashed" and random value stores. The men ogle as we make our way back to the apartment with bags in tow. I would love to know what woman has ever met her husband from unwarranted street harassment turned to love. I doubt it has ever happened. Yet you couldn't avoid the advances.

Pushing through our door, I place the bags I'm responsible for on the breakfast bar. Talia's going on and on about contract negotiations and this class she's excited to take this semester. I nod and smile as I gather the papers sprawled across the counter. Before we left, I was going over the songs I plan to perform at Palomar's on open mic night. It was my process to test out my songs with a crowd. See how they re-ceived them and to work on my performing chops. It is a sweet place, a refuge from being on the go in the city that never sleeps.

"Are you coming to Palomar's?" I interrupt her, essentially think-ing out loud at this point.

"Oh, uhm, yes, that's the plan, but I'll have to let you know for certain." She opens the fridge as I hand her groceries.

"Okay, cool. Let me know. I'm going to stash these papers in my room."

I take my phone out of my bag, remembering that I should tweet about the open mic too. This time around I decided to share the event. It was so hard for me to put myself in the forefront, but I knew it was something I had to do if I ever wanted to get any further in my music career than writing songs in Red's studio. Malik got his start at

Palomar's and now he was a guitar player for Tau. Maybe my talent would be discovered there, too.

You're still coming to Palomar's Friday, right? I send a text to Dylan.

Wouldn't miss it, he hits me right back.

His response calms some of the nerves I already feel bubbling up. I sit on my bed covered by a printed quilt from Jungalow and toggle to my Twitter app. There staring back at me is the DM from Tau. I wonder if I'll keep running into him while he's in the city. I mean, New York is this huge place, but the industry, well, it's so small. Over and over, you see the same jerks. The ones who told me to send them records and then I never heard from them. The ones who told me the music wasn't good enough. Folks always ducking and dodging while trying to maintain appearances.

I sit with my thoughts for a minute before placing the papers in my notebook and on the wooden nightstand for safe keeping. It rests on top of an overflowing dish full of costume jewelry and the Jesmyn Ward book I'd been trying to get to. There were a few new tunes I was looking forward to trying out but in the interest of friendship, I turn my musical mind off along with the gold table lamp.

"Hey! Did you get lost?" Talia yells from the living room.

"Sheesh, can I have a minute?" I throw the phone on the bed and hustle back out.

"So, what are you thinking?" I ask.

"Well, you know Netflix has tons of B movies we haven't gotten to yet," Talia offers.

She curls up on the couch under a purple quilt. The smell of processed cheese heating on our frozen pizza in the oven invades the air while we scroll through titles.

"Well, there's one with Larenz Tate." I grin wide.

"Carlisa Henton, that man is a million years old." She rolls her eyes.

"I wasn't a fan back in the day but it's like he gets better with time." I settle down into the large orange wing chair.

"I can't. Who else is in this? Oh okay, yeah, I can watch, look at the costar, it's Lance Gross." She play-humps the air and I toss a throw pillow at her.

"Let's start this thing, puhlease!"

At various points we yell at the screen, delightfully sickened at the awful story line yet somehow we're still entertained. The plot is predictable, the drama actually comedic, and the acting a little subpar but not terrible enough to quit the movie.

The pizza crusts stack up on our plates and the half-eaten bag of popcorn is as fragrant as when we took it out of the microwave. As the credits roll, Talia pops up from a mountain of pillows and begins gathering our mess to take to the kitchen.

"I knew it was him the whole time."

"You didn't know, that actually shocked me."

"I knew, believe me," she laughs. "You're always oblivious."

"Well, sue me for wanting to enjoy the movie without having to try to figure the whole thing out." I grab our wineglasses and follow closely behind her to the kitchen.

"How was the thing with Dawn last night?"

"It was cool. Aminah is amazing. Super-dope artist, so it was nice to see her. Oh, and Tau showed up."

"Oh, and Tau showed up," she mimics. "You gonna say it nonchalantly like that?" She puts her hand on her hip.

"What did *you* do last night?" I ask, leaning over the counter.

"Changing the subject, I see. Anyway, talked to Mama Reddington."

"How's she?"

"Good. My sister wants to explore Rome for a year. My parents aren't having it. Which is a whole thing. I listened to her fuss and then got about a few lines written and was out. I was thankful for a night to go to sleep at a reasonable hour."

"Ha! Tiff is definitely the wild card."

"Deadass! Tyler is getting his PhD, I'm in law school, and she wants to explore. She thinks she's white." She shakes her head and turns off the lights.

Laughing, I bid Talia adieu as I head to my room for the night. I consider messing around with the guitar but decide to aimlessly scroll apps on my phone instead after tying up my hair and putting on a pair of sweats.

As I read through the day's events according to Black Twitter, a small red notification pops up on the bottom of my screen.

I got in the studio with Aminah today. She's incredible.

A remix to "Pop That"? I reply sarcastically without thinking.

You got jokes. What you doing up so late?

All of a sudden, I'm in a full-blown conversation with Tau Anderson via DM. And it's actually about great music. Surprisingly, we have some similar tastes. We agree that Jay is the GOAT, Miguel's *Kaleidoscope Dream* was a perfect R&B album, and he puts me on to a new artist named Khalid. We do, however, get stuck on J. Cole vs. Kendrick for a bit.

All I'm saying is people sleep on Cole because he doesn't do a ton of interviews and whatnot. He's not so in your face, I write.

We all know how lyrically sound Cole is. But come on, Kendrick is . . . Kendrick.

As the DMs fly I can't help but remember his faint aroma of mint and cognac as he whispered in my ear. I toggle between apps and field a few random thoughts from Dylan on some lyrics we're working on together but find myself awaiting Tau's next response. I even pace back and forth in my room before snuggling under the covers with the phone situated on my chest.

Every time I feel it buzz, I find myself loosening up. He mentions his hopes about actually winning a Grammy after being nominated multiple times. I try to assure him that as much as we all want to be recognized, myself included, a trophy doesn't validate the art. The art is what gives those institutions any type of relevance. I consider whether I should tell him that I'm a songwriter too, but I don't want to sound too thirsty, like I'm fishing for an opportunity.

Before I know it, I drift off in awe of our exchange.

Friday comes faster than a Usain Bolt race. Developing shoot concepts kept the days full. We were planning looks, the shot sequences, and working with agencies to book talent. It felt like it was just yesterday that Tau sauntered into the office and here we were hustling to get things ready for his first shoot with us. Still, I found some time to scribble out my set list in the small notebook always homed in my backpack. I'd written a brand-new tune last week and wanted to throw it into the mix. The chords to one of my favorite Lauryn Hill songs had stopped evading me so my set was shaping up nicely. I skip out of the building on time today in anticipation of the evening.

Although I'd been doing the Palomar open mic for a bit, this was the first time I invited people I know aside from Talia. I've always been a little shy about singing my own songs but trying out a few new tunes in front of an audience was worth the nerves. That was a part aspiring songwriters missed about the process. It wasn't just personal therapy, the words needed to resonate with other people to generate revenue and an audience. I never thought of myself as an artist, but I couldn't deny the feeling being onstage gave me.

I'm so sorry I can't make it tonight.

A text from Talia. She was trying to get a head start on an important review with the hopes of her school selecting it for publishing, so she needed to put in a few more hours at the library. It was our dance, Talia and me. I was usually tied up with Dawn and she was trapped in the library cramming for a big paper or presentation.

Thankfully, I'm able to get home from work with enough time to change and get my mind right but not much else. I put my things together and head toward the door with my guitar in tow. The air had a chill now, so I grab my motorcycle jacket, lock the door, and duck into the rideshare waiting at the door.

When I walk into Palomar's, the place is already full of patrons eating. Some folks occasionally look up when someone worthwhile hits the stage. Between acts, the DJ plays a few songs. Kendrick Lamar's and Rihanna's voices consume the place with their song "Loyalty." I spot Red and Dylan at a table in the corner.

"Yo, Hollywood!" Red smiles and gets up to give me a hug.

"You look amazing." Dylan takes in my bright orange satin shirt revealing just enough cleavage with my delicate nameplate chain centered. It's tucked into a funky pair of blue pants with maroon and orange stripes.

"Thanks! You guys want a drink?"

"You buying? Oh yeah, we want a drink." Red downs the drink in front of her. Dylan shakes his head in dismay and watches me as I walk toward the bar.

I make my way back before the next act starts. Placing the drinks on the table, Dylan pulls out the dark cherrywood chair next to him for me to sit.

"This guy can really blow," he says while leaning in.

"He's no you." I bump shoulders with him.

He wasn't Dylan but the tall, bearded brother is definitely hitting all the notes. He stands in front of the black backdrop with draped fairy lights, laying it all out on his rendition of "Prototype."

I'm up next. I say a prayer under my breath. Singing in front of people is all about pushing myself. The first time I ever stepped into a booth at a recording studio, I was mortified. Nothing came out. I couldn't get past the mental aspect of being comfortable enough with my own voice. Tagging along to a couple vocal lessons with Dylan proved helpful, but I'd been singing all my life. Finding my voice taught me everything I wanted was outside my comfort zone. Singing at open mics was the start. Covering some of my favorite songs live helped me dig into the important things I wanted to say in my own music. Embodying the performing, writing, and being completely vulnerable onstage helped me discover a new level of artistry.

"Next up, we have Carlisa Henton!" The emcee for the evening introduces me and all the nerves shoot through my body. But that's the thing with adrenaline—when you learn how to use it, it's an asset.

I grab my guitar and walk up to the side of the small stage. The applause is comforting as I sit on the stool and adjust the microphone in front of me. I search the crowd for a place where I can keep my eyes so I don't get too nervous, and I settle on the large clock above the door. It was a trick my dad taught me. Looking down at my guitar, I pluck a few strings to make sure I am in tune.

"How y'all feeling? Are y'all all right?" The crowd cheers and some respond with "Yeah!"

The small stage lights are bright, but I see a thin figure with a hood over their head walk in the door and slide into a corner of the bar.

"I'm gonna sing a few songs for you guys, I hope that's okay." Cheers erupt from the intimate room. There are a few folks on dates, a couple groups of ladies hanging out, and the stragglers populate the bar. It's warm and inviting. The dark wood gives Palomar's character, and the aroma of smoked barbecue wings reminds my stomach I haven't eaten since lunch. "This one is called 'Catch Me.'"

From the first chord, I relax into my set. Everything else melts away at that moment. My hand strums the strings and the words flow out. Being onstage is a natural high a nonperformer may never understand. It's a conversation between my guitar and me and the audience.

"See I started off chasing dreams / but fell into reality / realized you wasn't next to me / and was it all worth it?" I sing from my diaphragm, as I was taught.

It was a song I was hoping would find its way to Rihanna. I never recovered from *Anti*. That album had me obsessed with working with her someday.

"You ever felt like that?" I offer to the crowd. "Like sometimes you're just running so fast after a dream without taking stock of all you're losing on the way?" A few audience members give me some love.

As I finish my last song, the hooded stranger from earlier claps enthusiastically in the back. Dylan and Red stand cheering and clapping on my right. It's so satisfying to be well received.

"That's my time, guys!" I wave and take a short bow. I'm greeted by a couple of people as I walk off the stage.

"That was phenomenal. How can I follow you?" a short guy with full cheeks asks.

"Oh, uhm, I don't post much, but my handle is itscarlihenton." He nods as he hits Follow on his phone.

"I'll be looking out for more stuff," he says before heading back to his seat.

"'Ex-Factor' is one of my absolute favorites. I so needed to hear that tonight," a young woman says. Her expression is reflective of the solace Ms. Hill's music so often brought me. "Can we take a picture?"

I'm so flattered by the fanfare. Who did they think I was? The wonder in their eyes though, it was like how I would feel if I were meeting

Diane Warren or something. Instead of running for the nearest exit, I relax and give each person the time and attention they deserve. Their smiles are warm and their passion genuine. I make my way back over to Red and Dylan; they have the biggest grins on their faces.

"I gotta pee."

"TMI. Why do women always have to announce that?" Dylan shakes his head.

"Sorry," I laugh.

"We'll wait for you to get back so we can cut out," Red jumps in. "You killed it. You're getting more impressive by the day, girl."

"Red! Thank you!" I'll always owe Red for being the first person who took a chance on me. We like to think we can do it all on our own, but in this business, you need other people. She's definitely on my list of names to thank when I give my first acceptance speech.

"Yeah, what you tryna be, my competition?" Dylan scrunches up his face playfully.

"Ha! Never." I couldn't hold a candle to Dylan. And I had my heart set on writing. The spotlight terrified me.

I turn to walk toward the restroom opposite the bar. As I approach the hallway, someone whispers my name. I turn around, following the voice. Tau sees the shock in my eyes and puts his finger to his mouth.

"Shhh."

"What are you doing here? How are you here? What the—" He puts his finger close to my mouth now. We're standing in the narrow hallway that leads to the restrooms.

"I said shhh . . ." he says with a laugh. "You posted it on your Twitter. I follow you, remember? You know Twitter is a public forum, right?"

I shift my feet, looking past him to see if Dylan and Red are looking this way.

"Yes, yes," I stammer. "I did post it on Twitter."

"But you forgot to mention it during our direct messages." He pauses. "So, I figured we could finish our conversation tonight. This, you as an artist, that's a new development."

I take a step back. I'm suddenly leaning against the wall. Tau takes a step toward me and he's too close for comfort. I can smell his scent, taste it even. What was that damn scent and why was it so intoxicating?

"You left this whole part out of your Ms. Professional routine the other day."

"That's because I'm not an artist, I'm a writer." I cross my arms.

"What I just saw up there? That was something special." He lifts an eyebrow dramatically, like The Rock. "Let me guess, you're heading home after this? I've asked enough times." He laughs. "You should let me drop you off there. Maybe we finish this healthy musical banter. I mean damn, shawty, I liked those records. You're hella talented."

I don't let that part sink in. Tau Anderson said he likes my songs. "First of all, how are you here without anyone?" I reach for my chain.

"Mark is right at the corner. He can drive us to your spot."

"My spot? We've been through this already. How do I know you are not actually a crazy stalker?"

"Let's be honest, I could have any girl in here let me take her home, but I guess you're more interesting to me. And your boss ain't here tonight, so I figure you may be out of excuses."

As annoyingly cocky as it sounds, he's right. He reaches for my hand, which I let him hold for a split second before I yank it away.

"I'm not sure what I wasn't clear about here. I can't do this with you."

"I'm not asking you to do anything but let me take you home. You have to get there, right? You rather some strange Uber driver than me?" He smirks.

"So you want to be my Uber driver?" I squint, hunching my shoulders. "You're trouble."

"Well, you keep saying no, but your eyes are saying yes." He keeps inching closer and I have nowhere to go. "You seem like you like a little trouble."

I look over at Dylan and Red. Red shifts her weight from her left to right foot and Dylan looks at his watch. What would I even tell them? Why was I considering this, knowing it was likely a recipe for disaster? But there was this nagging feeling that he wasn't quite what I assumed he was.

"Look, if I can guess your favorite album of all time, then will you let me take you?" He smirks.

"The chances are slim, so go head," I say with a shrug.

"All right, so look, outwardly, it's Lauryn. Since you play, you sing, you write. Of course, *Miseducation* would be it to the naked eye."

"That's an easy guess, I covered her song."

"Aht, I wasn't done," he says, holding his index finger up to his dimple. "That's outwardly, but really, it's Bianca's debut, *Painted*."

"What makes you say that?" I try to keep a poker face.

"The red Chucks. You've had them on every time I've seen you."

"Lucky guess. I am not impressed."

"That's cool. But a deal is a deal, so figure it out, baby girl," he says, before taking a step back. "I'll be waiting in the big black truck outside." He reaches up and grabs one of my curls and lets it bounce back. I feel a chill in my body. He pulls his hood farther over his head and walks toward the exit.

I lean my head back and bang it softly against the wall. What am I about to do? I couldn't ignore what a huge opportunity this was for me if Tau was serious about my music. I take a deep breath and walk back over to Red and Dylan, hoping I think of something that doesn't sound completely like a lie on my way back. I don't. I give them some lame excuse about needing to head to the store to grab a few things for the apartment before heading home after we get outside of the venue.

"I maybe thought we could catch up." Dylan's posture deflates.

"I know, I'm sorry, we'll link I promise," I assure him.

"Look, Rob is waiting on me so we out, Dylan. Our guy is pulling up," Red says, looking at her phone.

"It's all good, guys, really. I so appreciate you guys coming out and supporting me tonight. Means everything." I reach out for hugs. Dylan throws me a look.

I wave as I head in the opposite direction where the big black Cadillac Escalade waits at the corner. While Red is far up ahead, Dylan lingers. I turn back and catch his eye. He tosses his head up slightly. As I turn back toward the truck, Tau lowers the window.

"So you figured it out?" He smiles and opens the truck door for me to jump in. Mark comes around to grab my guitar and puts it in the trunk.

"That's your homeboy?" Tau nods toward Dylan, who is finally walking to catch up with Red.

He watches Dylan disappear into the door of a Camry.

"Yeah, we make music together. He's a really talented artist." More important than explaining who Dylan was, I had to figure out what the hell I was doing riding home with a client.

It was about a twenty-minute ride to Brooklyn from Palomar's. The inside of the truck is warm and luxurious. All Cadillacs seem to smell the same. Maybe it was the smell of money. I study Tau's face as he mouths the words to "Colors" pumping through the speakers. He has tiny lines that form near his eyes when he smiles and his pink lips poke out enough to be enticing.

"Amos Lee? What do you know about Amos?" I ask.

"Love Amos Lee." He raises his eyebrow.

"Hmmm."

"What? I'm only supposed to like freaky R&B songs, right, or hip-hop? Y'all kill me," he says, laughing.

"Y'all?"

"You this feisty all the time? I mean, I like it, but I want to prepare myself." He takes his wallet and phone out of his pocket and places them in the cup holder between us. Mark is up front looking like he's not paying attention, but I can't imagine he's not listening to our conversation. I wonder what it's like to never be alone.

I try to dial it back. I did decide to let this man take me home, so I should show that I have manners.

"So, you feel like people put you in a box?" I ask while pulling on my hair.

"All the time." He pauses. "I'm a whole person. But it's like you get frozen in a frame that's one album out of your life. One thought. I like a lot of music. And I want to do a lot of different music." He looks at me and his gaze is piercing.

"If I am going to be able to talk to you, I need you to stop looking at me like that." I look out the window as we whiz past shop after shop. The lights are all a blur. The city is alive, and I am reminded of why I love New York so much.

"Like what?" He leans his head back, exposing small moles on his neck. "I've never seen someone who looks like you. I mean your beautiful skin and that hair."

I might be blushing, but I am not light enough for anyone to see it.

"I get it from my momma." I pump my arms in the air imitating Beyoncé's Uh-Oh dance and he rears back and laughs.

"Where you from?"

"Not far from you, actually. I grew up in Severn, but my mom is an Afro-Latina. So that's part of the look, I guess?"

"Oh, so now who's the stalker?"

"Except your life story is plastered on the internet and you're my boss's client who I've had to research. So, I know you grew up in Maryland too. Eastern Shore, right?"

"I was born in Virginia. But yeah, Moms moved to Maryland when I was still young." He nods while contemplating his next thought. "I want to play you something. Something new."

"Oh. All right, let's hear it."

He searches through his phone for the track and tells Mark to turn it up. Closing my eyes, I try to get even more comfortable to listen. The music pumps from the speakers and Tau's falsetto echoes throughout the truck.

"Bend over, touch your toes, crawl to me, telling me you want more." When I open my eyes, he's nodding along to the beat and inside I'm cringing. This sounds like every other Tau Anderson record from the last few years. Nothing special. I'm humbled that he would play something new for me, but this just wasn't it.

The record fades out and I nod slowly without saying anything.

"What?" He looks over and I see it. The vulnerability. That doesn't seem to change no matter how far in the game you get.

"I mean . . ." I have no idea how to say it. But being me, I find a way. "It's cool, but it's nothing special. It's the same old Tau. You said you were working on some different things, right? I mean, I remember listening to the *Black Light* album and thinking, *This project is so thoughtful and honest. I have to write for him someday."* I fiddle with my chain.

"That was a good album, but damn, that kind of hurts," he says, rubbing the scruffy hairs on his chin.

"Look, I know the game. *Black Light* might not have sold like the label wanted it to, but that's where you built your core. Don't forget about them. You said you don't want people to put you in a box, right? Don't let them."

"Hmm . . ." he says pensively. I'm sure that I've offended him and look out the window.

Mark takes the corner sharply and without being able to brace myself, I end up halfway in Tau's lap. I pull myself up and push my hair back in place. He finds it hilarious, so much so that I have to laugh too, which breaks the awkward silence.

"So she does know how to laugh."

"Sometimes the boxes we're in we create ourselves, is all I'm saying."

"Or the label. But that's a whole other beast."

"I can imagine."

We pull up on my block and I tell him it's a house two doors down from my actual apartment. This could still be stranger danger.

"When can I see you again?" He reaches out and strokes my arm, and all the hairs on the back of my neck stand up.

"You seem really cool, but I can't. I mean, I'm kind of flattered, but I can't hang out with a client."

"Well, I do also like your songs. I'd like to hear more of them sometime. You know, you might be able to help me get out of the box." He draws a square in the air as he says it.

He was going to try to play that card. I mean, getting a record on one of his projects would be everything. But I didn't want to get that chance based on him finding me attractive. I thought about Dawn's warning and quite frankly, I knew better.

I pause to think about whether I'm crazy for not giving in to his advances. He is probably one of the most beautiful men I've ever seen. His persistence was throwing me off. "Look, I'll see you at the Merlin shoot, okay?"

"I told you, I'm not here long. I'll only have about two weeks after that."

Mark looks up in the rearview mirror as if saying *Your move.*

"I'll have to let you know."

"Ha! That's crazy. Shawty got me out here working. I have to say, it's been a long time but I'm up for the challenge. Especially after what I heard tonight."

I open the heavy door of the truck. Mark walks around to grab the guitar and hands it over to me. He smiles and shakes his head.

I close the door and walk slowly, as this is not actually my building.

"So, when can I at least get your number?" Tau asks from the open window.

"You seem pretty active on Twitter. You can always find me there."

"Solid." He shakes his head and throws up a peace sign as Mark hops back in the front seat.

"I'm good, you don't have to wait."

"Oh, so I can't see your real spot?" he yells as Mark pulls away slowly. I watch the large Escalade emblem get smaller down our street and laugh to myself. Hustling down to my building, I run up the stairs to see if Talia is still awake.

Talia was knocked out when I got home last night, so I decide to keep my special Uber ride to myself. The more I thought about it, the more I realized I should probably keep it close to my chest. My mom used to tell me, "If you want to keep a secret, you keep it to yourself." As much as I love Talia, I don't want it getting out to anyone that I may have had a moment with Tau. Too much was at stake.

I get up early so I can head to Red's spot. She has some exciting news she didn't want to tell me over the phone. The plan is to finish up the last record we worked on with Dylan.

Red is waiting for me at the door to the studio when I arrive. Her red hair is pulled up in a tight bun. Ushering me in, her eyes are wide with excitement as she closes the door and takes her seat in front of the board. I look around for Dylan.

"Is he late again?" I ask, putting my bag down and taking a sip from my large green tea that I stopped to get on the way.

Red wanted to talk to me first. She gave us staggered times so she could get me alone. When Dylan wasn't late, a lot of times we'd link up to come together. I didn't like the idea of keeping this secret. We were a team and he was my friend, but I figured it was for a good reason. As she turns around in her chair, I peep her exclusive crushed velvet Jordan 11s.

"Where do you even find these sneakers?"

"Oh, these old things?" She turns her foot from side to side.

"Oh yeah, those old things," I mimic and shake my head, lifting my red Chucks in the air.

"You know me." She pulls her chair in closer and her eyes get serious. "So, I got a call about a recording session with an artist tomorrow. Their producer wants us to come in and work on some songs and they're going to pay us for our time."

"What?" I say, confused. "Well, who is it?"

"They wouldn't say. Said they're kind of big, so they didn't want to let anyone know who it was. I don't ask questions when there is cash involved. We do so much of this work for free trying to get on."

Her words are coming in slow motion as I do my best to process. This never happens. I mean, as a writer, you literally do all the work up front and hope that somewhere down the line maybe you'll see a deposit from BMI or ASCAP one day. The big-league writers, they were the ones who were paid for their time.

"Well, I'm in. This freaking sounds amazing. I wish I knew who it was so I could prepare. I mean, how did they even hear about us?"

"They mentioned Dylan's records," she says, turning her gaze over to the board in front of her. "Anyway, we need to be there at four tomorrow. That gives you enough time after church, right?"

"Yeah." But then it sinks in that Red must have called me in early because they didn't ask about Dylan. Not sure how well that was going to go over. "So, no Dylan?" I ask carefully.

"Nah. Well, I mean Dylan is an artist. As much as he writes, they kind of only asked about us because they liked the records we did for him. So, I mean, let's go in and find out what we're working with first before we tell him. Gucci?"

"I guess so. I mean, it sounds like a great opportunity."

"It is a great opportunity, okay?" she emphasizes. "It could be the break both of us need and this will only help what we're doing with Dylan in the long run."

A quick knock on the door commands our attention and I swallow the excitement that had been stirring in my chest.

Dylan walks in ready to get down to business. He squeezes out a "hello" with little enthusiasm as he heads directly to the booth. No candles, no oil, no small talk. Red looks at him puzzled because that's never quite the way it goes. Dylan tried to waste at least thirty minutes at the beginning of every session.

"You coming in trying to get straight down to business?" Red asks before he opens the booth door.

"I'm trying to focus. Is that a crime?" He puts his bag down and pulls up his jogger pants.

"Come on, what's up witchu?" I chime in.

"That's kind of funny because you definitely gave us some BS after the show last night. I mean, we came out for you, and you ditched us." He closes the door and sits down in the chair before throwing Red a look.

"Aww, come on. I told you it wasn't that serious last night." Red rolls her eyes. "Dylan seems to think you met up with someone that you didn't want to tell us about. I mean, it ain't none of my business, but you were a little evasive." Red shrugs and looks for the song we're supposed to be working on.

"I just, something came up. Why are you making a deal about it?" I ask.

"Nothing." He grabs his phone and heads into the booth.

The tension in the air is suffocating. Making music comes from an emotional place. It's nearly impossible to do good work with Dylan's attitude in the way. It's all about synergy in the studio so I walk in after him.

We're practically on top of each other since the booth is so tight.

Red's voice comes through Dylan's headphones. "Imma let y'all work that out." She turns up an episode of *Snowfall*.

"What's the deal, Dylan? I don't want you to be upset with me."

He smirks and turns to face me. "Did you or did you not somehow meet up with Tau Anderson last night?"

"What?" Shit, how did he know? He must have seen me get into Tau's Cadillac.

"Yo, be honest. Like why are you lying to us? It's us. It's me." He takes the headphones off and looks at me.

"I . . . didn't, I mean, he kind of showed up at the spot and wanted to talk about a few things from our meeting earlier in the week."

"Oh, really?" He could see right through me.

"Dylan, I'm trying to understand, why would that make you pissed at me? We were all going home."

"Nothing. You don't get it. Two years we've been working to-gether." He mutters something else but I don't catch it. "You know what, never mind. It's all good. Just don't be *that* girl, Carli," he sneers.

"What girl? I'm about my business, Dylan, and if anyone knows that, it's you." I get serious with my credibility in question.

"Right, that's what you say, but I guess it takes a dude that's on to get you to change your mind. Now can we work?" He places the head-phones back over his head.

Why was he tripping on me so hard? I mean, I heard his story about his friend, but I wasn't going there with Tau. He took me home. Why was my professionalism in question when nothing happened? It would be my mistake to make if anything popped off with Tau.

I walk out of the booth and plop down next to Red. I don't even feel like working anymore, but I don't want to be *that* girl who can't put her feelings to the side either. Red looks at me.

"Y'all good?"

"Not really, but let's get this song done." I hit the spacebar and the record plays.

Somehow drama had found its way into my safe haven. The one place of peace I didn't have to try so hard to put on my best face. One of my best friends was pissed at me for lying.

We bang out the finishing touches on the record without saying much to each other. It never felt like work when I was in the studio with Dylan and Red, but today definitely felt like I was punching a clock. After the session my mind is all over the place. I decide to head straight home instead of stopping in the park. I have to meet Red at Stadium Studios in Times Square tomorrow. As much as I'm looking forward to it, this falling out with Dylan feels like a little gray cloud over such great news.

On the dusty train, I scroll through my phone and see I have another DM.

At this meeting and all I can think about is your smart ass. They love this record I played for you last night. But I can't help but think you might be right.

You seem to somehow be getting me in trouble with everyone I know. That can't be a good sign, I send back.

I don't know what that's about. But I know when I used your pitch about Black Light building my core, it felt like they were hearing me for the first time in a long time. We might be able to help each other. Send me your number. For real. Being in these DMs has me feeling mad thirsty. There's a laughing emoji at the end of his message.

I smile to myself on the train. The thought of us being able to help each other aside from the flirting lingers. Why couldn't I get something out of the deal as well?

Feeling emotionally drained from the day's events, I oblige.

Good morning, Carlisa! I'm not sure which one I like better. Carli or Carlisa. Tau's text message is the first thing I see in the morning.

Morning. You're up early, I reply.

Photo shoot for an interview.

Nice! I'm headed to church. But have a good shoot.

Church. Aw man, I really gotta straighten up and fly right, huh?

Don't. They barely let me in, I send back and kick my leg out of the covers so I can make my way to the bathroom. Talia is going to kill me if I make us late another Sunday.

We make it on time but the coolness of Dylan's greeting before he rushes toward the stage irks me. But I can't let it get me down. Two consecutive days in the studio is like solid gold. I made sure to put all my random ideas together so I would have some things to throw out there in the session.

After what feels like an eternity, Pastor Marsh gives the blessing and we're out. We head to brunch with the usual crew. I take down a few mimosas so I'll be a little more relaxed for my big session with the unknown high-ranking artist. Thankfully, we keep the conversation away from dating. Fred is discussing politics. He's speaking passionately about the numerous violent murders of Black men and women at the hands of police. That wasn't really up for debate, as we all agreed something needed to be done. When they killed Wesley Gates earlier this year, you would think New York would have been turned upside down, but life just went on. Whenever I dwelled on it, I couldn't help but feel angry about the lack of care for our people, but I mostly felt helpless. Powerless. I grab a beverage napkin and scribble a note on it.

How Can We Go On? An idea to explore through a song.

After we settle the bill, I gather up my stuff and give hugs to Fred, Mari, and Talia as she reminds me that Dylan was supposed to join us for brunch today. It totally slipped my mind after our exchange or lack thereof at church.

"Yeah, I think he had something else to do," I lie. This was becoming a terrible habit. But I had no time to make up something about why we were beefing.

"Okay, cool. Well, have a good session, Carli! Can't wait to find out who it was with!" Talia says with a wave as I depart from the crew.

I wave back at her before hustling to the train. Normally, I avoided Times Square at all costs, but there were a few different studios in this area. After walking shoulder to shoulder with a family from Pittsburgh, I get to the studio about five minutes early. I take the elevator up and I'm greeted by an older woman who holds up a weathered index finger, the phone to her ear, sitting behind the reception desk.

I'd been in a lot of studios but none as impressive as this. Scanning the room, it's as if a glow radiates from the glass case with Grammys, actual Grammys, in the middle of the reception area. The red walls are filled with platinum and gold plaques including one for *Painted*. I smile at the picture of Bianca in a black tutu and red Chucks. This is the studio her producer, Ige, calls home, though he's rarely ever here and is always traveling.

When I was younger, I always read the liner notes that listed all the personnel who worked on the album. I would rip open the CD covers and scan the booklets not only for the lyrics but for the producers and musicians, hell, even the background vocalists. I wanted to know who the people were who came together to create something so masterful. Ige's name was inside so many of those covers. Right out of the gate he was scoring singles and number one records. Now I was standing in the reception area of his studio.

"Good afternoon, how can I help you?" The receptionist's voice puts an end to my daydreaming.

"I actually have a session here today."

"Hey, Hollywood." Red creeps up from behind me.

"Oh hey! Yeah, I'm with her." I point.

"Great, you're in the A-Room. They'll be out in a few to grab you." She goes back to her computer as Red and I sit down in the plush chairs in the waiting area.

"Carli, Red." We both look up and my face drops. Meck is standing with his arms open wide in a puffy bubble vest with a gaudy chain dripping with diamonds. His pants are baggy, which reminds me of the nineties. Clearly, his fashion sense seemed to have taken a detour.

"Meck?" I say and the sound of his name coming out of my mouth makes the hairs on my arm rise.

"What's up? Y'all ready to work?"

I look at Red, hoping that she comes up with something to say because it's like Ursula from *The Little Mermaid* came and snatched my vocal cords.

"Always," Red says. She starts to walk down the hallway toward Studio A and my brain goes to follow but my legs don't move. She looks back at me, confused. "Carli?"

My brain is firing a million things at once like a stalling car engine. I grab my things slowly and walk toward her to keep from looking completely insane. When we get inside, I try to take in the beautiful studio even though I can't believe the person who called us in is Meck. I put my book bag down on the red couch across from the board.

"I need a minute." I push open the heavy door and start toward the bathroom, but right as I step out I hear the studio door open and close behind me with force. I look back over my shoulder. It's him.

"Hey Carli, I wanted to get you alone for a second." His words corner me as he points to the kitchen off the waiting area.

"Meck, this is bullshit," I start before he even gets a chance to say anything. "Why would you call us? Why would you call me? We're not cool. This is not cool!" I cross my arms and glare at him.

"Whoa, whoa. You're still pissed from years ago?" He's smirking, which incites me.

"Are you serious?" I raise my voice.

"Shhh . . . please don't be all rowdy in this establishment. I came out here because we have an opportunity and I want to make sure you can keep your shit together for us to all get this bag." He steps back and turns his lips up at me.

"I've always been professional. Have you learned to be?"

"Look, you need to relax. Shit happens in this business. It's the business. So either you're going to act like a grown woman or a little girl who can't pull it together for the work."

"Fuck you, Meck." I spin to head to the restroom. "Fuck you!"

I let out a shaky breath once I'm safely behind the door. There's no way I'm giving Meck the satisfaction of seeing me cry. I did have to get my shit together if I was going to be productive in this session.

A few seconds pass. I settle on a plan. I psych myself up to tell Red I'm not participating in the session. In the hallway a short kid with starter locs and a black hoodie with a broken heart on the chest smashes into me. He stumbles backward and checks the large camera hanging around his neck before rushing out a "Sorry" and disappearing down the hallway, with another group of artists that I assume already passed by, toward one of the other studios. It wasn't a painful collision, but I take it as a sign that today just isn't my day. Taking a deep breath, I pull open the door to the A-Room to grab my stuff.

"Carli?" Tau is standing at the board, his arms folded across his chest, talking with Meck when I walk in. He stops midsentence, leaving Meck in the middle of whatever trash he was probably spitting.

Walking over, Tau grabs me up into a hug and gives me a kiss on the forehead. "Hey," he says before holding on to me a little too long. Meck's stare is piercing. His mouth is practically hanging open as he looks from me to Tau.

Red gives me wide eyes as she talks to Frankie K. Mark is seated on a stool in the corner doing a crossword puzzle. I cannot believe that this session is with Tau.

"So Tau is looking for some different sounds and I thought of you two. After Dylan played me some of his new stuff. We wanted to get some fresh takes." Meck pulls two chairs across the hardwood floor close to the board. He sits down in front of the vast array of knobs and faders, facing a huge double-paned window with the live recording room on the other side. Tau is still looking at me intently and I break his stare, focusing my energy on twirling my nameplate chain.

Operation Get the Hell Outta Here doesn't feel so easy all of a sudden. I'm dumbfounded but compose myself for a moment to greet Frankie and Mark before sitting next to Red on the couch against the wall.

"Did you know this session was with Meck?" I say to Red in a hushed tone.

"Meck, yes. Tau? No. He said you guys had peaced it up and I probably should have known not to believe him but . . ." She casts her gaze downward. "Carli, my fault. I thought it would be something good, but I should have talked to you first."

"Yeah, I was about to grab my stuff and leave."

I'm pissed. But I'm also in the studio with Tau. The range of emotion has me all over the place. I needed to be smart about where work like this could take my career.

Meck was the worst kind of industry guy. We were working with Kyra, who was an up-and-coming artist with some buzz, around the time I met Red three years ago. Meck cornered me in the studio one day telling me how beautiful I was and how he couldn't stop thinking about me. I remember feeling so small at that moment. I felt as if everything I had done with Kyra, and in the industry in general, didn't matter because all Meck saw was something to conquer. I've never forgotten the phone call I got the next day.

I practically ran into the Garter bathroom stall when I saw the call come in from Meck, only for him to tell me my writing services for the Kyra project were no longer required. He was clearly upset with me for turning him down.

When he hung up, my dreams of being on a major project evaporated with the dial tone. None of my songs saw the light of day and that project put everyone who worked on it on the map. They replaced me with another writer. I sat by and watched everyone else who worked on the project benefit because I wouldn't compromise my integrity. I was too embarrassed to tell Red what really happened, so she chalked it up to creative differences. Dealing with Meck was my wake-up call to how cutthroat the music business could be. I had to learn how to move smarter. So many men in the business were collecting protégées like trophies.

I try to get my head in the game while we listen to some of the other new songs that Tau recorded, including the latest with Aminah. He sounds amazing. Much different than what he played for me the other night. This sounds special. Less 808s and more guitar- and piano-driven. He's fusing some of his hip-hop roots with the singer/songwriter elements he apparently likes. I remember us listening to Amos Lee. I know that Red and I can fit into this sound.

"You sound great. Now this I like," I say, lost in the rhythm flowing from the speakers. Red has her eyes closed and I know that her mind is working with what she can add to the sound.

"Thanks!" He looks up and smiles, nodding his head to the music while locking eyes with me.

"Tau, you're good, right? I'm gonna head out," Frankie chimes in. "Good to see you again, Carli." He gives me that thirsty look from the concert.

"Yeah, I'm good, Frank. See you tomorrow." Tau turns back toward the board showing Meck where he wants to do some ad-libs on the record playing.

"We wanted you to hear this stuff. I mean, if you want, we can work on something. I have the studio until about ten." Tau leans back in his chair looking confident. He's dressed in black sweats with a fresh white pair of Adidas.

"I'm down," Red says enthusiastically. "I probably have to skip out around eight though. I have to go to a family thing with my husband."

"So how do y'all know each other?" Meck asks slyly. That question must have been burning inside of him since I walked back in and Tau seemed so familiar.

"Oh, I'm working with Dawn on some business shit at Garter Media," Tau explains. "But also, remember the new writer I was telling you I met at that spot?"

"Oh yeah, at Palomar's?"

"Well, apparently, you and I have great taste. In writers." Tau grins and winks in my direction.

"Oh, shit. Well, yeah." Meck nods as I stare at him. Amid my rage at having to be in such close quarters with Meck, I realize Tau mentioned me. Not as some girl he was trying to get to know better, but as a writer he was interested in working with. Maybe he could actually see me, unlike the rest of them who got so caught up in fulfilling their physical desires.

"Red, you have your laptop? We can vibe out and see what happens," Meck says.

They jump right in. Red starts working on the drums while Meck lays some keyboard parts. The chords are beautiful. I must admit, he was a scumbag, but he was also talented. Unfortunately, that was how it often went.

Tau nods along to the music as he starts mouthing some words. He's lost in the rhythm, and I am lost in amazement that I am in the studio with him. Two nights ago, he told me he liked my songs. Now we were here. The circumstances were dreadful, but I was still thankful it was happening.

The afternoon gives way to evening faster than I'd like. Mark heads out to grab dinner while the rest of us listen to what Red and Meck put together. It's a ballad, very cinematic. The stuff I love the most. I can even hear them adding strings to the bridge to really make it big.

"Cool, so we can put some finishing touches on it once y'all come up with the lyrics." Red starts packing her bag to go. "I really wish I could stay. I'm excited about this."

Tau stands to hug her. "Me too. Nice meeting you. I'm here for about three more weeks, so we'll bang it out. Tell hubs you need a clear schedule for a few." He smiles and reaches up to grab the top of the doorway, stretching his slim but muscular body.

Red laughs and nods as she makes her way to the door. Before heading out, she ensures that I'm good sticking around and I am. I don't want to leave. I would stay and write twenty songs with Tau if I could.

"I actually have to head out too. Gotta get with this DJ about playing some of my artist's new records," Meck says.

"Oh man, okay cool." Tau turns. "I'm glad you really went different here. Tired of working with the same cats all the time that are so busy chasing the charts that the music has no soul. Omar is always pressing me about these charts, but I'm like when has that ever been the bar for our music? You can have a hood classic all day and eat good."

"Right. Mar is just Mar, you know? He's a record man and that's what they do. But you know I'm always connected to the next new sound, I wouldn't steer you wrong," Meck boasts. "Imma head out."

Meck's exit is my chance to have the huge console to myself. Tau walks Meck out while giving him the rundown on their recording schedule. I push back the unpleasant memories seeing Meck brought up and focus on the music.

Tau is gone for a minute, so I start playing with some lyric ideas. "Early morning the light filters through the blinds," I sing. Ah, I love that. "Illuminating this perfection I call mine." I nod and write the second line in my book.

The heavy door pushes open and Tau looks strangely serious when he returns. Trying to read him, I close my book but set my pen in it to keep the page. His face is stoic.

"So, you've been pushing this whole 'I'm not an industry girl' with me but—" He stops.

"What are you talking about?" I put my book onto the board and turn to face him.

"You and Meck were a thing and you didn't think you should mention that? You had to know I know him. We've worked together." His words feel biting. "I'm trying to tell him that this is not a place for his bullshit and he's telling me new information."

"Hell no!" I start. Meck must have a death wish.

"Oh . . ." Tau sits back in the black chair waiting for an explanation.

"Is that what he told you? He's the scum of the earth. He tried to freaking come on to me years back. And kicked me off the project we were all working on when I wouldn't give him the attention he was looking for."

"Shit, my fault."

"He's a liar and a pervert. He's lucky I didn't punch him in the nose tonight."

"Whoa, tiger." He shakes his head. "My fault. I've known Meck for years, I know he ain't shit. But it hit me for some reason when he started talking about you. I don't like being the only one that doesn't know something. I was thinking, *Damn, she was kicking all this 'I don't mess with guys in the industry' stuff.*"

"Not normally my thing at all. I've made my mistakes. It's messy, nine times out of ten. Exactly like that situation and I wasn't even involved with him romantically," I say.

"It's hard to know who's for real out here. Just like I know some dudes make it hard for women with real talent."

"Clearly. I mean, Meck took my power at that time and now I have to play nice for a shot at getting my music heard. How crazy is that? People who work with him always excuse his behavior. Like everyone knows he ain't shit but his talent matters more than the women he degrades."

We sit face-to-face in stillness as my words seem to settle.

"Look." Tau pauses, picking his words carefully. "I'm not Meck. I want you to know that. I think you're talented and also gorgeous. But I never want to make it uncomfortable for you. My bad if I came on too strong. And Imma check him about that shit, believe me."

Meck was an absolute jerk. But something felt genuine about Tau. Speaking with him felt easy, without all the celebrity pretenses I'd grown accustomed to. There was so much more behind the hard beats and sexy lyrics. I wanted to see more of that.

He stands up, grabbing me by the arms, and pulls me into a tight hug. Versace. That's the smell. With him this close, I figure it out. But there's something mixed with it that I still can't pinpoint. He brushes my hair back and stares into my eyes long enough for me to be slightly hypnotized before he kisses my forehead. This time, it's welcomed.

"Dinner," Mark says, standing in the doorway. I pull back from the hug and smooth out my ruffled T-shirt.

"Word," Tau says to Mark, unbothered. "I think we're going to split anyway. Right, Carli?" He looks at me.

"What about dinner?" I'm still hungry.

"We can eat in the car. I want to take you somewhere," he says, looking at his watch.

It was against my better judgment, but I still hear myself say "Okay, cool" before I have the chance to deliberate. We pack computers and charger cords and head out. We walk past the front desk that now houses a young, savvy twentysomething with his laptop open.

"Heading out early?" He peers out from behind black frames.

"Yeah, thanks, man," Tau replies. I follow close behind. He turns to me. "It'll be fun. I didn't think we'd finish in time, but you'll be a better date than Mark, anyway." He grins and Mark rolls his eyes as we head downstairs.

We pile into the Escalade with bags from Shake Shack in tow. I still had no idea where we were going, but I'm down for a small adventure, anything to take my mind off bumping into Meck. I chomp down on french fries with no regard to the glances Tau keeps throwing my way.

"The weather is holding up." He looks out the window.

"Where are we going?"

"It's a surprise."

It's not a long ride. Mark pulls up outside the Embassy Suites and I look over at Tau with a vicious side-eye.

"It's not what you think, I'm staying at the Carlyle," he says, laughing. "Damn, girl, it's like your thoughts have a megaphone sometimes."

I stop midbite of my chicken sandwich and laugh at myself because he's right. Mark pulls the car up to the valet. We get out and walk into the brightly lit lobby, which is buzzing. A few people look in our direction, but the thing about New Yorkers is they really didn't care who you are. Sure, Tau looked like someone they should know, but these folks were worried about their own business. My eyes land on a grungy kid hanging around with a camera around his neck. I realize he's the same kid I smashed into in the hallway at the studio. He's still in the hoodie and this time, I notice a bright turquoise ring. I take him in for a while wondering about the coincidence. I mean, photographers were often on the move. We follow a roped-and-stanchioned aisle to the elevator that goes straight to the rooftop.

We get out of the elevator with Mark leading the way. A young woman with a bright and bubbly smile stands at the entrance next to a basket of blankets. Mark takes out his phone and she scans it with her own.

"Welcome, Mr. Anderson." She hands us two blankets and the smell of buttery popcorn invades my senses.

"What is this?"

"You'll see," he says.

We walk out onto the rooftop and the bar is buzzing with patrons. Rows of popcorn boxes line the bar and to the right is a huge screen with rows of chairs in front of it. I look at the sign with a poster of the film *Love Jones* starring Larenz Tate and Nia Long from back in the day.

"Rooftop Cinema Club. This is one of my joints!"

"*Love Jones*, really?" I laugh.

"Have you ever seen it?"

I pause and look up at the sky because I know what's going to come next when I reveal the truth.

"Awwww, shawty, come on, okay, this will be good." He's almost giddy about it, which is such a change from his always-cool demeanor.

"I was young when it came out."

"No excuses, you grown na!"

"All right, all right." We find a few empty lawn chairs at the back. In the darkness, it's hard to see anyone. Mark goes to the bar to grab a few drinks and we settle in under one of the blankets as the film begins.

"All I'm saying is, how she gon go to New York on my boy?" Tau asks as Mark drives.

"He needed to say he wanted her to stay," I say, mindlessly looking out the window.

"Okay, so stay."

"What?" I look over at him confused.

"I don't want this night to end, so stay." He looks right into my eyes and I have to break his stare or else I think all my insides would have melted. "We can get dessert and go to my hotel."

"Tau, I . . ." I start, while reflexively shaking my head from side to side.

"Not like that, I just want to finish this convo. It's very important whose side you're on here or else I don't know if we can keep working together."

"Oh really? It's like that?"

"It's like that. Come on," he pleads, and this time I can't resist. If I was honest with myself, I was enjoying his company too. We pull up in front of the Carlyle after swinging by a small ice-cream shop. The hotel is impressive. I've read about places like this but never stayed in one. I was still on an Airbnb budget when it came to traveling. We pull around to a private entrance to avoid the small group of people gathered up front.

"Aight, Mark!" Tau gets out and closes the door behind him. A doorman greets us right outside the door. We walk through the massive lobby to private elevators that take you to the suites.

"So he does leave eventually," I say.

"Ha! Yeah, I mean, we're together twenty-four-seven. He's literally in the room next to me. But the suite, that's me. Me and you tonight."

"Oh." I wasn't at all prepared for anything to go down tonight. I think I have Minnie Mouse underwear on. I was feeling adventurous for sure, but not that adventurous. I kind of forgot what this was like, hanging out with someone I was attracted to, interested in. I had been so focused on Dylan's project and crushing it at work.

He hits the button for the twenty-seventh floor once we're inside.

I focus on the lights above the doors that indicate each floor we pass. He's sneaking glances in my direction and I pretend not to notice. I follow closely behind him as he navigates the hall. He opens the door and it's the most breathtaking hotel room I've ever seen. Through the large windows, Central Park is visible below. Madison Avenue looks immaculate from this high up. The sky is brightened by lights from the streets and buildings. The pillows are monogrammed with large *C*s on a beige tufted couch and the chandelier makes the living area look like it is sparkling. *How the other half lives*, I think to myself.

"Look, get comfortable. I'm going to take this stuff off."

I'm mildly interested in what I know is happening under those clothes. The tattoos, the six-pack. I slide out of my Chucks. The floors seem too nice to drag my dirty sneakers across. I head to the small dining table and start unpacking our sweet treats.

"Damn, you gonna start without me?" Tau reappears in gray sweats and a loose-fitting tank that exposes his small chest tattoo.

"Saved by grace," I say out loud. "Didn't take you for that type."

"What type? That don't know Jesus? Name an R&B singer that didn't start singing in the church?" He folds his arms and waits.

"Well . . ." I have nothing.

"Yeah!" He laughs. "I'm definitely not a saint. But I know that God saved me. I've been in some shit that could have gone completely left if not for the man upstairs. You can't live like I do, be from where I'm from, and not acknowledge that it's from God."

I nod. Impressed. It's quiet for a moment and I proceed to make a dent in the ice-cream sandwich in front of me. He opens up his sundae and takes a spoonful.

"So, did you really tell Captain Scumbag about me? That you met a writer at Palomar's?"

"Yeah, why would I lie about something like that?"

"I don't know. Why do men ever lie? It's not like y'all need a reason."

"Aw, come on, that's unfair. I meant it when I said I liked your

records. And that you were talented as hell. I was planning to bring up
your performance to Meck during the session but then, there you were.
Kismet."

"Mmmm." I try to take it all in. "Well, just know that I am only
here for the ice cream. And tea if you have some."

"Oh really? That's it, huh?" He strokes his scruffy chin hair before
venturing over to the kitchen area. He holds up a generic tea bag and
I nod. It would have to do. He sets up the small coffee maker to heat
the water.

"I'm not sleeping with you."

"I'm not sleeping with you." He smiles. "I told you it's dessert. I'm
an adult. I can control myself. I know you think I'm a sex-crazed ma-
niac." He shakes his head.

"I don't. I'm sorry. I just say what I think, it's easier for me. I like it
all out on the table."

"I respect that." He heads back over to my seat at the table and pulls
me up by my arms so that our eyes meet. "I want to kiss you. That's
what I'm thinking right now. And I mean, technically this is what, like,
our third date?" he jokes.

He pushes my hair back, leans in, and lingers long enough to see
if I will meet him halfway. There's a glimmer in his dark brown eyes
right before he closes them and kisses me with a delicate peck on the
lips. He retreats to the chair on the other side of the table with a look of
satisfaction. We finish the cold treats.

"Come on." He leads me through French doors to where there is
a king-size bed. He pulls a Big K.R.I.T. T-shirt and a pair of basketball
shorts out of the dresser. "You might as well stay here tonight. It's late.
I can have Mark drop you off in the morning." He sits on the edge of
the bed.

I stop, trying to figure out exactly how I got here. From telling him
that I can't hang out with a client to standing in his bedroom.

"You're thinking too much. Go change out of your clothes and come on. We'll watch *Ballers*. I love that show."

"I want to. I'm enjoying myself, it's just—"

"You need someone to get you out of your head. That's all," he says, without looking up as he searches for the remote.

"Some of us have real jobs, you know?"

"Oh, aight, bet." He stops his search and looks up at me, warming my whole being.

I wanted to tell him no. To have him call Mark or an Uber or whatever for me to go back to Brooklyn. But "Fine" betrays my lips.

Once in the bathroom, I lean back against the closed door before exhaling. This was playing with fire and I knew it. Yet somehow I pull off my jeans and shirt and lay them neatly on the side of the Jacuzzi tub. The Shake Shack taste is offensive so I lean over the sink and swish some water around in my mouth. My phone vibrates on the counter, causing me to flinch. A heart animation from my mom saying she misses me.

When I emerge from the elaborate bathroom, Tau is lying on the covers in his sweats. A steaming paper cup of tea is on the nightstand beside the bed. The Rock's voice blares from the TV. His eyes dance taking in the sight of me standing in his clothes. I climb onto the bed next to him and he pulls me in close with a strong grip and places a kiss on my forehead. I breathe him in.

Creeping up the rickety stairs at 7 a.m. is not as quiet as one would hope when trying to slip past Talia without having to answer twenty-one questions. But each creak of the stairs reminds me how noisy everything is in this building. You could always tell when someone was approaching the door. Maybe a text last night would have been the better move but I wasn't sure what to say. I resolved to tell Talia I stayed at Red's since our studio session went late. That was my story and I was sticking to it.

I place my key in the door slowly and spin the lock. The shower is going when the door opens. *Great*, I think to myself as I pop off my shoes and tiptoe to my bedroom. As I pass Talia's room, she's standing in the doorway in her robe.

"So, that's what we're doing? Staying out all night with no text? You trying to be on *Dateline*?" she asks with her arms crossed.

"My fault." I try to keep moving. "Thought you were in the shower."

"I'm about to hop in. Listen, I'm not judging, just shoot a sister a heads-up so your parents don't run up on me."

"I'm sorry." I definitely wasn't thinking straight.

"So, where *did* you spend the night?" She moves her shoulders up and down playfully.

"Red's." It comes out firm and calculated like I practiced. It's hard for me to lie to Talia. As much as I wanted to share with her how exciting it was to spend a night with Tau, I knew better.

"Wait, so who was the session with? Anyone exciting?"

That I didn't anticipate. "Oh, a young artist signed to Def Jam."

"Oh okay. Well, that is not as exciting as a date or something." Her eyes narrow. "We're on the way to being lonely biddies!" Talia yells out as she slips into the bathroom. Through the closed door she adds, "Just let me know next time so I have details for *Dateline* if you come up missing!"

Talia had too much going on to read into my lies. I fall onto my bed with my arms spread open. The Big K.R.I.T. T-shirt Tau let me sleep in came home with me and it has his scent all over it. We literally slept. So, I guess I technically did sleep with him?

We talked a little after watching *Ballers*. He told me about how his mom still insists on living in Maryland, and how he let it go once he bought her a nice spot in the burbs out there. I divulged my mom's incessant worry about me living in the city. I fell asleep while talking and felt him pull the covers over me and snuggle close. It was the perfect ending to a day I couldn't have predicted. Mark was waiting for me bright and early so I could head home to get ready for work. The shoot is fast approaching so I need to make sure everything I'm responsible for is in order.

My phone buzzes.

Tonight I have a club appearance. What time you off? Goodness. He wastes no time. Had to respect him leaving no room to wonder.

I may be late tonight preparing for your shoot next week, I send back.

Well, hit me. It starts late, we can get dinner before.

I can't even focus when I get to work. I'm low-key intrigued by the thought of hanging out with Tau again. All my assumptions about him were wrong. Charming, kind, and easy to talk to definitely weren't on that list. Based off what I had learned about Tau the night before, we vibe to a lot of the same music, we're both close with our moms, and feel really passionate about being creatives. He was also sexy as hell up close and personal, which didn't hurt. I'd be lying if I said it didn't take a lot not to jump all over him last night.

"So, you get me here?" I look up and Dawn is standing frozen, waiting for me to respond.

"Yes, exactly!" I pop back into the conversation. "I'll make sure everyone has call times and that wardrobe is set up and ready to roll."

"Perfect." Dawn nods toward me. "Looks like we're on schedule. Let's make sure we tie up all our action items this week and we'll re-convene Friday."

The team consists of two senior account managers and Siena, who works as the admin taking notes and making sure we all have our follow-up items. She stops me as I start to walk out of the conference room.

"Do you know Tau is going to be at Frenchie's tonight? I think I might go," she gushes while flipping her hair.

"Oh no, I don't really keep up."

"Seriously? Did you see that man when he came here?" She pauses for a second, thinking something over. "He could definitely get it."

"Oh, well, okay," I say, shifting my eyes.

Siena and I didn't talk much but I guess she thought fangirling over Tau was something we had in common. She's been at Garter about a year, but she might just work here to see who she can snag from the client list. I could be more social with the people in the office, but between being Dawn's go-to girl and my music, I don't really see the value. I kept them at arm's length not on purpose, but Siena always tried to reach out. Meanwhile Ryan's invitations to lunch were slowly dis-sipating the more Dawn seemed to lean on me in meetings. It suddenly occurs to me that I can't go to Frenchie's with Tau if Siena's planning to be there. I can't risk someone from work seeing me with him.

Hey, something came up, I text Tau.

Nah, it didn't. Get out of your head. Mark will get you around 7, he sends back. How did he know how to read me through a damn text message?

As six thirty rolls around I creep into Dawn's office. "Hey, I wanted to see if you needed anything else?"

"Rushing off tonight? That's not like you." She looks out over the top of her glasses.

"Oh, dinner plans with a friend. But you know, I'm here if there's anything you need. No problem," I say, biting my lip.

"No. No worries. I'll see you tomorrow then." She pushes up her frames, barely looking up from her computer.

Thankful that she oddly doesn't have anything extra for me to do, I rush to the bathroom to freshen up before she can change her mind. Fluff the hair, shove a little more deodorant under my arms, and roll my amber and sandalwood oil over my wrists and neck. My Biggie sweatshirt kept me warm in the frigid office air-conditioning. It falls nicely over my pencil skirt that hugs my generous hips, so I decide to let it rock, hot temperature be damned. Adding a little lip gloss, I smile to myself. It's been a long time since I was this happy about anything other than working with Red and Dylan and it felt good. At ten before the hour, I hop into the elevator so I can meet Mark a few blocks from the office.

"Evening," Mark grunts as I hop into the back of the Escalade. We sail up the avenue heading to Le Méridien.

"You're so warm, Mark, I love that about you," I blurt out sarcastically.

"Ha! I try not to get too attached." He looks at me in the rearview mirror.

His statement hits me like a ton of bricks. And what did he mean by that? How many girls did Tau have Mark picking up and dropping off in the middle of the morning? *Shit, you're so much smarter than this, Carli. What the hell are you thinking?* I'm quiet the rest of the ride.

Everything is grandiose in Tau's life. The high ceilings of Le Méridien, the lavish tables and private dining rooms. I feel grossly underdressed, but I try to walk in confidently. He's waiting in a side room with a propped-open door marked with a large *L*. Mark sits at the bar while I walk over to the table. Tau stands and kisses me on the cheek, before pulling out the chair for me to sit.

"Hey." His whole face lights up and I forget all about Mark's comment.

"Hey yourself." I feel like I'm back in high school with a crush.

"How was work?"

"Wild. Your shoot is taking over our lives. But I'm used to it."

He signals the waiter. "My friend here clearly needs to unwind a bit." He laughs as the waiter pours a dark liquid into our glasses. "I'm sure it'll be perfect."

"Oh, it has to be," I say with a smile. "That's what working for Dawn entails."

"I can see that. But you seem on top of it."

The waiter reappears and places fresh arugula salads in front of us. He takes our entrée orders. I can barely wait to eat. I lift my fork and catch Tau's eye. He reaches for my hand and bows his head.

"Thank you, Father, for this food we are about to receive. Let it be nourishing to our bodies. And excuse this heathen who was about to dig in without first giving thanks." He opens an eye and my mouth drops open. I squeeze his hand and we laugh.

I sip from the wineglass and savor the taste of oak and blackberry. I want to absorb the moment, truly let go.

"My uncle Russ, he always taught me the value of hard work, you know? When I was a kid, he used to always say talent could never beat hard work. So, I know it might seem crazy now, but the hard work will pay off. I always believed that when he said it."

"Oh, he and my dad must be cut from the same cloth." I nod while taking a forkful of salad.

"Yeah, yeah man, Russ is everything." I can see Tau disappear in his thoughts.

"Where'd you go?"

"Oh, nah, just thinking." He fiddles with the napkin on his lap. "Gotta get my mind in party mode. This stuff was a lot easier when I was younger."

"Really, old man?"

"You're funny." He waves me off. "I'm glad you made it."

Our meals arrive; he gets the filet mignon and I do the smoked salmon with a side of fries. On a few occasions, I look out of the room only to see some of the female staff walking leisurely by the door and whispering to each other. At one point Tau waves and they walk off giggling and embarrassed.

This time, I do a little preventative measuring and tell Talia that I'm going out with Dawn on Garter Media business. Meanwhile, Tau and I ride to Frenchie's.

"We got that brand-new Tau Anderson. He's in the city, ladies, and he's at Frenchie's tonight if you want to get down," the radio DJ announces and spins Tau's latest record.

"*I like it when you pop that, pop that, pop that . . .*" pumps through the car speakers, and Tau shakes his head.

"You can hit that, Mark." He turns to me and threads his fingers through mine.

"Insightful lyrics," I jab.

"Ahhhhh, funny."

We pull up close to Frenchie's to a line forming around the building. The same type of MAC Makeup Girls from the concert are waiting outside. The dresses are just as short, showing out for the last few weeks of summer. Somehow it slipped my mind that there would be an audience waiting and I needed to figure out how to walk into this club apart from Tau's fanfare.

I rack my brain and blurt out, "I have to pee!"

"Uhm, well, okay." He cuts his eyes at my abrupt revelation. "I mean, it should only take a second for us to pull around."

"Well, can I go through the front? I have to go like bad."

"Carli?"

"Okay, look, there are a lot of people out here and I . . ."

"Want to make sure no one sees you walk in with me?" He looks over at me with his head resting on the seat.

"I mean, it would be helpful." I bat my eyes to soften the blow.

"Shit, okay. Look, uhm, let me call my contact quick and they'll have someone meet you out front."

He pulls out his cell phone and dials. After a quick call, I see a woman in a gray bodysuit hugging every one of her curves. She waves from the entrance toward the truck. I hop out quickly to the stares of everyone and they are immediately disappointed when they don't recognize me as someone famous. They instead turn their attention back to the bouncers as I follow closely behind who I assume is an IG model of some sort.

"I'll show you to the bathrooms near the VIP. And we can meet them right up the stairs." She has an accent I can't quite pinpoint.

Taking my time in the bathroom, I check myself out one last time. The VIP looked like it was out of the way enough, but I was still going to have to keep my eyes open. Meeting back up with the young lady, she shows me the way. At the top of the stairs a dark Middle Eastern man with a ponytail greets us.

"Tau is right this way. We have a few chilled bottles for you, and the house is filling up. Let me show you to your section."

Tau waves from the balcony area that overlooks the club. Couches are arranged in a square with rich-colored pillows. Burnt orange fabric is draped from the ceiling creating a canopy, and there are bottles on the table along with carafes of orange juice, cranberry juice, and soda.

"You good now?"

"Perfect." I give his arm a squeeze. I appreciate him being understanding. "Hey, you should make sure they bring you some Ace of Spades bottles. A few flicks will probably make them happy. And you can release them after the shoot when they make the official announcement."

"Always working." He laughs and kisses my cheek.

The club is dark and smoky and the music blares through the state-of-the-art sound system. A few people start filling up the VIP area. The bass is thumping, and the lights are flashing all around, illuminating the faces of partygoers eager to have a good time. Scantily clad women dance on raised platforms placed throughout the downstairs area. I see Angela Yee from *The Breakfast Club*, and is that Remy Ma?

"Nice shirt," Angela comments.

"Thanks." I grew up following Angela's career. There was that small period of time I thought I wanted to be on the radio. Until I did an internship my freshman year and realized how not glamorous it could be.

"Tau, hey boo."

"Ang!" He opens his arms wide.

She greets Tau with a huge hug. She's been one of his biggest supporters since his start. There were rumors they dated. I wonder if they were true.

After one of Angela's people grabs a few photos of them, she and her squad make their way to their section, which is adjacent to ours. Frankie K appears soon after and gives Tau a handshake. He looks at me and whispers to Tau, patting the small pocket of his shirt.

"Nah, Frank," I hear him say. "Relax."

"Oh, she got you on best behavior?"

"Frank." Tau's eyes are serious.

Looking dejected, Frankie slinks over to Angela's section drinking straight from a bottle and holding it up over the balcony as the onlookers cheer. His eyes are already a bit crazed. Either he started drinking early or he's on a little something extra.

It's interesting, the setup of these situations. You come to a club to "party" with celebrities, but meanwhile they're above you, having their own party, and you're literally beneath them on the bottom floor.

"What was that?"

"Frank just being Frank."

"Okay . . ." I wait for the rest of it.

"He gets stuck sometimes on who I used to be. I've done a lot of wild shit in the past, Carli. Sometimes people try to keep you there, is all. He means no harm. Frank's been riding since day one though," he adds sincerely.

"Wild things like what?"

"Like, I don't know, young rich nigga shit."

"Got it."

"I was young and dumb. You know what that's like, right?"

I nod, trying not to linger on what Tau was implying. The industry was a wild place. It had an allure for sure, but it could also be extremely dark.

"Come on, man, you can't sit back all night, you're getting paid to be here!" Frankie motions for him to come up to the railing with him. Tau looks back at me.

"Do your thing," I say.

Looking relieved to have my approval, Tau immediately goes into entertainment mode. He grabs a bottle from the silver bucket with ice before walking over to join Frankie as fans scream down below. "Free Smoke" by Drake plays as he raises the bottle in the air. Frankie shoves a vape pen in his direction as Tau waves him off smoothly while continuing to dance and celebrate. I slide out of the VIP past Mark to get some fresh air.

"Carli! You came out?" Siena and two of her girlfriends are dressed scantily and searching for the VIP entrance as I emerge. Shit.

"Hey, I was in the neighborhood, so I decided to stop in. But I'm probably going to head out soon."

"Really? I mean, it's just getting started." She pouts.

"Well, I have to finish preparing for the shoot, you know?"

"Oh, okay. Well, I guess we'll see you later."

Siena waves as one of her friends snuggles up close to try to whisper, although they've clearly been pregaming and her whisper isn't exactly quiet.

"Who wears Chucks to a club?" They laugh as they walk up the steps where Mark is perched. I look up and he catches my eye. Reeling from the smartass comment, I shake my head slowly and Mark nods.

Mark has his arms folded as I see Siena's mouth moving. He shakes his head, and she starts talking more emphatically with her arms and hands. She even looks around for me but I slide into a hallway at the bottom of the stairs. Mark points to his wrist; they don't have any bands on for the VIP. Siena and friends march back down the stairs looking like hurt puppies. I run back up quickly once they're out of sight and Mark gives me a low five. Mark was definitely more down than I gave him credit for. I guess you couldn't guard someone like Tau without picking up a few maneuvers.

With a quick glance, Siena turns her attention back to the VIP entrance and I swiftly dash inside, completely unsure whether she saw me head back up or not. Following their moves, I walk to the front of the section and see Siena and crew move through the crowd drawing the stares of men along the way. I back up from the balcony and sit back on one of the couches so I can try to stay out of view.

"Where'd you disappear to?" Tau turns.

"Oh, I, uhm, had to run to the restroom," I say, pulling out my phone as a distraction.

"Again?"

"It's the wine from dinner," I reason.

"Well, there's one up here too, next time." He searches my eyes. He swirls his drink in his hand and leans over me on the couch. He grabs the top of my hair, pulls my head back, and kisses my neck. I feel my whole body jolt and forget that we're out in public.

"Pop That" thumps out of the speakers and he laughs while giving me a quick kiss on the lips. My eyes follow him as he walks over to the balcony to show his face and dance to his song. His frame is chiseled, and his long tee falls perfectly over his fit butt. Frankie grabs him into a side embrace and bops from side to side while the whole crowd sings along.

Making his way back to me after his song plays, he guides me up from the couch as a little reggae begins to play. Turning me and placing his arms around my waist, he whines slowly against me. It all goes quiet. I no longer see anything around me, there are only sensations. The bass vibrating through my body, the smell of sweat and cologne, the thick smokiness in my chest, and the rhythm of his hips. I close my eyes in surrender.

I don't want it to end, but the DJ switches it up to trap, which isn't so much my speed. We both plop down on the couch exhausted as he pours me a drink. I sip it slowly, taking it all in and listening to the sounds of folks below singing the words to "Mask Off."

"Come on, we fitna go. I did my time," he says, reaching for my hand and pulling me up toward the exit.

"So how does one get used to this?" I ask as we shuffle back into the car.

"You make a lot of mistakes first." He closes his eyes and leans back against the headrest.

Moving in closer to him, this time I initiate the kissing with one on his neck. He looks down at me before I tilt my head up. I close my eyes and lean forward, pressing my lips against his. As I bite his top lip, his hands find their way to my waist.

"You coming back to my spot?" he asks, our lips still entwined.

I rummage through my drawers looking for a shirt to throw on. My hand lingers near a black shirt that reads NO, YOU CANNOT TOUCH MY HAIR. A forever mood.

"So ma'am, I know that I've been busy, but you have been sneaking in and out of here all week like a ninja in the night." Talia bursts through my door with her arms crossed and chin pointed down.

"Never mind me standing in my bra, right?"

"Nothing I haven't seen, and stop avoiding the matter at hand."

"Oh, it's been crazy at work and working with Red at the studio. I'm heading to her spot now, actually. I'm running late." In actuality, I've been staying at Tau's on one too many occasions. I pull on my T-shirt and shake my hair back out from getting stuffed through the neck hole.

"Uh-huh." She nods but rolls her eyes. "I love how you're treating me like I don't have a degree and I'm not close to another. But I won't break out my interrogation tactics yet. Live your life, B!" She waves, heading back out the doorway.

Red is going to kill me for being so late. We're supposed to be finishing the song we started at the studio the other day for Dylan. And dropping the Tau collab bomb on him since we were officially working on his new project while he was in town. I was not looking forward to that part at all. He was barely returning my texts as it was.

As I rush to the door, Talia is sitting in the living room. "You look vibrant at least. Whatever you're doing, you look vibrant." She smiles and sinks back into her reading.

After some hustle to get out of Crown Heights, I arrive and hit the steps over at Red's. I shoot her a text that I'm on my way up. She meets me at the door. I walk in and see that Dylan is already there.

"Hey," I say, searching Red for some type of clue as to what's been going on before I got here.

"Welcome, glad you could make it."

"I know, I'm sorry. I woke up late." Hitting the streets with Tau was taking its toll. I toss my book bag on the floor and sit next to Dylan.

"Hey, D."

"What up?" he says unenthused.

"So, I wanted to get together so we can figure out how to finish your project," Red says, interjecting the awkwardness. "We got pulled into another project, Dylan, that we kind of need to focus on at least for the next two weeks, which may push us back a little bit."

Dylan shifts in his seat and rubs his hair. He glances at me while fiddling with his earring. "Hmmm." He nods slowly. "What project?"

"Well." Red looks at me. I raise my eyebrows and nod toward her to tell him. Dylan's eyes shift from Red to me. "We got pulled into recording with Tau Anderson through Meck, actually." She rips off the bandage.

"Hahaha!" His laugh is loud and obnoxious.

"Look, Dylan, I know that no artist wants to wait, but a few weeks is not going to make a huge difference," she pleads. "We're in control of this. We don't have a label breathing down our necks."

"Perfect." He stands slowly, towering over us. "Okay, cool. You said I was the priority, Red, and now I'm getting pushed?" He uses both hands for emphasis, pointing to his chest.

"You know it's not like that." Red is calm. I watch, trying not to get read like I did the last time all of us were in the studio. I'm going to let Red handle it.

"It feels like that. Especially since I played Meck the records we all worked on, which is probably why you got the call. Am I right?" he asks, stuffing his hands in the pockets of his hoodie.

A thin veil of silence covers us.

"Right. Okay, cool. You believe in me. You say you do and then this pretty boy gets to come in, take my writer and producer, and take—you know what? Never mind."

"My dude," Red says, clearly irritated. "We all have to eat. We have to take work that pays us too, so we can do things we love. I have a husband counting on me to make shit work."

"You think I don't have a lot riding on this too? Shit, this is all I do. I don't have one foot in and one foot out like some people." He cuts his eyes at me. "Hit me when you're ready to finish."

In a huff, he grabs his bag and heads toward the door before I even know what's happening. The door slams behind him.

"Really?" I look at Red. I wasn't expecting that to go well. But I wasn't expecting it to go quite like that.

"Look, you ain't making this easy for us," Red blurts out, looking past me to the door to ensure Dylan is out of earshot.

"Me? What do I have to do with what just happened?"

"Dylan has a thing for you, Carli. I don't know how you missed it over the last maybe year or so, but he does. And that's making this whole situation a little more complicated," she says, rubbing her temples.

"Seriously?" I let out a deep sigh and roll my eyes.

I jump to my feet to try to catch Dylan. All I wanted to do was make records. I wasn't so great at navigating the intimacy it required.

But things were different with me and Dylan. We had a connection. I didn't want that to change.

"Hey!" I yell as I get to the bottom of the stairs and open the front door. Dylan had cleared the front steps and made it midway down the block. I step out onto the landing.

"What's up?" He looks back.

"Why haven't you ever said anything?" I ask, clunking down the rusty steps. He walks back to meet me.

"About what?" He looks at me with uncertainty.

"Being into me. I mean, I thought. At Palomar's. But Red just said—"

"Red? What? I mean—" he stammers. "I've been trying." He stops.

"You're treating me like shit and that's not fair, Dylan. I didn't know. I thought we were, well, friends."

"Look, it's all good, man. I'm good. You got your boy now, so don't worry about me." He adjusts his book bag on his shoulders, looking past me.

"My boy? I told you the Tau thing was for work."

"At Frenchie's too?" He leans in, anxious for my reply. If Dylan was at Frenchie's I completely missed him. Hell, if he saw me there, I wonder who else did. I look down, hoping some words come to me.

"I-I . . ." I had nothing. There was no denying our chemistry, but I chalked it up to our similar creative energy.

"Look, you said you don't date musicians, right? You never would. Which is why *I* tried to play the background. But I see that was contingent on the size of the bank account, right? 'Cause you can't tell me that somehow Tau *fucking* Anderson is the one who changed your mind. Homeboy has run through half the country probably," he offers as a finishing blow.

I tilt my head to the side trying to comprehend the words being hurled at me like daggers.

"Is that what you think of me? That I'm some gold digger?" My voice cracks. "Dylan, you know me."

He was affirming everything I figured people would assume if they ever got wind of me hanging out with someone like Tau.

"Yeah, well, perception is reality." He shakes his head. "Look, hit me when y'all are done with Pretty Boy so we can finish up this real music and move on. I'm sure you'll have some good material after homeboy screws you over like he does everyone else."

"Dylan!"

"Oh, and you can have these." He reaches into his bag and pulls out an envelope that he hands to me before bumping my shoulder and disappearing down the desolate block.

He leaves me standing in the middle of the sidewalk. I gather my pride and walk back up the stairs to finish up with Red.

Even the bird-of-paradise plant in the corner of my bedroom seems to mirror my mood, drooping at the sides. The leaves sway from the breeze through my cracked window covered with sheer curtains. I snuggle under my weighted blanket and stare at the cracks in the ceiling. Red and I had made some headway on the song for sure, but my heart wasn't functioning at max capacity. The fact that I missed it with Dylan and couldn't spare his feelings gnawed at my subconscious. It hurts to be on the brink of losing someone I care about. Two years of working, building, learning from each other, finding a creative rhythm, and it could all be down the drain just like that. This industry was full of mourning, and somehow, you had to keep picking yourself back up and doing it all over again.

I pull the envelope Dylan handed me out of my book bag. Inside are two tickets to see my favorite artist, Bianca, on New Year's Eve. I'd tried to get tickets, but they sold out in minutes. I reach for my phone, hovering over Dylan's name. Nothing I seem to type in the text message box feels adequate. My thoughts are interrupted when my phone vibrates, and Tau's picture appears.

The sun is beating down on us, but the breeze from the water gives a little relief. Honestly, for the end of August in New York, it could be much worse. We wrangled a few of the Giants players to give the set a full look and create the party atmosphere Dawn imagined. It was shaping up nicely. Merlin Santana was excited to have this star power on one of his company's yachts, and Dawn was happy we finally got to this day.

A few reps from Ace of Spades, camera crews juggling lights and equipment, and the makeup crew idle along the path to Dawn. Her long duster is dancing in the wind, and she adjusts her shades, looking majestic standing on the pier as her short bob mimics Beyoncé's infamous fan-blown hair.

"Are we good?" I ask, shielding my eyes from the sun peeking between clouds.

"Lesson twenty-six: Always bring shades." She laughs and reaches into her purse to pull out a Fendi eyeglass case. "I have an extra pair."

Of course she has an extra pair of Fendi shades, because they're so easy to come by.

"Thank you! I always forget." I had a pair of Ray-Bans that I loved, but rushing out of Tau's hotel this morning, I left them on his night-stand. With two weeks left to his trip, I was staying at his hotel more nights than I was home and making up new things to tell Talia each time. He dropped me off around the block from work so I could ride to the shoot with Dawn, since she insisted we go together the day before.

Tau suddenly emerges from one of the decked-out trailers parked in the lot of the marina, where he was conducting an interview with a reporter from *Essence*. A few photographers snap nonstop from be-hind a small barricade set up off the beaten path. They clamor over one another to get the best shot of his fresh white pants, a pair of black Ferragamos, and no shirt under a robe with multiple gold Cuban link chains sparkling in the sunshine. Meanwhile, Tau looks unfazed. One of the makeup girls dressed all in black walks over to shine him up with baby oil and the producers load the girls, jocks, and crew into one of Merlin's biggest yachts. A flying bridge yacht from what Merlin explained a bit earlier in the day, with multiple levels and about five cabins inside.

"This is great!" Merlin walks up to Dawn. His large belly, which definitely knew luxury and good food, is accentuated in his Gucci threads.

"Yes, I love when a plan comes together, Merlin. Couldn't have done it without you!"

"Should I check in on our talent?" I ask, motioning toward Tau.

"Yes, yes, of course." Dawn smiles and turns back to Merlin, pump-ing his ego a bit more.

I run over to the start of the pier where Tau begins walking down to board the boat. My hair blows all over my face and I bat at my unruly mane with my hands.

"I like this vision of you running over to me in the wind," he teases.

I throw him a serious look. "We're at work," I say through clenched teeth.

Completely ignoring me, he pushes the hair out of my face, linger-ing at my temple. "I like the glasses."

"They're Dawn's, who is probably watching us right now along with all these other people, so I need you to pull it together." Sure enough, Dawn is still talking to Merlin, but I can see her posture turned toward Tau and me.

"Good to go?" I say with a friendly and dramatic pat on the shoul-der as I head back down the pier.

"Good, especially from this view." I catch myself smiling when I look back at him. Then I force a frown to show Tau I mean business.

As we reach Dawn and Merlin, they both greet Tau like he's the center of the universe. "All set, superstar?" Dawn asks.

"All set!"

We load onto the boat and set sail a bit into the East River. Shooting in Miami like we'd hoped wasn't in the cards for coordinating everyone's schedules, so we had to pivot. The boat is elaborately designed with recessed lighting, crown molding, and white furniture with blue-and-white-striped pillows. The girls cozy up next to the players and Tau. A twinge of jealousy bubbles up in my throat. They're laughing and living it up, having a good time, which is the point of the shoot, but I can't help but find myself wondering, Is this real? Is he really into me? Why would a guy like him be into me? Dawn catches me staring intently.

"It's like we thought, right?"

"Right. Looks great. The girls are beautiful."

"They are. I'm sure it's what these guys are used to." She crosses her arms and rears back on the heels of her loafers.

"Yup." I swallow hard.

"You can cozy up a bit more, we need you all in the shot," the slinky director instructs from behind the main camera. The girls move over, serving even more dramatic face, and Tau stares into the camera. For a second, he peeks over at me with what I decipher as a reassuring glance.

The shoot is grueling. *Move over this way; no, this way; cross your legs but not that much.* All types of instructions are being thrown from behind the camera while twenty or so people look on. There's nothing natural about it, but it's all about capturing a natural-looking image.

The director finally cuts, and I'm surprised no one is seasick yet from the gentle rumble of the water beneath us. The crew heads out from the cabin onto the deck to get a few still shots with the New York skyline in the background. All of the work, preparation, coordinating clothes and looks and staff, and just like that the day comes to a close without a hitch.

As we head back to the dock, Merlin and a few of the brand execs are going over the schedule with Dawn for the release of the ad. Tau finds me standing near the Jacuzzi that sits at the back of the boat, gazing thoughtlessly at the river.

"That's a lot coming at you at once."

"It can be. But I'm built for it. Been doing shoots and videos and all that stuff a long time. You learn to work like they won't so you can live like they can't," he says.

It was only seven, but the Garter team had been here since about seven a.m., going over every detail to ensure things went smoothly. I understand why they call this the golden hour as the dwindling light from the sun illuminates a path to the unforgettable New York skyline. The city where dreams come true. That's what always drew me to it. That hope. Tau spins me around to face him and pulls me close by my waist. He rubs his hands up and down my arms to warm me up as I shiver a little from the cool breeze. The remnants of his Versace cologne mix with the salt water, creating its own savory aroma.

"I don't think about it much. I have to take care of my family, you know?" He nuzzles my nose and I forget all about where I am. "They're all depending on me to stand tall. This is nothing compared to my grumma working in the crab-canning factory or my mom picking up diner shifts when I was little."

"Yeah . . . that's the hope, one day. That my mom can quit working at the law firm, watching other people live grand lives." He pulls me into his chest and I exhale. His embrace is becoming a lot more familiar.

"Yo, Tau!" one of the players calls from the open door of the cabin. "We're docked. You trying to come with? We taking a few of the ladies down to Pergola," he yells before seeing me dip out from behind Tau. "Oh, my bad, man, I see you good!"

"I'm good, Dell!" Tau yells through a smile.

He gives him a salute and disappears back inside the boat.

"Gah, I have to go find Dawn." The fact that I'm at work rushes back to me and I hustle to my post by Dawn's side.

Thankfully, she's chatting with one of the players about some upcoming meetings. Merlin and I find ourselves standing together and I thank him for an awesome experience. Totally fulfilled and handsomely paid, he hands me his card in case I ever want to come out and take a gratis ride. I can totally see me living it up on a yacht.

"Hey!" I say to Dawn. "Are we about wrapped here?"

"Yup! Amazing shoot today! I'm looking forward to the final cut. This was a great tie-in, Carli. I'm close to disappearing on an island and sipping mojitos all day. I feel like the company may be in good hands with someone like you."

It was flattering. And on the best days, I considered what it would be like to fully commit to the idea of following this work as a career path. But I mean, Dawn was going a hundred miles an hour at all times, which might be why she never really settled down. Although my mom was always rushing me, I did want to have a family someday. I think of Tau's words of working like some people won't and that's exactly what working at Garter is. A means to an end that hopefully involved creating beautiful music.

"Thanks again, Dawn, this was great!" Tau pops up as we all exit the boat back onto Pier 42. "You ladies good getting back to the office?"

"Oh, I forgot we came together, honey. I actually have to hop over to Midtown for a late meeting. Do you want me to get a car for you?" she asks.

"Oh . . . uhm, no worries. We're actually closer to Brooklyn now, I can get home from here."

"I can drop you off where you need to go," Tau offers innocently, and I can see some of his acting chops at work.

"Hmmm . . ." I pause.

"I'm headed that way, no big deal."

"To Brooklyn?" I ask, raising an eyebrow.

"Yup, I have some things to pick up from Kith."

I look at Dawn, who looks a little skeptical, but she seems to buy Tau's act. I have no idea how to play this, but I don't want to overdo it, so I agree.

"Okay, well, I guess so."

"Great, it's all settled." She gives Tau a kiss on both cheeks. "I'll see you tomorrow then, Carli. Make sure the interns get everything packed up in wardrobe, please. I don't need any designers calling me this week. And text Ryan to make sure he's coordinating all our social efforts for this launch. I want the plan on my desk by Friday!" She shifts her bag from one arm to the other and walks toward the parking lot with her duster trailing in the wind.

"Really?" I turn and hit Tau. His devious grin is telling, and he gives me a quick slap on the butt while waving to Dawn's back down the pier. She turns and waves one last time as I swat Tau's hands moving all around behind me.

We stopped to grab a few margaritas after the shoot at a Mexican spot not too far from the pier. He spent part of dinner catching up on emails and fielding calls from Frankie about upcoming meetings and new deals on the table but I didn't mind. It was nice to take a load off after being around so many people. He went seamlessly from one thing to the other while managing to entertain a few folks that came over wanting to grab photographs. I felt like my eyes were playing tricks on me when one guy came up who I know I recognized. His hair was wrapped in a tight do-rag so it was hard to tell, but I think he was the same kid from the studio that night. He was acting like a fan, but something told me he was up to more than that with his bulky DSLR camera instead of an iPhone like everyone else. I couldn't help but start to think that maybe he was following us. I was happy to get back into Tau's truck to head over to his hotel. Just the two of us, and well, Mark.

I wrap my arms around Tau's waist as we walk down the long hallway to his suite. Feeling pretty buzzed, I laugh, tripping over my own feet as we stumble into the living area. Everything is artfully arranged and smells fresh as usual.

"You're silly." He grabs my arms, letting me fall gently to the couch.

"I'm not. I'm together, I promise. I'm not drunk, just relaxed for once in my life." I giggle through a hiccup. Okay, maybe I am a little on. The tequila had me feeling warm inside. I'd never say it out loud, but I liked how the alcohol seemed to dull my brain. No work or Dylan, no anxiousness, and no wondering if I was headed down a road of absolute and total destruction.

He looks down at me on the couch and shakes his head. "I'm gonna get this baby oil off me and take a shower right quick. They got me out here shinier den a mug." He pulls off his white V-neck T-shirt revealing his bare chest that I spent the whole day staring at. I watch him intently as he walks toward the bathroom.

My phone rings and I grab it from my purse.

"Dad?" I try not to sound inebriated.

"CC, how are you?" A piano is playing in the background. His voice is thick and a little raspy as he tries to talk over it.

Carlisa Candice. My dad always calls me CC.

"Uhm, I'm good, out with a friend," I say, looking over at the bedroom door. I wonder where he is now.

"I'm in Dallas. Playing tonight with a few cats from Badu's band." A loud voice yells that sound check is in five.

"Sounds like you don't have a lot of time."

"I know, never enough time." He sighs into the phone. "Hey, I'll be in New York soon for a gig. When I get the dates I'll let you know. I can't wait to see you."

"Oh wow, okay. I didn't think I would be seeing you this soon," I say softly. "Was talking to Mom about seeing you at Christmas."

"Well, I'm lucky to get to the East Coast. I've been overseas the last month. You know they appreciate the music better. And they pay. How's your writing going? How's your mom?"

"She's good, always worrying about me. And the writing is really good, actually. I'll tell you about it when you come."

Managing my excitement has become a bad habit of mine. I've survived a lot of broken promises about visits so it was easier to keep the real emotions at bay. The shower stops and I rush to get my dad off the phone.

"My girl is coming back, Dad, I have to go. Keep me posted."

"I love you, *mija*." He always said it as if he was apologizing.

"Love you too, Papa." I hang up the phone and stare at it. He likes to resurface out of the shadows when I least expect it. I should be used to it by now. But it was like a ghost appearing. Tau comes out of the bedroom wearing basketball shorts. Small beads of water on his chest catching the dim light.

"Were you talking?" he asks.

"My mom." I take off my Chucks and stand, looking up at him.

"Oh cool. Moms is bad, right?" A wide grin spreads across his face.

"What?" I push him in his chest but allow my hand to linger.

I reach up to run my hands over his hair, uncertain whether it's the margaritas or if I'm trying to turn the page on my phantom father's call. Whatever it is, I'm feeling bold. These last couple of weeks have been so intense. Every day I was getting more and more comfortable with the idea that somehow this was my reality and not some fantasy. All day I had to sit and watch him with other women, and I wanted to have something over them. I wanted to feel like I got a piece of him that no one else did today. Placing my hands on the back of his neck, I stand on tiptoes to kiss him. First soft, then more aggressive. We push back through the French doors. As we enter the bedroom he lifts me off the floor effortlessly so we're eye to eye.

"You drunk, aren't you?" He puts his forehead to mine.

"I'm a little drunk. But I know what I'm doing," I whisper. I did. I even remembered to wear grown-up underwear. We'd been spending every moment we could together. Between meetings and after I got off work. It was easy with him. Easier than it's been with anyone before this. It wasn't just the physical attraction for me, but I had to say, I did want to know if all the hype was true.

"Hey," he whispers between kisses. "You know we don't have to do this."

"I want to," I say, holding his gaze.

Laying me on the bed, he unbuttons my boyfriend jeans before pulling them off from the bottom. He reaches for his phone and fiddles with it until *Kind of Blue* plays out of the small clock/speaker on the night table. He reaches for my top and pulls it over my head. His fingertips graze my body, and with my eyes closed, they feel as light as a feather duster tantalizing all my nerve endings. When I open them, he's on his knees looking over me.

"What?" I ask.

"It's even better than I was picturing. I want to admire what's always hiding under those big clothes."

He grabs my leg and kisses up to my thigh. It's like lightning is striking all over my body and the more I try to control it, the more electric the feeling. It had been a long time since I let anyone touch me. I couldn't believe it was him. I wasn't sure if I even still knew how to do this with someone. A part of me was anxious, as always. How many women had he been with? I couldn't turn off my brain. Damn, I probably should have had one more drink at the restaurant.

He lowers his body onto mine while kissing my neck and all over my face. Our lips meet and I feel myself let out a low groan. He stops and rolls off me.

"What now?" I raise up on my elbows and look over at him.

"Nothing." He looks straight up at the ceiling.

"Really?" I brush my hair back, all of a sudden feeling very naked.

"It's just—" he starts and laughs, placing his hands behind his head.

"What is happening right now?" I frown at him.

"I'm . . . I'm kind of nervous. And I've never been nervous." He lets out a full-on chuckle. "I don't know. Something feels different with you."

"You're nervous? I haven't had—well that's not important—but I'm saying, what are you nervous about?"

"I'm sure you have pretty high expectations." He grabs one of my curls and lets it pop back.

I guess I'd never thought about it that way. The pressure to be mind-blowing. So many songs about pleasing women in different ways set the tone for this moment. And I did have high expectations. You can't talk that talk and not be amazing.

No pretenses, no flashing lights or screams from a crowd, but an intimate moment where he was nervous. Not at all what I would expect. But it felt good to be wanted, to know that I wasn't the only one trying to live up to something here.

His vulnerability gives me the confidence to climb on top of him, conjuring the spirit of all the sexy Yoncé songs I've listened to in my lifetime. I love the contrast of my deep red undertones next to his fair complexion. I bend and kiss his chest tattoo and trace the others that make up the sleeve on his arm. Angels and script, so much intricate detail. He reaches over to the nightstand that houses my sunglasses from the night before and his hand reappears with a condom.

I can feel him, and he grabs onto my hips. Miles's horn wails in "Blue in Green" as we become entangled in each other's arms. He rolls me on my back and his face is illuminated by the waning moon outside the large windows. My body relaxes into our rhythm. The strong grips of his hands are possessive of every soft part of me. His warm breath in my ear invigorates me and every part of me responds. I pull him in close and allow my mind to completely shut down as Tau Anderson proves every lyric in his songs to be true.

A while later, both of our bodies are still. Only the sound of our shallow breathing is audible. His head is nestled against my stomach. "Hey, I want to ask you something." I'm so rattled by the aftershock of the experience, I barely hear Tau's request. "Hey," he says again, reaching up and tracing my lips with his finger.

I had been lost in my thoughts. "Oh sorry, what's up?"

"Come to Vegas with me for this BET thing Wednesday. It's some honors thing and they want me to do a tribute but I'm flying back right after."

"Like, be your date? Like at an event with media?" I ask, hoisting myself up and forcing him to move. I pull the covers up over me and scoot to the top of the bed.

"Yeah, like out in the open, where people can see us. It's not that hard to understand," he says, sitting up.

"Tau, you know I can't with Dawn and—"

"How long you think that's going to really work for me?" I can see his eyes cut at me in the dim lighting. He strokes his beard and laughs. "I'm a grown-ass man sneaking around with you."

My senses return and my skin gets hot. "I didn't ask you to. I told you what it was from the gate. Yet you pursued me. I have—"

"A career. And a reputation. It's cute and all, but we're adults that get to make our own decisions."

"This is my life," I say quicker than I have time to think. "I'm supposed to risk what I've been building for a few fun nights?"

Tau looks taken aback by my tone. "No one is trying to step on what you're building, shawty. Look, I've been out here taking down more chicks than I care to mention, acting reckless, drinking and not even remembering the shit I got into the night before and it gets old, fast. And it's lonely. Not the way people think but like being trapped in a glass box where everyone sees you, but no one can hear you scream. But then I see this gorgeous girl at my show and actually like kicking it with her, we have great conversations, and she doesn't want to tell anyone? Has me picking her up around the corner from work? I've been playing along, but that's not me."

"Right." I get where he's coming from, but he doesn't understand. "You're not always trying to prove your worth and trying to be more than some tits and ass. Sorry if that's offensive to you that I'm not falling all over myself to be out here running the streets with you publicly." I get up and start looking for my clothes. Something about arguing naked does not feel right.

"It's only been a couple of weeks, Tau, think about it," I say with a more centered tone.

"Some things don't take that long to know, Carli."

"It's not smart." I sigh. "I can't do that. You know I can't do that."

"Aight. Don't go," he says calmly. "But don't expect me to sit on my hands waiting for you to be ready." He tosses my underwear and shirt at me and I catch them close to my face.

"Take me home."

"It's the middle of the night." He stands and pulls on his briefs.

"And?" I stand with my arms crossed, glaring at him.

"No." He pulls the comforter from the bed and grabs a pillow, walking out through the French doors, leaving me standing in the dark.

My phone vibrates on the nightstand. I see it's a media alert on the lock screen, which is odd because those rarely pop up for me. After clicking the post on the *Daily Spread*, an entertainment media outlet, there's an image at the top of the page of Tau on the pier. Scrolling to find my name while my heart starts beating violently in my chest, I stop. My name is next to a photo of us farther down the page talking closely near the back of the boat. The caption reads *Tau Anderson and Garter manager Carlisa Henton connect after a campaign shoot. The question is, business or pleasure?* I lie back on the bed with the phone on my chest, staring up at the wood-trimmed ceiling. This could not be happening.

I had become accustomed to hearing from Tau in the morning. But on this dreary Tuesday, I hadn't heard a peep. My phone was dry. But I wasn't planning on backing down. Tau was in the wrong. He pursued me knowing the situation at Garter and then decided he didn't want to play by the rules. And yeah, I don't remember the last time I had as much fun as I've been having spending time with him. But did that mean I had to be willing to sacrifice my life for it? My mom had done that. She worked her ass off to make sure things were stable at home when the gigs weren't flowing for my father. Women were always the ones whose aspirations took a bullet. Why couldn't he understand that I needed my reputation? I needed to be taken seriously. I needed to show the Mecks of the world that they couldn't crush me. And then there was Red. I don't think our friendship could withstand a fallout from both Dylan *and* Tau.

The key, I resolved, was to be undeniably exceptional. A great song was a great song. I grab my headphones. Listening for ways to improve upon what we did the other day in hopes that Red and I could still win, whether Tau hates me or not. A girl had to have hope, even though getting a song placed after someone's ego was bruised went against everything I knew to be true in the industry. It would change everything to be on a new Tau Anderson record. I hope I hadn't jeopardized that.

Pacing around my room, I sing to myself, thinking of ad-libs and harmonies that might make the record sound bigger. I flip through a white bookcase that holds my vinyl records. I run my fingers over the covers of Teddy Pendergrass, Chaka Khan, and Sarah Vaughan albums. Being one of the greats was the goal. I wanted to write songs the whole world would sing. How was I supposed to do that and build something with Tau at the same time?

Tau heading to Vegas would give me some time to think. I love being wined and dined, the incredible sex was pleasantly disruptive, but when I played things out in my head, it was easy to see how unrealistic we were being. Tau lives in LA and is barely even there. What was going to come from a monthlong rendezvous? Last night left me wondering if Tau was actually serious about whatever we had going on.

I needed to get ready for work. Dawn was just as tapped into the news cycle as I was. She had media alerts for Garter too, so there was no way to avoid this photo. It wasn't necessarily incriminating. We weren't touching or holding hands or anything suggesting intimacy. It was all in our eyes if you really focused in on it.

I scribble a few small notes about the song and will shoot them over to Red a little later today. Grabbing all my things, I look around my room, turn off the light, and head toward the door.

Coming up the grimy subway stairs, I dodge the sea of traffic on the sidewalk to get on the right side of the pavement. The clack of women's shoes, incessant horn blowing, and the random yelling on the street corner provide the morning's soundtrack. Talia and I have a date to watch the BET Legends event this week and I'm looking forward to it. We've been ships passing in the night for the last couple of weeks, especially now that school was in full swing, and I always felt more grounded after our time together. I needed her.

I take a deep breath before opening the Garter suite door. Right on the other side of it is Siena, bright and cheery. "Morning, Carli! We haven't caught up really since Frenchie's. Wasn't it a movie?" she asks while organizing a stack of papers on her desk.

"I was only there for a bit. It probably went up a little more after I left."

"Oh, right." She nods, tapping her long nails against the keyboard. It's hard to read whether she's being sarcastic. Maybe she saw me head back up the stairs at the club that night. The ping of the interoffice messenger draws my attention but she keeps talking. "How did the shoot go yesterday? It looked amazing in the *Daily Spread*."

"It was great." I can't help but wonder who in the office has seen the photo of me and Tau. I decide to play it cool.

"Ughhh, I hate that you are not even moved by it. Like, spending a day with Tau Anderson would be everything." Her face is expressive. "I mean, even the insinuation of us having a thing would make me crazy."

"It's actually pretty uncool. I'm a woman at work. Just trying to do my job."

"Uh-huh, I get that. Look, I can put in a call to a friend I have there, woman to woman, about what they're insinuating. You know, women have to stick together." She scoots up in her chair a bit closer. "But there has to be someone that makes you tick. Come on, who is it?"

"Nah," I say in a whisper, shaking my head. She looks hopeful, but I can't indulge. "But if you could put that call in, I would appreciate it."

"No one's perfect, Carli."

She crosses her arms with a pout as I walk past her to get to my office. Her computer pings again and she laughs before I hear the tapping of her acrylic nails on the keyboard. In my peripheral, I see movement in Dawn's office, and she appears at her door as I get closer. I brace myself.

"So, a ride home from Tau Anderson?" Dawn looks at me squarely.

"Yeah, he dropped me off. Nice guy." Every mention of his name was making my stomach tighten. I was so in over my head.

"Only a ride, right? I mean, I think I saw you two catching up a bit after the shoot. Like in that photo, but then again, my eyes aren't what they used to be, right?" I let the rhetorical question hang in the air. "You remember what we talked about?" she whispers.

"Absolutely. I remember very well!" I say, trying to muster up some enthusiasm. "That was me doing my job. Checking in on the talent, tying up loose ends. It's a shame how these sites can paint us all out to be something we're not." Dawn is all about female empowerment, so I try my best to play into that hand.

"Right. Well, great, because I'd hate to see anything get in the way of my plans for you here." She meets my eyes. "I am thinking about promoting you after this last campaign. We'll see how pleased the folks at Ace of Spades are but I think you nailed it, Padawan." She smiles wide with her bright red lipstick exaggerating her small lips.

"That's amazing, Dawn. I can't thank you enough for even considering me." I look toward my office door where I want to sit and process for a minute. But I'm trying not to rush off after Dawn drops what should be great news.

"You've come a long way since being my assistant is all I'm saying." She smiles and turns to head back to her desk. "I'll see you at noon to catch up and figure out life now that the Ace of Spades shoot is over."

I was trying to figure out life after Tau Anderson. I walk into my office where Ryan is already furiously typing away at his keyboard. He seemed to be trying to step it up since his last fumble.

"Hey." He looks up from his computer screen.

"Hey," I reply with a vacant stare. I plop down in my chair, tossing my book bag beside my desk, and wait for my computer screen to illuminate.

"Everything okay?" he asks, raising an eyebrow.

"Great. Looks like Dawn is considering me for a senior position." I force a smile.

"Oh, that sounds awful!" he pokes and rolls his eyes. "You don't sound so excited. Man, maybe after you get promoted, she'll actually notice the work I'm doing," he says.

"Oh, Ryan." I feel like a jerk complaining about someone acknowledging my work.

"It's all good, girlfriend." He tries to sound hip. "I know you're killing it. You know the rest of us frivolous peons are taking lunches and, God forbid, having real lives outside work." He says it with a straight face so I can't tell if he's joking or not.

"Trust me, I know how demanding Dawn can be. Don't let her get to you."

Ryan sighs. "I'm trying. Besides, there will be an opportunity to step up once you're in your new position." He rears back in his chair with his hands behind his head.

I think about how this is it for some people. Ryan wants to work his way up and eventually move over to a larger firm. I wish I could be satisfied with being Dawn's golden-child employee who worked her way up. But I want so much more. It felt like the walls were closing in on me with this job. I needed air.

I trudge my way through the rest of the workday; quitting time can't come fast enough. I was knee-deep in client proposals and emails. Ryan and I pound away at our keyboards as if our lives depend on it. I'm constantly glancing at my phone. This time I don't even ask if Dawn needs anything else on my way out. I'm still thankful for dodging a major bullet earlier.

The week felt so intense, and it was only Wednesday. Even though no one brought up the photo again, I was still so paranoid. I needed to take the edge off for sure, so I stopped to get a bottle of wine on my way home. Talia beat me to the apartment and is right there to greet me as I rush through our door.

She smiles as I walk through the living room. "I am so glad to be somewhere other than the library. Next May cannot come fast enough." She walks to the kitchen and returns with a huge red bowl of popcorn.

"I bet. I admire your academic prowess." I bat my eyes at her. "I finished undergrad and convinced myself each year that passed that I didn't need a master's." We both laugh.

"Oh, you grabbed wine? You read my mind."

"Yes, long day!"

"Seems like you've had a lot of long days. Look, I'll grab us some wineglasses. You go drop your stuff and get comfortable. The show is coming on soon. I can't believe you were at a Tau Anderson shoot two days ago and now we're about to watch him on TV!" she squeals as she jumps up.

"Yeah." I pull out my phone to see if Tau texted. I even resort to checking Twitter and there's nothing but a generic tweet about watching BET tonight.

Walking slowly, I head to my bedroom to put my bag down, kick off my shoes, and gather myself for a moment.

Hey, did you make it okay? So I caved. Another way to look at it was being the bigger person. Was it stupid of me not to take the chance of a lifetime and fly out to Vegas with a sexy superstar? But there was no way to resolve sabotaging my career when I had no other means of income. Music was everything, but if I was being honest with myself, working with Red and Dylan didn't keep the lights on. Tau had come in and completely disrupted my world. It was hard to tell which way was up.

As I rummage through my dresser looking for a pair of sweats, I spot the shirt Tau gave me the first time I spent the night at his hotel. There's a sudden sinking feeling in my lower abdomen. It was terrifying liking someone this much so soon. I wasn't the heart-on-my-sleeve type. I prided myself on leading with my head. Being calculated, logical. Nothing was logical about this.

I head back to the living room, and Talia and I get comfortable in our respective chairs as the red-carpet coverage starts. All the stars are dressed in expensive tuxes or couture gowns. They pose and strut their stuff as a lead-up to a brief interview with Terrence J, who asks them the usual questions—what designers they're wearing and who they're excited about seeing tonight.

"I can't wait to see what Jazmine Sullivan is performing. She is sick with it," Talia says while shoving a handful of popcorn in her mouth, some rebellious crumbs finding their way into the crevices of the couch.

"Right, she is such a freaking beast." I reach for my phone on the side table and check to see if there is a text notification. My lock screen is dull except for multiple Slack notifications from work. I decide to set the phone screen down to stop torturing myself.

The countdown in the bottom left-hand corner of the TV screen is getting closer and closer to showtime. As we're watching and giving our yea or nay on outfits, I immediately recognize Tau's walk. It was always as if he had somewhere important to be. He's clad in a dark blue tux with a white shirt and black tie. His lapels are black, and the suit is a European cut and tailored to perfection. He poses for cameras and reaches his hand out and on the other end is Aminah. Blair's Aminah, who performed at S.O.B.'s and whose account was on my desk for Garter. Her black sheath dress hugs every curve. It's sequined with a boatneck and a low-dipping back. My internal temperature skyrockets. I pull off my hoodie.

"You good?" Talia turns from the screen, glancing at me stripping off my clothes.

"Uhm . . . yeah."

"Tau looks freaking amazing. This is the man you had to act normal around? But wait, I didn't know he was dating Aminah," she says, bumbling on and on. "Doesn't she have that song called 'Focus'?"

What the fuck? echoes in my mind. He got someone else to go with him that quick. Was this chick sitting on reserve somewhere? He had twenty other women he could call to go with him to this thing. I was in no way cut out for a man with that many options.

"Carli!" Talia yells, staring at me. My thoughts consumed me for a moment there.

"Shit, sorry. I was just—"

"Okay, look, what the hell is going on with you? You haven't been yourself lately. We're best friends and I try not to pry, but damn, girl, we're supposed to be able to talk to each other. You've been so unavailable lately." Her eyes are filled with concern.

Everything I'd been keeping to myself the last couple of weeks is finally past max capacity. I open my mouth, unsure of how to start, and it all comes spilling out. "I've been hanging out with Tau." Saying it out loud brings immediate relief. Well, before a beaded throw pillow whizzes past my head.

"Seriously?" Talia grabs another pillow and instead of throwing it literally swings it full force at my head.

"Ouch," I yell. "Please stop assaulting me."

"*Why* wouldn't you tell me this?" She falls back onto the couch.

"I was planning to. But the night he gave me a ride home from my show you were sleeping. And then I decided I shouldn't tell anyone so that it didn't somehow get back to Dawn. Which it almost did yesterday." I reach for popcorn as I watch Tau and Aminah saunter down the rest of the red carpet.

I give her the rundown about seeing him at Aminah's show and him popping up at Palomar's. And the fact that he's the artist Red and I are working with.

"Oh girl, so you been living a whole double life? I mean, that's a lot of lying you were doing." She rolls her eyes so hard I'm not sure if they'll come back around. A light bulb goes off in Talia's head. "Wait, so why is he at this show with Aminah?"

"He asked me to go, but I didn't want people to know, and he shouldn't either, from a PR standpoint. We've only known each other for a couple of weeks. Running around the city together has been crazy enough."

"Let me get this straight. This fine, well-off man asked you to fly to an awards show, likely private, and you politely declined? What is wrong with you?" She imitates a gun to her head and pulls the imaginary trigger.

"Look, I know! And you're not helping right now because I am freaking out over him going with Aminah. She is freaking perfect!" I whine. I lie down on my side and put my head in Talia's lap. She strokes my hair and sighs.

"You're freaking crazy."

"Dawn was kind of onto Tau being on my heels and literally warned me about messing around with him. I wasn't going to be able to talk my way out of being at an awards show with him! Then, the *Daily Spread* thing. There were all these photographers at the shoot. Did you see it?"

"You know I don't have time to read that kind of trash. But hold up, did you—" She purses her lips together and I know exactly what's coming next.

"Yes, and it was everything." I smile and the remorse is immediate. I also explain to her the dilemma with Dylan divulging his feelings, which added another layer of complexity to my life.

"He was legit pissed, like I knew he was checking for me in that way. Cussed me up and down the sidewalk. And in my mind, I'm like, *Am I making a mistake?* Dylan's a great guy and I feel like he makes so much more sense in my world."

"I hate you. But I love you at the same time. Look, I could have told you about Dylan and I've only been around you all on Sundays. Girl, I've seen the way he looks at you." She laughs. "I'm so freaking jealous right now. You have multiple men pissed at you. Meanwhile, there is like one nerd in my civics course that keeps giving me the eye and I am so lonely I've literally considered it."

"I can't," I giggle. "So what do I do? You always have the best advice. I mean Dylan is amazing. And we have such a good time together as friends. But I haven't even considered us as a couple. Then there's Tau, with all the baggage of stardom." I laugh nervously. "But we connect. It's easy with him. I like that he's so confident and doesn't really care what people think of him and yeah, the sex, well . . . Gah." I cover my face with my hands.

"We get one life. It's time you start making some grown-woman decisions. As flighty as my sister is, I love how she just goes for it, you know? Like she knows somehow she'll always land right where she's supposed to."

"I don't want to hurt anyone or be hurt myself."

"And I get that, girl. But love, well, at least the way I see it with my parents, love is about taking chances. Love is about risks."

"Well, right now, neither of them are speaking to me."

"Dylan will come around. At the end of the day, you all are friends and I don't think he'd be willing to give that up so easily. And Tau looks a little busy. But try him when he's back. He's coming back to the city, right?"

"Yeah, he's flying right back. He's here for like another week and a half. But what happens after that? He lives in LA."

"You hurt his pride a little. You think men like that are used to women telling them no?"

"I know. Which is why he didn't take no for an answer the first and second time."

"One should have such problems, my dear." Talia rolls her eyes and gives me a hard pat on the forehead. Her eyes shift past me as she stares off into the distance.

"Are you good?"

"Yeah, it's just . . . You know I'm also working on my review note, which is a big deal, and I know you've been caught up, but I'm out here struggling too."

My heart sinks a little. Here I am rambling about boys while Talia is working on her whole future. She explained it to me over dinner one night: basically, getting published and being selected for your law review's executive board was an amazing résumé builder. It would help her get the corporate law job she really wanted, which was why she had become a library addict these last few months.

"It's just, my note. I know it's amazing because duh!" She laughs. "But I feel like my counterpart is going to get the first publishing spot and she's not even that great."

"So . . . why would she?"

"Because she's like some fifth-generation Boudreaux. There might be a building on campus named after them."

"Oh." I take a deep breath. "Well, that's normal. We work twice as hard to get half the credit, right?"

"But I did the research, and they haven't published a person of color over the last six years since this new professor took over the review. I even found a forum of Black and brown students comparing notes. All of them felt like the notes published above theirs were subpar."

"Damn. So how do you all change anything?"

"That I'm still working on. Fred and I are trying to arrange a meeting to discuss real options. I'm just so tired of having to fight for our place in academia."

"Hey, you can't get tired. You're going to be the most amazing lawyer ever. One that really cares. One that's smart as hell and passionate and has cats," I joke to lighten the mood. "But really, Tally, whether you're first or second getting published, the cream rises to the top."

"Thanks. We all need to be encouraged in our greatness every now and again. I appreciate you, girl." She mulls over her next thought. "But getting back to you, Carli. You need to be honest with the people you love and, most importantly, with yourself. You believe in your writing and the opportunities you have in front of you, right? Maybe it's time to stop using Garter as a crutch. And stop all this lying."

The show blares on. They come to the Ronald Isley tribute and Tau steps onto the stage and sings his ass off. He should do more records like this. People probably have no idea how good a singer he actually is from songs like "Pop That." I wanted to write a song that would showcase those riffs, runs, and harmonies he was truly capable of. Hopefully, what Red and I created was it. Hopefully, he would respond to my texts at some point. All I had were hopes.

Late at night while I'm lying in bed, my phone vibrates. A call from Tau.

"Hey," I say into oblivion.

No answer on the other end. In the background, shuffling and muffled voices are all I hear. Then loudly the laugh of a woman and Tau's drawl emanate from the phone speaker.

"Hello!" I say into the phone, irritated.

Nothing.

"Tau." I sit up to see if I can hear actual words but it's indistinguishable. Only a bunch of swishing around and giggles. The phone beeps as it hangs up from his end and I stare into the darkness, wondering why he is still with Aminah this late into the night.

TRACK 16

I pull my hair up into a high pouf, adjusting my curls so they frame my face right, and wrap a tribal scarf around it that Talia gave me from her trip to Cape Town with her family. Looking pretty always helps when I feel so crappy. I reach for my highlighter, fill in my brows, and throw on some red lipstick. And just like that, I feel a bit better.

I'm scheduled to play at Palomar's, but with everything going on, my heart isn't in it. I haven't written much outside of the record that may or may not see the light of day for Tau. Red had a date night and Talia was visiting her parents. It would just be me. Maybe that's what I needed. Me and my guitar.

Still nothing from Tau aside from the infuriating butt dial and I know he's back in the city. One more week left to his trip. I heard him on *The Breakfast Club* yesterday after his performance. My pride drew the line at one text after getting crickets the last time I reached out. Red asked me this morning if I heard anything about the session for this weekend and I didn't have the guts to tell her there may not be one. I reach for my guitar and head out to catch the train.

Palomar's is packed as usual on a Friday night. I find the promoter to let him know I'm here. It's hot and the smell from the barbecue is thick in the air. I feel better. I feel ready. I feel at home.

The familiar rush of adrenaline comes over me as I hear them preparing to introduce me.

"Carlisa Henton!"

The crowd applauds and I approach the stage. As I sit down and adjust my guitar and feel the familiar heat of the lights on my skin, nothing else matters. I envision those moments with my father on our porch in Maryland and backstage at his shows, plucking the guitar strings, learning the notes, and remind myself that no matter what, this is where I belong. No, nothing even matters. Not Tau, Dawn, Dylan. All that matters is this moment. I decide to start with a rendition of "Nothing Even Matters" from Ms. Lauryn Hill.

As I finish my set, I stand up to thank the crowd and hear a clap that echoes loudly over all the others. I squint to see a tall, thin figure with hair reaching for the sun.

I walk off stage to lingering applause and head toward Dylan.

"Hey," I say while grabbing my guitar case from a small table in the corner to tuck my acoustic Ibanez away.

"Great job. I don't know, it really seems like you're gearing up to be an artist someday. I'd buy a show ticket."

"Nah, I love writing songs. Feels good to play here. But only here." I stand my guitar case upright to lean on it. Our last encounter was harsh. I had no idea how to act around Dylan.

"Look, I'm sorry about last weekend." He gets right to it. "Can we talk? Maybe go somewhere a little quieter?"

"Uhm . . . okay. Talia made a huge dinner before she left. We can grab some leftovers at my place if you want?"

I lift up my guitar, which he takes from my hand and carries out the door. We stand outside Palomar's in the warm night breeze while he requests a ride on his phone. Cars whiz past and couples walk briskly to their destinations. There's an awkward silence.

"I overreacted. I know." Dylan turns to face me. His eyes have a veil of remorse.

"About which part?"

"Both. You guys working with Tau and whatever you have going on with Tau."

"Well, the work is just work. I mean, you know that. It's how it goes. Red believes in you. And I think you're a star."

"Yeah?"

"Really." The car pulls up and we jump inside and greet the driver.

Dylan is to my right; I angle my body toward him so I can look him in the eye. "You're an incredible artist, Dylan, and a few weeks is not really going to make a difference. You know that. I think you were mad about the other thing so you blew up about the new project." I glance out the window. I wasn't sure if the other thing was actually a thing anymore.

"I don't get what you see in him," he says, searching my eyes for answers. "Like, all these dudes try to get at you and you block them left and right, and this guy? The panty raider, or whatever his songs say. Definitely didn't think it would be a dude like that." He shakes his head.

"You can judge me, that's cool. I get it. But something was—I mean, I don't want to talk about it if it's going to make you uncomfortable." I'm nervous to make things worse.

"I'm cool. I just really don't get it."

"Something was different, like sincere. Even though he has this whole playboy persona, I guess. He sees me in this weird way. Beyond the physical attraction. Maybe I'm stupid, who knows? Nothing feels as sure to me as it used to," I say, sighing.

"At the end of the day, my feelings aside, I don't want to see you get hurt. I mean, the Aminah Matthews thing?" The wrinkles in his forehead grow more pronounced.

"I'm sure he has tons of girls to take to awards shows," I say, shrugging.

"That's exactly what I mean, that ain't fly. I don't care how many girls were around, you would be worth sacrificing all that." I let his words sink in. We both look out of our respective windows until we pull up in front of my apartment building. As we both wish the driver good night, Dylan grabs my guitar and follows me up the steps. My phone vibrates in the pocket of my denim jacket.

Studio tomorrow at 8. It's Tau. I breathe in the night air slowly, relieved work is still on his mind. This was a first, a man who didn't let his pride get in the way of the work. Who still thought I was talented enough to work with.

"Good news?" Dylan asks as I slide my key into the building door. We make our way up the stairs to my place.

"Oh yeah, Red telling me about our session tomorrow." I push open the door to my apartment and toss my keys on the coffee table. I grab my guitar from him.

"I *am* happy for you guys," he starts. "I'm only an artist who's sensitive about my shit."

"I know." I pat him on the shoulder.

I tell Dylan to head to the kitchen while I go to my bedroom and return my guitar to its rightful place in the corner near my overflowing hamper. I need to get to that laundry. The brevity of Tau's text hits me. Nothing in regard to us personally, only a date and time for the studio. He's been in control of this thing the whole time and the fact that he couldn't screw me into wanting to be seen in public with him bugged him. I wasn't stupid enough to jeopardize the work though, so I send back a simple Okay cool after deleting and retyping countless other options.

I walk into the kitchen to find Dylan humming a tune to himself. His voice is pure and his runs flawless. He's always been attractive with his full lips and artsy swag, but after frivolous dating escapades early on, I was in a place where I just wanted to focus on my career when Dylan came into my life. And that's what I have been trying to do until this point. I had tunnel vision.

"Your tone is the best."

"Thank you. You know, I've heard that forever. After a while you start to think you're special until you get out there and there's twenty million other special singers and you're trying to stand out." He pulls at the vintage jersey he rocks under a hoodie and adjusts the rings that adorn every finger.

"I hear that. I mean, I thought knowing guitar and being able to write would be a fast track to the top. But this business is about so much more than the talent. Navigating the waters, making good connections, hell, learning how to move in a room full of vultures."

"Exactly. People always ask me, 'Well, why isn't so-and-so more popular?' And it's like, it could be a lot of fucking reasons. If I knew, I'd figure the formula of popularity out for myself."

"Dylan—" I start and then stop.

"What?" He steps closer, putting his hand on my shoulder.

"Sometimes I hope God wouldn't be so cruel that you could work so hard toward something for it not to happen. That you could see something so clearly when you close your eyes but for it to never be tangible."

"For real. Sometimes you feel close but so far. You guys working with homeboy threw me for a loop. Someone else special, you know? Something else in the way of the finish line. I don't have a plan B. Without music, I don't know what I would do with my life."

I place my hand on his and reassure him with a small pat. Nodding in agreement, I go to the refrigerator to grab leftovers. We were all trying to be something, to be special, and hoping that we could believe it long enough to convince the rest of the world.

"And the answer is no," he says.

"Wait, what?"

"God is not that cruel. But it's his timing, not ours. That seems to be what trips us up most times." He runs his hands over his hair. "But look, what is up with you and Tau? I mean, I've been quiet long enough. You're funny, hella sexy without even knowing it, dumb talented, and ambitious. Does he know that?" He looks up and our eyes meet.

Breaking the intensity of his gaze, I start pulling out containers and spread them across the breakfast bar. I'm not sure what to say. I'm not used to Dylan speaking his mind when it comes to me. He does about every other thing, which is why it's shocking that he's held this in for so long.

"We were just kicking it. No pretense," I say while sorting through the containers. "And I'm not a gold digger."

"You know I know that. I was pissed. My fault, yo. I never should have said that shit to you. I'm really sorry," he offers.

"But I'm as confused as you about the Aminah thing, so can we drop it?" I plead.

"For now," he retorts as he steps over to help me make plates from the vast amount of Tupperware. "So, what's this new record y'all been working on for this dude?"

"Ahh, I love it. I think it's really dope." I light up and start to hum the melody and Dylan nods along. I get to the bridge and he starts to sing with me and catches some of the harmony notes. "Yup!" I say in between mumbling out the last notes. He laughs as I finish the idea.

"No cap, it's *Billboard* status."

"Thanks!" I'm warmed by Dylan's smile. Maybe he was the better guy. Kind, sensitive, and thoughtful about the world and all its shortcomings.

After doing damage to the leftovers, we head to the living room to watch one of the comedy specials on Netflix. We argue over whether we should watch Bill Burr or Mike Epps and end up watching both into the wee hours of the morning. As the credits run, Dylan looks at his phone, which reads 2 a.m., and we both agree we should call it.

"This was fun," I say as I walk Dylan down to the ground floor.

"Very fun, Carli. Look, I'm sorry, okay?"

"It's all good, Dylan. I'm sorry too. We're good."

He pulls me into a tight hug and nestles his chin in my neck. I smell the frankincense that permanently wafts from his being. He lingers close while still holding on to me and our eyes meet. I can feel his heart beating under my hand, which rests on his chest. We pause and he leans slightly forward with his eyes closed, and before I can think, I feel his lips on mine and we kiss. I pull away when I realize what's happening. Not only was I being a shitty whatever I was to Tau, this would only complicate the things Dylan and I just peaced up.

"We shouldn't."

"I know." He looks more intense than I've ever seen him. He searches my eyes for the truth.

"Dylan."

"Carli, I've wanted to do that for a long time."

He hops down the front steps and looks back at me. I wave to him as he gets into the gray Hyundai he called. A truck pulls up behind him on our one-way street, the bright lights distracting. It's late and Future's voice blares from the speakers rapping about commas and fucking them up. Dylan shakes his head and closes the car door. As the Hyundai starts to pull off, the vehicle behind speeds off as well. Brooklyn has its share of crazies. I close the door and head back up to the apartment. I can still taste his kiss. Part of me wants to wash it off, but the other part can't stop savoring it.

Staring deeply into the bathroom mirror, I realize no answers are going to come from looking at my reflection. Tau was someone special, but I hadn't anticipated the jolt of electricity I felt when kissing Dylan.

Red is pumped about presenting the song we created. I'm anxious as hell. This Saturday will be my first time seeing Tau since he's been back from Vegas. Then there was linking with Dylan, which scrambled my brain. I'm not going to let man trouble mess up this opportunity. This is make-or-break. We had one more week to get it right before Tau was back on a plane to LA. If Tau records one of my songs, it has the potential to change everything for Red and me.

After tackling an inordinate amount of laundry, enough to see the shag rug in my room again, I gather my things to head to the studio. Humming the melody as I skip down the stairs, the title comes to me. "Good Morning, Love." That was the name. They normally came to me after the song was complete.

The same receptionist from last time greets me when I arrive at Stadium Studios. She informs me we're back in Studio A. I push open the soundproof door and Meck is on the other side.

"What's up?"

I look at him and toss my bag near one of the chairs closest to the wall. I trace the strings of the guitars set up in the corner. He stares at me as I completely ignore his greeting.

"Really? So she's fucking Tau Anderson and now she's too good to speak. Funny," he says while making a sucking sound with his teeth. He straightens his ugly chain and adjusts his polo shirt. "Your man says he's running late."

His verbal assault is jarring and the wild look in his eyes reminds me of the last time we were alone in a studio. My skin starts to crawl. Okay, Tau was late, but where the hell was Red?

"I'm out." I turn to hit the door and he closes the gap between us fast and grabs my arm. "Get off me," I yell back at him while trying to snatch my arm from his grip.

"Maybe now I can see what's so fucking special about it. Does glitter shoot out of it or something?" He's so close his hot-ass breath is violating my nose.

"Get the hell off me, Meck!" I shout, but I'm sure no one can hear me through the thick soundproof door. My skin is flushed. The door is maybe seven steps away, but that's practically the distance of a stadium from end to end in my position. I've never in my life had someone put their hands on me and my mind is racing about how to escape. He grabs me tighter and pushes me against the wall, knocking one of the gold plaques off-center. He pins both of my arms against the wall. I'm writhing in his grip but he's so much stronger than me.

"You let him hit it and not me, huh?" His eyes are wide and glassy. "I get you into a good situation and you still want to act like a bougie-ass bitch!"

I can barely hear him, though I realize he's calling me every name under the sun. His voice is this low buzz while I literally search for anything I can grab hold of to knock him over the head. What makes a person like this? What makes a person think they have some type of entitlement to a woman? His crazed look is terrifying, his whole face distorted.

His grip gets tighter and sweat is starting to form on his forehead as we tussle. I desperately yank and pull to free my wrists, but it only makes my skin burn. I kick at him, and he dodges until I stick one right in his balls like my dad always taught me. He grabs for his junk and reaches back for me with a balled fist, but I sidestep him and the door swings open.

Red. Mark. Tau.

Tau's eyes dart back and forth as I smooth out my disheveled hair and look down at my wrists. He moves with swift precision across the room and stands between Meck and me. Meck's eyes water as he doubles over. I readjust my cropped hoodie and rub my wrists. The pressure of his fingers digging into them persists.

"Carli? You cool? What the fuck just happened?" he asks, pushing Meck to the floor.

"Yo, for real, Tau? Over this bitch!"

Tau uses his foot to keep him down. "You should shut up. You know that, right?"

Red makes her way over to me and hugs me before pulling my face into her hands. "You good? What happened? Did he?" She looks from Meck to me.

I'm frozen. The words are stuck in my chest like the wind has been knocked out of me.

"Yo, get this dude the fuck out of here, Mark, before I kill him." Tau presses into Meck's side harder with his sneaker. "I let you slide the first time with the shit you talked. But you put your hands on her? On my girl?"

Mark rushes over and lifts Meck off the floor like he's a child. Hoisting him up by his arms, he drags him toward the door.

"Let me get my stuff at least," Meck pleads as he's twisted up in Mark's grip.

Tau grabs his bag and tosses it at his head. "We done. Like never again."

"Ain't shit, man, I was just fucking with her. I wasn't going to do nothing. Her stuck-up ass think she can treat people however," he says through his crooked mouth.

I cringe at his voice.

"I hope it was worth it, Meck. I told you this wasn't the place for your shit. We done."

"Over a groupie-ass bitch, huh? You throwing away years?"

"Ain't gon' be too many more bitches, homie." Tau starts to head toward him and Red moves to block his way. Opening the heavy door with Meck in tow, Mark pushes him out and disappears into the hallway.

"Wait, did he say 'my girl'?" Red whispers, still stroking my hair.

"Well," I say softly. I had no idea what we were. "We'll talk about it later."

"This dude really tried it? Like I really would have killed this dude," Tau says to us, but kind of to himself as well. He paces the floor before walking over to me, and Red takes a step back.

"Did he hurt you? My fault, man. I never thought he would pull a sucka move like that." He shakes his head.

"No. He gripped my arms up a little. If I was lighter, I might be bruised," I say, trying to laugh.

"That shit ain't funny." He shakes his head. "Mark is going to fuck him up. Discreetly. Just know that. And I would too if I didn't have this whole image shit to care about," he says. "You don't have to worry about him."

How silly to think that maybe something would be different this time. Putting an opportunity before my safety.

"We should just reschedule, Carli. I'm so sorry this happened." Red looks at me, concerned.

"Yeah, I'll bite the bullet on this one, let's get back up later."

"No, I don't want that bastard ruining my night," I interrupt and walk over to readjust the plaque on the wall.

"Carli, it's not that deep, we can do this another time," Red reassures me. "I was a little sick myself, which is why I was late. I'm sorry."

"No, fuck him. Just give me a second."

I walk out to the restroom and notice the receptionist is bewildered.

"Do I need to call the police? Is everything okay?" she asks.

"No, we're good. Sorry about the commotion. But we're good."

Once in the bathroom, safe from view, I take a deep breath and lose it. My body heaves as the tears dig tunnels down my cheeks. What just went down with Meck had unleashed the floodgates. Pacing back and forth I try to decide if I can handle being in the studio right now. I splash water on my face and adjust my curls. My hands were still shaking but I meant what I said. Meck had taken enough from me. I was going to play this record for Tau and spend the night making heartfelt music. Going home and feeling sorry for myself wasn't going to get me any further. I had to prove Meck wrong. I wasn't a piece of ass to Tau. I was a talented songwriter who knew her stuff.

I walk back into the studio to Red's and Tau's stares. Nothing is turned on and the room is quiet.

"I said we would work, y'all. For real. Please don't take this moment from me."

Tau looks at me intensely as I walk over to pull my notebook from my bag. Everything is still for a few seconds.

"Aight," he finally says.

Red grabs the auxiliary cord so she can plug in her laptop and play the music out of the speakers.

"Carli killed the lyrics, man. She brought what we did to life."

"Early morning the light filters through the blinds, illuminating this perfection I call mine. How lucky am I to have her by my side?" my voice booms through the speakers. Of course, I can hear all the imperfections in my vocals, but I try to block it out and vibe. The song is so soft and it's talking about love instead of sex, which would definitely be a turn for Tau. He's taking in every word.

"Pull her back into my arms, kiss her cheek and say to her, 'Good morning, good morning, good morning, love.'" The hook is my favorite part. It's this

mix between John Legend and Stevie Wonder. It's the type of song that makes you look forward to falling in love one day with the hope of finding someone who makes you relate to the lyrics. I get lost in the music. The arrangement is so light and airy, and the guitar is the perfect lead sound that drives the whole thing.

"Stop it," Tau says.

Red and I exchange a look. Tau strokes his beard and taps his foot on the floor. Mark walks back in with a simple nod to Tau. He cracks his knuckles before taking his seat in the corner and pulling out his crossword.

"What's the word?" Red asks.

"Run it back."

When she plays it again, this time until the end, there's a long pause when the record finishes. Tau finally makes eye contact with me.

"This shit is amazing."

A wave of relief washes over me. I was tugging on my necklace the whole time, waiting for his response. I'd imagined hearing him say those words about the track over and over in my mind. We try to decide if we should cut it tonight, and Tau assures us that he has the room locked in. But they both still have a look of worry in their eyes for me.

"I told you I'm good. Better than ever knowing that you like the record."

My phone rings.

"Oh, let me take this," I say to no one in particular.

Tau's eyes follow me across the room. I step out into the hall and walk back to the waiting area.

"Papa, hey? Everything okay?" Hearing from him again so soon has me worried.

"Hey CC, are you okay? You don't sound right."

"I'm okay, Papa. What's up?" I would never tell my dad what happened with Meck. He would go crazy, as in hunt down Meck and hurt him. We barely spent enough time together as is. Prison would complicate things.

"I'm in your city! I have some time until my ten o'clock hit. Where are you?"

Of course, he never lets me know ahead of time that he's coming. I'm in the studio session of a lifetime after another traumatic run-in with Meck. And Tau Anderson is about to cut one of *my* records.

"Uhm, I'm at the studio, I'm not sure I can meet you. We're literally just getting started."

"All good, *mija*, I'll come to you. Where are you?" I can hear the excitement in his voice. I miss him. I always wanted to be seen as a serious musician, to make him proud of me.

"Well, let me check, Dad. I mean, it's kind of with a big artist." I shift my weight, anxious to get back inside to cut.

"Ohhh, too Hollywood for your own papa? Let me know, *mija*, I don't have too much time, but I want to get there."

"Okay, Papa, give me a minute. I'll text you."

I breathe in deep. With the evening's events, I don't want to rock the boat. When I step back into the studio, Tau is already in the booth practicing the lines for the first verse. I bite my lip and push open the booth door letting it close behind me.

"I need to ask you something."

"Hey, mute my mic real quick," he says to Red, who gives him the thumbs-up through the thick glass.

"My dad is in town and I don't know how long he's here. Can he stop by the session? He has a show at ten, so he won't be here long."

"So your dad is a musician?" He nods. "Yeah, whatever."

"Okay, thanks."

I shoot my dad a text letting him know it's cool for him to stop by. Meanwhile, Tau is killing the performance on this record. I love this texture of his voice. It's rich, meaningful. The work fills the ache Meck left behind.

My phone buzzes about thirty minutes into the session. There's a text from my dad letting me know he's arrived. My heart flutters as I pop out of the studio room to head to the elevator. I jump out at ground level, open the door, and there my dad stands about six feet two, adoration all over his face. His hair is grayer than when I saw him sometime last year. His skin is an olive tone and tanned to perfection, making his green eyes stand out that much more. His hair is cut short, and the guitar attached to his back towers over his head. All the albums, late nights, and tours, and he was still so handsome, so fly.

"Papa!" I say and melt into his arms.

"Wow, look at you! CC, you're so beautiful," he says, patting my hair down and kissing the top of my head.

I pull back and look up at him. "We're cutting one of my songs, Pop."

"Well, let's get in there." We head upstairs and through the doors of Stadium Studios.

Red is at the board going over the background parts with Tau in the booth when we get in. The lights are turned down low to set the vibe, so it's hard to see him. I twirl my nameplate chain.

"You still wear it?" My dad looks down at my chain in my fingers. He bought it for me when I was about ten years old.

"Of course. Had to get a few more links put on it," I say, smiling. "This is my dad, James Henton," I say to Red. "He's passing through before his gig later."

"James Henton is your damn father?" she says, looking at me with her eyes so wide, her eyebrows raise. "Now it makes sense why Carli is so damn talented," she gushes to my dad as she stands to shake his hand.

"Wow," he says in his thick, raspy voice. "That's always good to hear. Listen, I'm a fly on the wall. You guys do your thing."

"What's up?" Tau interjects through the speakers.

"Oh sorry, Carli's dad came in," Red says, pressing the talkback button.

"My fault," Tau says through the mic. The headphones slam against the music stand and he emerges from the booth.

"Tau Anderson." He leans in after they shake hands.

"I know you. My boy Dex plays keys in your band." My dad nods and smiles. "I'm James, James Henton. CC didn't tell me she was writing with Tau Anderson."

"CC?" Tau smirks.

"I'm sorry. Carlisa." My dad looks over at me nervously, knowing that I hate when he lets "CC" slip around anyone but family.

"But wait, *the* James Henton? Like played with Rico Stone and the Nasties, James Henton? My mom was trying to get me to play guitar so bad because of those records!"

"Ha!" My dad clasps his hands together. "Aw man, yeah, that was when things got fun."

I was used to people geeking out over my dad, but watching Tau have a fanboy moment was extra fun. Even if folks didn't know *the* James Henton right away, it was always the Rico Stone stuff that they remembered. That's when things took off for him, and my mom and I became a liability. It was a sore spot. I was proud of him, of course, and his work helped me become the musician I was now. But his stardom left a gaping hole in my family.

"Well, yeah, so Dad, have a seat. We're just digging in here." I shake my head. Tau lingers and looks at me, smiling cynically. He turns to head back into the booth to pick up where we left off.

We get right back to it. Tau is such a professional. Dylan is a great vocalist, but Tau has a way of stacking vocals for the backgrounds effortlessly. It's easy to tell he's been doing it a long time. The precision is uncanny. Clearly, he was a student of the school of Brandy.

"This is really good, CC—I mean, Carlisa," my dad says quietly, as Red works some of her magic adding reverb and compression to the vocals.

"Thanks. Using what you taught me."

"I feel like we could recut some of these guitar parts." Red is essentially thinking out loud.

"Oh, well, I guess maybe my dad could do it, since he's here." I look over at him.

"Ha!" My dad swats his hand in the air. "I'm an old man these days. This is your moment, CC—Carlisa. I don't want to impose."

"Dad, no, it would be great. Live guitar would really kill this. I didn't even think of that," I plead.

"I don't have much time," he says.

"You don't need much time. You're a professional."

"Come on, I'll plug you in real quick." Red grabs the instrument cord to plug his guitar into the compressor.

"We're going to try something. Record Mr. Henton on guitar," Red says to Tau.

"You're in charge." His voice echoes through the speakers.

My dad pulls out his guitar, Bella as he calls her, and plugs in. Red hits Play a couple of times so he can get familiar with the music. He noodles around to get the chords and does what I've known him to do. He plays beautifully. Tau steps out of the booth nodding along to the tempo. After a few takes, we get it down and Red even makes room for a short solo.

"Wow, I mean, the man, the myth, the legend," Red says with a reflective nod. "My dad used to run those Rico vinyls into the ground before he died. Mr. Henton, that was extraordinary."

"James. Call me James." His laugh makes his chiseled cheeks all the more pronounced. "And yeah, Carli's a pretty good guitar player herself. She could have played this, but I bet she doesn't say that. Still doesn't hit that F chord correctly though."

"I get it done," I say, rolling my eyes.

"I hate that I have to go so soon. I have to figure out when we're flying out. I'll give you a call to let you know for sure." He stands up, wrapping up the cord to hand back to Red and placing his guitar back in its case.

"James, good to meet you," Tau says in awe.

"Good meeting you, too. Thanks for giving my daughter a chance. She's always been too proud to let me help her. Independent. Taking it all on her shoulders when she didn't have to." He shakes Tau's hand firmly and looks him in the eye. My dad is so old-school. He's all "always look a man in the eye" and "your word is all you have." I can't believe I got to share a piece of this moment with him.

"Dad," I say through clenched teeth.

"All right, all right, I'm out." My dad nods as he hoists his guitar up over his shoulders. He and Red share a glance and she reaches out her hand but he hugs her instead. I take the elevator all the way down to see him out. Two cabs pass him by and finally one slows down. I cross my arms, as the late air is cooler than when I arrived.

"I'm good, baby. I'll call you tomorrow."

"That was amazing, Dad."

"It was. Thank you. That meant a lot to an old man."

"Maybe you can come to church tomorrow? Hang out with me and Talia?" I beg. He wasn't really the church type.

"Maybe," he says, before giving me a tight hug and throwing his guitar in the cab ahead of him.

"Gramercy Theatre, Dad. It would be great to spend a little more time with you," I say, giving him the puppy dog look. He waves and blows me a kiss. I linger as I watch the cab whiz down the block and maneuver in and out of traffic.

Red and Tau are listening to the playback of what we recorded when I get back into the session. She runs the record back from the top. The music blasts from the speakers and Tau's voice is smooth, captivating, and airy. The performance is seamless. It's better than I could have ever imagined. I thought I was a pretty good singer, but it was amazing to hear a real singer bring my words to life. He knew where to put the right inflections, when to pull back, exactly what timbre was best for certain words. There was nothing like that magic.

I look around the room waiting for feedback. It seems like they're in a daze still trying to digest what they heard. I can hear my heart beating in my ears. Right before I resolve that they hate it, a huge smile invades Red's lips. She wants to say something, but she's trying to let Tau speak first.

"This record will bring the whole project together." He looks over at me.

I'm realizing I've worked my whole life for these few hours in the studio.

Mark is downstairs with dinner. Red heads down to help him carry things up before we get started on another idea. My phone is on the board next to Tau, who is nestled in his seat. It vibrates violently against a fader. He looks up from scrolling through his phone and peeks over at mine. Picking it up off the board, he turns to me slowly.

"Dylan," he says, reading the notification on the screen as I walk toward him to grab the phone. "Dylan," he repeats with recognition. "That's your boy who was at Palomar's with you?"

"Oh yeah, he's probably wondering how the session is going," I say, scrolling through the text. I sit back down.

"Tall, lanky, right? High-top fade?" he presses.

"Yeah," I say, getting suspicious. What exactly is his current infatuation with Dylan?

"So the same guy that was leaving your crib last night?" He says it calmly, but I can see a fire brewing in his eyes. "The guy I asked about and you said he was your homie is the same guy I saw leaving your crib when I drunkenly asked Mark to drive me over there after my appearance at a club? I forgot about it with all the bullshit today."

I knew eventually we would circle back to where we left off before the awards show. But I wasn't prepared to be ambushed about Dylan.

"Dylan is my *friend*." At least he was before we kissed. Now, I was confused about all of it. "He was leaving my place because he came to my show and we caught up. He was pissed at me for lying to him about you," I say, scooting to the edge of my seat.

"Me?"

"Yeah, you. He saw me leave with you from Palomar's and saw you on TV like everyone else did with Aminah Matthews."

He laughs and shakes his head.

"What's funny?" I snap back at him.

"You're funny. You don't want to go with me. I see some dude leaving your crib in the middle of the night and you're questioning me. I can't make this shit up," he says, looking at the door. I'm thinking we have about two minutes to get to the bottom of this before Red and Mark come back into the control room.

"I don't know . . . what I want," slips out.

"That's clear. Look, I've been straightforward with you since the gate. But you, you've been throwing me crazy flavor one minute and then you're cold the next. I don't have the time, shawty. So, if it's business, you wrote an amazing record. Let's do that again and we'll be straight. You don't ever have to worry about me trying to keep you from a bag."

"There's nothing going on between me and Dylan," I say, swallowing the guilt. I needed to figure out what was happening between me and Dylan before trying to explain it to Tau. Looking for a place to expel my nervous energy, I pick up one of the guitars and practice my F chord.

"Aminah was a favor for Blair. And it's not like the girl I asked to go with me was available. It's not that complicated."

"Dawn warned me about getting involved with you, Tau. It's not that simple either." I pause for a second, remembering his late-night call. "Did you sleep with her? You butt-dialed me."

My heart feels clenched, bracing for whatever Tau says next.

"No. When I played her my new record, she liked it. And I couldn't believe she was being honest. And I thought about your ass and how you keep it real with me and I like that. We went back to my hotel, but with a few other people, late. And when she was hanging around like she wanted to stay, I told her I was tired and had an early flight." He rubs his temples and reaches for his bottled water.

Red and Mark push through the door with food.

"Hey!" Tau says, throwing his arms up in the air. "All right, we fitna bust this grub and then we can dig into this new track Red talkin' 'bout," he says, completely switching gears.

Mark distributes our orders while Red plays the new track. We play around with some vocal ideas while the music plays and Tau hits a groove that Red likes. She motions for us to head into the booth. He has the melody and I start mumbling words while she records. We come to a part where I take the harmony note and Red hears both of us through the mic. The music stops.

"Hold up, do that again," she says through the talkback.

"Wait, what?" We're both so lost in the moment.

"Sing that last line again, it sounded amazing together, I don't want to lose that."

Red plays it back so that we can get it better this time. We work through the rest of the record with some words and some nonsense. Red is in the control room trying to piece together an arrangement to make it make sense. While she's tweaking, I sit on the stool in the corner of the booth while Tau stands near the mic. The lights are low in the booth and just the light from the huge computer screen creeps in through the window.

"So, what happens now?"

"I think she's just mixing the vocals," he says, looking back at me.

"I mean with me and you."

"Look, I'm not tryna mess up your career. I just thought we had something going. You're dope as hell, honestly. At the end of the day, a career is something we do. It's not who we are. But if it's that important to you, I'm not going to stand in the way of that."

"The problem is I want it all. I want the life Garter affords me. But the music gives me fulfillment. I want to be able to let myself fully live in the moment, but that might land me right back in Maryland looking crazy."

"Well, maybe some things are worth the risk."

Tau puts the headphones on the mic stand and walks up to me. He stands close while I'm still sitting on the stool. He brushes my hair back and takes my face in his hands, which feel surprisingly soft. He guides my lips to his and they're savory.

"Ahem," I hear through the headphones. Red clears her throat waiting to get our attention.

"I think we got something here. Care to hear it?" she asks.

We worked pretty late into the night and ended up at my apartment instead of Tau's hotel. Two records were in the can. I couldn't believe how fast things were moving. His departure was creeping up slowly, only a handful of days left in the cocoon we created.

My tribal duvet from Urban Outfitters covers his body. The queen-size bed feels so much smaller with two bodies in it instead of just mine. I've been up for a while when he starts to stir. Blinking profusely to gather his focus, he turns and looks at me.

"I have to get ready for church before Talia kills me," I say, lying on my side to face Tau.

"She don't know you're a heathen?" he says quietly with a laugh.

I push him so he topples over onto his back.

"Really? One missed grace and now I don't know Jesus?" I shake my head.

"Hey . . ." His eyes turn serious. "I'm sorry again about yesterday."

"It's over. Really. It could have been worse. I'm glad you showed up when you did."

"I will never let something like that happen again."

"I'm fine. Really. It's over." I had barely slept. I wasn't okay and Tau knew it, too. But I would be. I always kept going because what was the alternative?

He reaches for me and pulls my head toward him for a kiss.

"Mark's on his way to get me. We can drop you at church and then meet me later? Where's your bathroom?" He gets up, slowly making his way to the door.

"It's across from the other bedroom down the hall." I ogle him a bit in his briefs and he crosses his hands over his chest.

"Uhm, excuse me?" He laughs and tiptoes out the door.

Leaning back into my pillows, I cover my face with one as I exhale slowly. When I look over at my phone, the time reads 6:30 a.m.

Shoot. Dylan. I forgot to respond to his text. He was such a big reason this was even happening. He played the records that put us on Meck's radar. If these records saw the light of day, I had to do something for him. Man, Dylan. I needed to be able to talk to him face-to-face.

Session went well. I know we still need to talk, I shoot back.

She does exist. I'll be here when you're ready. See you later, he replies.

Tau is singing "Love U Better" by Ty Dolla $ign over the running water in the bathroom. That's an inspiring sound to hear in the morning. I pull the covers farther up. Closing my eyes, I drift back to sleep and the footsteps heading to my room startle me. I open my eyes to see Talia in my doorway.

"Uhm, who is in our bathroom?" she asks with a smirk.

"Uhmm . . ." I twirl my fingers. "Tau?" I say nervously.

"Tau freaking Anderson is in our bathroom?" she says, her eyebrows raising inches on her face.

"Talia, I need you to stop freaking out and I need you to disappear before he walks back in in his draws," I say, mortified.

"Ahhh, right!" Throwing her arms in the air, she scurries down the hall to her room and the bathroom door opens. Tau reappears with his hair smoothed down and a hand towel on his shoulder.

"Why do women have so many products? It's like a beauty supply store in there." He looks confused.

"You can close the door. My roommate," I say, jumping up and grabbing my #blkcreatives tee from my dresser. I also locate a pair of basketball shorts. This is what it was like to have clean laundry.

"Oh . . . hey, roommate!" he yells as he pushes the door closed.

"Hey!!!" Talia replies from her bedroom.

"So I get to meet a friend? I don't know, maybe you're moving too fast, Carli," he says through a grin.

He makes his way closer as I gather his clothes to hand to him. Taking the clothes out of my hand and putting them on my desk chair, he stops and stares at the photo of my dad and me. It was a sound check for the ASCAP Awards in LA. When he was playing, he would always bring me along. I would sit in the shadows backstage and watch him. It was invigorating to see him play, how every note affected the crowd. I wanted to make people feel the way he did.

"CC," he whispers, and pushes me back onto the bed.

"Really?" I twist my face up. "No one calls me that but my dad's family. I hate it."

"I like it. And your dad is James Henton? You were holding on to that ace. You never thought about writing songs with your dad? Getting him to help you?"

"It's complicated. I resented him for a long time, you know? And then I just got stubborn, wanting to make my own way." I attempt to push myself up out of the bed but he leans his weight against me. "I thought you had to get ready to leave?"

"Yeah." He smiles and playfully bites my bottom lip.

"For real, Mark will be here soon."

"Mark works for me, remember?" He lifts himself up and reaches for his pants. "And I'm saying what's up to Roommate on my way out."

"Fine."

He winks at me before scrolling through his phone. We head out of my bedroom and Hillsong Worship music is blasting in the kitchen. Talia is jamming, hands raised and all, waiting for the toaster to pop.

"Talia, meet Tau," I say in disbelief that an artist of his caliber is hitting the walk of shame out of my apartment.

"Talia, beautiful! Nice to meet you!" He smiles and his dimples are deep.

Talia is giddy at the sound of her name. "Loved your performance the other night."

"Thanks!"

"Finally, I get to meet the person who has Carli looking vibrant." She smiles slyly.

"Ha! Yeah, I guess so. You looking vibrant, huh?" He laughs, looking at me, and reaches for a side hug from Talia. "Good to know."

Later, Mark is waiting outside and the Escalade is freshly washed. Tau, Talia, and I pile in. They cackled like two schoolgirls the whole time I was getting ready.

"We're going to run past Gramercy Theatre," Tau says as Mark gives him a nod in the rearview. "Would love to be able to come with y'all actually."

"You know we have a whole VIP section if you want to stay," Talia says.

"Ha! Yeah, I feel like all the churches in LA are like that. It's weird though to be all separated in church. When I go home, my momma has none of that. It's like, I'm regular as they come. I miss that part of it sometimes. It'd be great to get home while I'm on the East Coast." He stares off into the distance.

I instinctively place a reassuring hand on his leg.

"I have to get up with Frankie to go over some travel stuff. The dates for finishing the album in LA and all. The last show with Usher."

That reality sinks into my chest. LA. That's where his life is.

Mark pulls over to the side of Twenty-Third Street and we see people filing through the doors held open by greeters and volunteers.

"Okay, I'm totally cool with sounding groupie-ish, but we should take a flick!" Talia flashes all twenty-eight of her teeth.

"But of course," Tau assures her.

He positions his phone in the air and I push his arm up a bit more to get the best angle. As cheesy as we can we smile, and I see a text notification from Aminah pop up at the top of the screen. He flicks it up and snaps a couple more takes.

"Good meeting you, Talia. Come meet us later if you're around."

Mark walks around to open the door for us and Tau reaches over to give me a kiss. I turn and give him my cheek, searching his eyes to see if he knows what I saw. "I'll hit you when I'm free."

I jump out of the truck and the moment my feet hit the ground, I look up and see James Henton standing outside the theater doors.

"Papa!" I practically scream in excitement.

"*Mija*, Talia!" he says, giving me a huge bear hug. Then Talia.

"James, so great to see you!" Talia and my dad. The last time he was in New York, they sat and binge-watched episodes of *Planet Earth* together. They had a connection all their own.

"I'm surprised you're here," I say.

"Was that . . . ?" he says, looking over at the Escalade that pulls off, sailing down Twenty-Third.

"Tau Anderson? Yes!" Talia says with eyes the size of saucers.

My dad steps back from me and I see his eyebrows start to furrow. He puts his hand to his head and starts smoothing out his eyebrows. He shifts his weight and looks down at me with his piercing eyes.

"Wait a minute," he says with uncertainty.

I look over at Talia, who is finally starting to get that she maybe shouldn't have blurted that out. Her skin turns a little red. Bless her heart. My dear friend is so freaking clueless at times.

"We'll never find a seat if we don't get in," she says, motioning toward the door and grabbing my dad's hand. As she pulls, his attention is clearly still on the disappearing truck, and I walk in close behind them shaking my head.

I was hoping somehow the pastor's message may have distracted my dad from the fact that Tau dropped me off this morning, but I knew my father. He hated every guy I dated. It was ironic how overprotective he was since he had never settled into a healthy relationship of his own.

Church started out as something I did to get some extra time in with Talia. But I had to admit that being there week after week made it impossible for faith not to seep in.

As the band plays the final selection going into the altar call, I find myself standing on my feet. I'm swept away by the sentiment as I sing in a hushed tone to myself, the lyrics to an Israel Houghton cover, "You Hold My World." Dylan looks on from the stage and winks at me.

A gentle wave of emotion comes over me as I wipe at the tears invading my eyes and hold on to each lyric in the song. The praise team sings while storms that have churned inside me for years seem to dissipate. I'm moving toward the front of the church before I even realize it as Talia and my dad look on. The pastor greets me with a warm hug and whispers a prayer to me that I tuck down in the depths of my heart before crumpling into his arms. I'm thankful to be in church on this Sunday. I thank God for watching over me and not allowing that idiot to hurt me, before returning to my seat.

Since my dad is in town, after church the three of us head to Agnes Café instead of Marv's. The nicer spot. I order the famous challah French toast and Talia rattles on about the progress they're making with the school administration about the head of the law review.

My dad is quiet, nodding and eating his omelet. He smiles as Talia reenacts her presentation with Fred. He's kind and thoughtful with his responses, but I know he is brooding, waiting for the right time to attack.

We take the train back downtown to our place with full bellies.

I push open the door to the apartment and we all file in. My heeled boots drop to the floor with a thud as I pluck them off and plop down on the couch. Talia rubs my back when walking past, her eyes pleading for forgiveness as my dad sits in the burnt orange chair across from me.

"You are awesome company, James! So good to see you."

He motions for her to give him a hug and whispers something inaudible to me in her ear. She smiles at him then at me before disappearing to her room.

I reach for my phone and see a text from Tau.

Dinner at 7. I'll send a car. I smile until I look up and see my dad's stoic face.

"*Mija*," he growls, before sinking back into the chair with his arms folded across his chest.

"Papa, it's not—" I start.

"You can't be seeing this guy? This pop star?"

I run my hands down my face, trying to figure out what to say. I'm still figuring out what the hell I'm doing and now I have to explain it to my dad. He is no doubt going to ask my mom if she knows about this. I am the dog in the burning room meme right now.

"It's just, he's a really cool guy, Dad."

"Come on, I did not raise you to be that naive. I mean, is this how you want to go about getting your opportunities? You're a musician, *mija*, you don't—" He stops and wrings his hands. I can tell he's grinding his teeth the way his chiseled jawline moves.

"Okay, Dad. I love you. But it's not like that at all. I didn't even know we would be working together." I felt like I was ten years old again trying to explain myself.

"I can't. CC, you need to focus on you. Not this guy. You have the chance to be so much better than me. A guy like that . . ."

"Like you?" I blurt out without thinking.

He bites his lip and clasps his hands together. He stares into my soul with those damn eyes. I want to sink between the couch cushions.

"It's a bad idea. You're better than that guy. I have toured the world with jokers like that. You don't think I know what they're all about? Hell, Dex plays with him. I hear the stories. From city to city they leave a trail of broken hearts. Clubs, women, smoking, the whole nine. Does he mention that to you?"

"You don't even know him." I laugh and feel the boldness returning to my body. It's like the line used in every teenage romance movie. "He's honest about that. He's different now."

"And you know him? How long have you been seeing him? I'm sure your mother would have called me already if she knew. Is that what he told you, that he's different now? And you believe that shit, *mija*?"

"We're kicking it. Not getting married. I get to live my own life."

"Kicking it," he mimics. "What does that even mean these days? I've been out there. You kids don't know shit about how dark this industry gets. And here you have more opportunity than I could have dreamed of and you're willing to throw it all away for what?"

"I'm not throwing anything away. I'm living my life. Outside of what you and Mom tell me I have to do. Be the best musician, be the best writer, the best employee. I'm young, I don't have to have it all figured out. I'm having a good time."

"He will break your heart," he says calmly as his eyes lose some of their fire.

I stand up from the couch and look at him with my head turned to the side. He could be right. But for once, I want to do something not based on rationale.

"And if he does, I will survive. I have before."

I do my best not to let the hurt look on his face penetrate as I start toward my room. Growing up, my dad was always this superhero to me but the older I got, the more I saw the flawed man. One that was afraid. One that couldn't be the husband my mother needed. How dare he.

"Don't worry. I'll be gone in the morning."

"Yup, I've heard that before," I say softly, before disappearing down the hall and closing my door.

I grab my phone and see question marks from Tau.

See you at seven. I sit down on the bed and turn to the photo of me and my dad. The first man to ever break my heart.

I try to perk up as I pull open the glass door to Fig & Olive. Two host-esses dressed in all black greet me with warm smiles. Mustering up a faint grin, I nod as my eyes search the room and land on Mark sitting at the bar. He points to a corner booth close, and I see Tau. The sight of him immediately helps my mood.

His smile is settling to me as I take a seat across from him and for two seconds I forget about the complete blowup with my dad. He was working so hard to save me from someone like himself. But why couldn't he have been a better man?

"Glad you could make it. Thought I was about to get left on read." He smirks.

"Never that."

"You okay?"

"I'm fine. Hungry."

After ordering our food, I can't stop my father's words from echo-ing in my head. *He will break your heart.* Everything in me told me that was probably true. That I was playing with fire and in the end, I may not be able to avoid the effects of the smoke.

"Well, I'd say that skirt is wrinkle-free since you've been picking at it this whole time." Tau raises an eyebrow with concern. I had been absentmindedly smoothing my skirt with my hands while lost in my thoughts.

"I'm sorry." I pat my skirt one last time and fold my hands on the table while we wait for our entrées.

"For real, what's up with you?" He reaches for my hand.

"I just, I mean, it's too deep to get into right now."

"You can talk to me like I'm a real person, with real shit some-times," he says, leaning back and putting his arms on top of the booth.

"Real like what?" I squint my eyes at him.

"Real like the person I spend the most time with is my bodyguard, who I pay to protect me. Real like I almost killed myself last year from drinking and driving. So what's up?"

I take a deep breath. "My dad. We exchanged some pretty harsh words. He saw you drop us off at church. I didn't expect him to be there at all. He doesn't normally pay my invitations any mind when he's visiting."

"Ohhh."

"I seem to have this thing with my father, always wanting him to ap-prove of the choices I make, you know? Like everything I do I'm hoping it'll be the thing that makes me worthy of his attention. But it's silly, I'm a grown-ass woman." I look up at him, searching for reassurance.

"Damn, that's real. Music can be all-encompassing. It's not always kind to families. And that shit, the void you probably felt, doesn't go away with a birthday."

"Yeah. I'm trying to figure it all out. Things felt so clear for me before. And now there's so many factors. And my dad barging in and assuming things I already fear people will think about me, about us, and well, it's a lot."

The waiter walks over and places fried calamari and bruschetta in front of us. "About us?" He leans back.

I mull over how much more honesty he can handle. "He told me you would break my heart," I say.

Tau reaches across the table to take my hands in his. "Look, I don't make promises I can't keep. But I like you, Carli. I want to see where this goes. But he's your dad. It's his job to try to protect you."

"Protecting me would have been being there. Being a partner to my mom. Actually putting an end to the indiscretions."

"Hey, you were being provided for though, right? I mean, I don't have a kid, clearly, but I would love to be home more. I've literally been in New York for going on a month, you think I don't want to be home? Sometimes we don't see the sacrifice is all I'm saying. And the other stuff, unfortunately so much of that is just in the DNA of the industry. Even some of the best men I know have made some dumb mistakes. I damn sure have made my own."

It didn't seem fair at all, but he was right. Maybe my dad was doing the best he could under the circumstances. I bow my head slightly, closing my eyes to gather myself. Falling apart at dinner was not what I had anticipated. I just wanted good company and a meal. Tau's hands pull away from me and when I look up, Dylan is standing at the head of our table.

"Oh, hey," I say, wiping at my eyes. "What are you doing here?"

"Are you good?" Dylan asks me but looks directly at Tau, who stands up from his seat.

"She's good," Tau says, sizing Dylan up, who stands a bit taller than him.

"I was asking Carli."

Tau laughs humorlessly. As he's staring Dylan down I notice how much bulkier he looks compared to Dylan's runner's build.

"I promise you, if I say she's good, she's good."

Mark, over at the bar, goes to stand as Tau puts a hand up to stop him from coming over.

Finally realizing this could turn into a shitshow, I stand up between them, adjusting my off-the-shoulder top. The two of them running into each other was not what I needed to happen tonight. Not after Tau brought up his suspicions. I grab Dylan's shoulders, shaking him a bit to get his attention.

"I'm fine, Dylan. I was talking about some stuff with my dad earlier. What are you doing here?"

"My brother works here. We were heading out when I noticed you in the corner looking upset and I wanted to make sure you were cool," he says, eying Mark, who is still standing.

The waiters in our section start to stare as they handle their respective guests. The hostesses whisper to each other as the small scene feels like it's getting out of hand. People are already reaching for their phones in hopes of recording a chaotic moment that might garner them some popularity if they share it on the internet. Dylan's brother is just a few steps away. Tau's skin starts to redden, and I am trying to figure out the quickest way to diffuse the situation.

"Well, like Tau said, I'm good," I explain.

"All right, I'll take your word for it. Hit me later then," Dylan says.

"Ey, playboy, I feel like you being wild disrespectful right now."

I push my hands into Tau's chest, hoping he'll sit back down.

"I'm supposed to be scared, pretty boy?" Dylan's eyes are fiery. "Look, I was here before you touched down and I'll be around after. See you later, Carli."

"Dylan, please," I interject, hoping that my tone can break down the tough exterior. "For real, y'all are acting crazy here." Snapping back to reality, Dylan looks at me and finally turns toward the door to link back with his brother to leave.

We both sit back down and Tau sips from his glass, nodding to Mark to relax. "I'm just gon' drink my drink with this beautiful woman in front of me and try not to think too much about knocking his cap back. Let's see, that's two almost-fights in a weekend. I think *you* might be trouble." He gives me a small smile. I'm mortified.

Earlier in his career, Tau got in a lot of trouble for continuing to hang around the guys from his old neighborhood. His team cleaned up his image, but I definitely knew nothing in him was afraid of Dylan. I remember an interview where he talked about constantly having to prove himself because of the type of singer he was. A bar scuffle in LA with his crony Chad White got them both locked up overnight.

The machismo of it all was a little sexy but I'm so glad Dylan and Tau didn't come to blows in this fancy establishment. I could see the headline now: "Rapper/Singer Turns Out Fig & Olive." Somehow, they never knew the difference between rappers and singers these days.

"He never acts like that."

"Oh that? That was a man who's watching the woman he wants be with someone else."

"What? Tau." I shift in my seat. A flash of Dylan's big brown eyes a few inches from my face enters my mind.

"I know there's something you're not telling me about that night." He swirls the brown liquid in his glass and the ice clinks against it.

"Tau, I . . ." I feel like a piece of shit.

"I don't want to know. You're here, which I think means that you want to be here. I'm sure you'll figure it out."

This was the complete opposite of how I would be reacting if the shoe was on the other foot. No way would I have been this calm if I knew in my gut something happened between him and someone else. This only makes the knot in my chest tighter. Especially after I badgered him about Aminah.

"Tau, I'm sorry," I say without going any further. We both know there was more beyond my words. I try not to make it worse than it already is.

"But look, the good news is, you wrote two new bangers." He taps on the table. "I'm taking some records to the label this week to play. My man J-Dot is mixing them since Meck turned out a dud. I have a few other records from recording in LA, the duet with ol' girl. It's going to be lit. I feel like the new album is coming together nicely."

I knew better than to get my hopes up, but I wanted to believe in the music I helped Tau create. I needed to.

"That's amazing. You dream about something so long, and all of a sudden it's closer than it's ever been."

"Cheers to that. To being closer than we've ever been." He raises his glass and clinks it against mine. Our dinners arrive and I try to shake all the drama of the day. We finish and share pie à la mode before Tau and Mark drop me back at the apartment.

I creep up the stairs and try to put my key in the door softly. It's close to ten. My dad is wrapped up in a blanket on the couch, his long frame swallowing it up. I turn to push the door closed and my keys drop to the floor.

"*Mija.*" My dad looks up, startled.

"Hey, Papa," I whisper.

"I want to protect you. Protect you from someone like me," he says.

"I know, Dad. I know. But you just have to trust me." I walk over to give him a kiss on his forehead. "I love you."

"I love you too, CC."

Protect was starting to sound like another word for control and I didn't want to be bound by that anymore. He was going to have to learn to let me make my own choices. The exhaustion settles in, and the bed calls my name. With all my clothes on, I lie across it and drift off to sleep, completely missing a call from Dylan.

I had to run, until Christmas. Love, Dad, the scribbles read in a note on the kitchen counter.

I'll be gone in the morning. That was always the case.

Feeling super sluggish, I hustle to get ready for work after a long night. We're presenting the Ace of Spades shoot to their team today and my nerves are all over the place. After watching a ton of edits, I think we finally had something that everyone agreed showcased all the parties involved in their best light.

During the meeting, Dawn drones on and I find it hard to focus. I've been thinking about how much I need a Momma talk right now. When my mom is not pestering me about settling down, she is the comfort I always run to. She also knew when something was up with me, so I can't say I wasn't avoiding her the last few weeks. My mind is scattered, thinking about what I want. The last place I want to be this Monday morning is in a conference room littered with papers and small talk.

Lost in thought, I'm startled by the applause that erupts around the conference room and I realize everyone is staring in my direction.

"An awesome job taking the lead on this," Dawn says, smiling. "I look forward to seeing you grow as the managing director of accounts! A new role created just for you." She is beaming.

I stand up and take a small bow, holding up a hand to wave, and smile and nod at everyone. All the faces of the reps from Ace of Spades and the other account managers on the project wait enthusiastically for my response to the news that Dawn dropped. Ryan immediately exits.

"Thanks so much, Dawn. I'm really proud of this campaign and the other things we have in the works with our great clients. It has truly been a pleasure to work under someone as influential as you. I've been learning from the best and hope to continue to level up!" The words formulate out of thin air.

I should be happy, but a feeling of dread is heavy on my shoulders. I have a sudden urge to throw all my papers and notes in the air and run screaming for my freedom. Instead I sit back down, smiling graciously. Anyone else in my position would see this as a major win. I was learning a lot by working for Dawn. But I was afraid the more I gave to Garter, the more likely my dreams of writing would slip through my grasp.

All the reps congratulate me on the promotion on their way out the door, offering me their hands to shake. As the guests filter out of the conference room, Dawn walks by and squeezes my hand as she follows behind to escort them out. Gathering my things, I head to my office to count down the hours until I'm free.

Siena is sitting on Ryan's desk and they both stop talking as I enter. "And there you have it." Ryan smiles with one too many teeth showing.

"Oh, I didn't even know." I immediately want to kick myself for feeling the need to explain.

"Killin' it as always," Siena jumps in. "Oh, and that thing at the *Daily Spread*, I had my friend edit the caption in that piece, by the way." Siena pats me on the back before walking out the door.

•   •   •

After work, I walk into a small pizza shop in Hell's Kitchen and wave to Dylan and Red at an orange booth in the corner. A teenage couple sits across from each other holding hands over the table while waiting for their pizza. The cashier holds a phone to her ear taking an order while ringing up a customer. The walls of the shop are covered in murals and the smell of fresh pizza sauce and dough wafts in the air. My stomach lets out a small rumble.

I sit down next to Red and across from Dylan.

"Hey!" Dylan fiddles with the top of the Coke bottle in front of him.

"I thought we were good?" I say, looking directly at Dylan.

"What? We are," he says slowly. "Look, can we talk about the project first?"

Red looks at me, confused. "I thought you two figured it out?"

"We're fine," I say to spare Red the drama.

"Yes, let's talk about *my* music," Dylan says and takes a sip of his Coke.

The project we had spent the last three months on was almost complete. We were in the middle of planning a release event for folks to hear Dylan's latest and we needed to go over the logistics. There was no label backing, or well-connected manager. We had to put all our resources together to make something happen. As we talk, Dylan begins to slump in his seat and crosses his arms in a pensive state.

"Are we sure it's something special though?" Dylan asks, twirling his tight curls.

"Dude, relax. You bodied this. And I don't touch nothing whack." Red rolls her eyes.

"We just need to get the right people in the building to hear it. So let's put our heads together on that," I say while chomping on a plain slice.

"That's a plan." Dylan nods.

"You not eating?" I look in Red's direction. She looks a little green.

"Nah, the smell of this pizza is no *bueno*," she says, putting her hand to her mouth.

Red reaches for her notebook and starts scratching down a list of everyone we know from press to a few label execs. Dylan was set to release his video for the first single the night of the party. They had a few more scenes to shoot but it would be ready by then. The promo photos were stunning, and it felt like he was ready to play at a much higher level.

We could do this. We didn't need major backing. With so much at our fingertips, if we just got it to the people, it would be undeniable. I rear back in the booth and smile. It's all happening. Every opportunity that hadn't panned out was leading to this, the life I dreamed about every night, the one I could see so clearly every time I closed my eyes. I needed it to catch up with how fast things were moving at Garter.

"It looks like we're in good shape. I'm gonna head out. I could use some rest," Red says.

"All right, cool. Feel better," I offer.

Dylan and I wave as she walks out into a sea of pedestrians. I take in Dylan's handsome face, wondering what to say next. I decide to rip the bandage off.

"Last night at Fig & Olive was out of line. I was upset about a family thing, and you came barging over like a crazy person."

"You looked upset and I—I just lost it, man." Dylan talks with his hands. "Like I don't trust this dude and I definitely don't trust him with you."

"I know that you and I, well, that night at the apartment, maybe it confused things."

"Carli, look, I know where I stand, so it didn't confuse me. I can't seem to read you because that night it felt like maybe you felt something too. Then I saw you with homeboy."

"Dylan, I don't know. The night when we kissed, I didn't anticipate feeling the way I did." The choice should be simple. Staring back at me was my friend, someone I could trust, someone who I knew cared for me genuinely. "And I did feel a lot of things, it's just . . ."

It was right there on the tip of my tongue. As perfect as Dylan was, something was pulling me to Tau. If I was in my right mind, there would be no competition. And yet, Tau still had a strong hold on my heart within such a short amount of time.

"Look, whatever you decide, we'll always be friends. I meant that the other night. I'll be around." He places his ringed fingers over mine.

"I just think that I started something with Tau that I need to see through. I don't want to take a chance on risking what you and I already have." I say as my hands retreat from his. "I feel like maybe I should give these back." I reach for the white envelope with the tickets for Bianca's show I stuffed in my bag.

"Well, I feel like we've got time." He stands up from the table. "There's a lot of time between now and then. You hold on to them." He kisses me on the cheek before throwing a peace sign and heading out the door.

As we pull up to a warehouse Wednesday night, the red carpet is bustling and the cameras flashing. The event is in Williamsburg, the highly gentrified part of Brooklyn with tricky train service from my Crown Heights apartment. Not to mention it was far.

Tau invited me to come out with him for this VIP night at 29Rooms, an interactive art and social experience hosted by Refinery29, and I finally felt ready. The end of his New York visit is closing in, and we only have a few nights left to enjoy. On opening night, they invite a bunch of celebs to check it out first before opening to the public. It wasn't an easy get. I'd been trying to go for the last two years, since it had been on my radar, and I couldn't snag tickets because they went so quickly. Proximity to celebrity had its privileges, it seemed. Mark walks around to open the car door for Tau, and he, in turn, walks around to let me out.

"You look gorgeous," Tau says, eying me up. "I miss my curls, though."

The black-and-white sequins on my dress catch every reflection of the lights. It's a Tracy Reese dress one of Talia's friends from church let me borrow that she recommended I accentuate with red pumps. Not the Chucks I was used to, but my favorite color nonetheless. Talia persuaded me to straighten my hair even though I tried to live a no-heat life. It was the first time I was showing up somewhere extra public with Tau, so my A game was necessary. My stomach is uneasy knowing it's against my better judgment to be here, but I can't keep playing double Dutch, which is clear.

"Thanks," I say shyly. I'm feeling out of my comfort zone of sweatshirts and jeans. He reaches over, brushing my hair out of my face to kiss my ear.

"You ready?" He exhales before adjusting his Tom Ford jacket and straightening out his chains. As he reaches for my hand, I take a huge breath and we dash into the lights.

This isn't really Dawn's thing, so I probably wouldn't run into her. I was doing my best to put the fear behind me. No worries about who is here or what people will think. The plan is to enjoy a night at an exclusive event I'd been trying to get to with a gorgeous man on my arm.

Frankie waves over the crowd lingering at the entrance. There is a huge exhibit filled with paper lanterns that people are painting with doodles and signatures.

"Ey!" Tau shouts and throws his hands up. "What up?"

"Not much. You shouldn't have to work too much, but there are a couple of outlets here that want to grab a few pics. Nice jacket," he says, completely ignoring me and quickly walking farther into the venue.

"You remember Carli, no?" Tau says, squeezing my hand while quickening his step to keep up with Frankie.

"Oh shit," Frankie says, turning briefly. "You look so different. Damn." He sizes me up with the same slippery look that totally creeped me out the first night I met him.

"Okay, Frankie." Tau pushes his shoulder backward playfully. They both laugh.

I stand off to the side while Tau speaks with a few people. Venturing out of the press area, I check out an exhibit that's full of branches and flowers. It's massive and beautiful with blooms that are pink, ivory, and multiple shades of purple. It looks like a scene straight out of some type of whimsical place like Wonderland or Narnia. There's a long line of folks waiting to walk in. Then I see her.

Aminah.

She's with a small group of MAC Makeup Girls who all look like they might actually be models because it's Fashion Week. She has on slinky nude heels with a long colorful kimono and a tightly fitted tank with high-waist jeans accentuating her figure. Her makeup is flawless, encapsulated by a long weave that graces her back. The text comes to mind.

Before I know it, they're all walking in my direction.

"Tau." She shrugs and smiles. Then I realize he's emerged from the press area and is walking up behind me.

"Aminah, what up?" They hug briefly as she stands a few inches taller than me. I want to shrink. I don't belong in this world, but I do my best to stand up straight and look engaged as he makes his way to my side.

"Not much, you never hit me back the other day."

The hairs on the back of my neck stand up. He swiped that text away so fast. What the hell was she still hitting him up about?

"Oh yeah, my fault." Tau shifts his stance.

"Well, when you listen to the record, let me know if you want to hop on it. The label is loving the first duet we did together, so don't go all Hollywood on me."

"Nah, I just been busy." He turns to me. "This is Carli. She's an amazing writer. We've been working together while I'm in the city."

"Hey, sweet pea, I love those shoes." She smiles and reaches out for an air-kiss thing. "Wait, we met at my show a few weeks back, right? You work at Garter?"

"Oh yeah, I, uhm, you know that's my day job. I write as well," I squeak out.

"Well, maybe we can write sometime. I'm still thinking about that chord progression you helped me with. I've been wanting to work with some new writers. And women writers aren't always easy to come by, if you can believe it."

"Yeah, I'll send her the record so she can get an idea of where you're going," he says.

"I can get in touch through Tau, right?"

"Oh, uhm, yeah." Is she serious? Or making small talk to impress Tau?

"Okay, great! See you guys around."

"Wait, can I grab a flick of you and Aminah?" There's no missing it this time. The photographer has on the same black hoodie with the broken heart on the left-hand side. I check for the turquoise ring. This kid is literally everywhere we go. My brain runs through the random run-ins with him from our first collision at the studio. I'm glad his focus is on them as I take a couple steps back.

Once they're done, Aminah floats into the press area with her entourage following close behind and all the press perks up to grab more flicks.

Maybe I'm losing it, but something feels off. I want to ask Tau about it, but I get distracted thinking about Aminah. "Well, that was, uhm, interesting," I say as Tau searches for his next move. We start walking toward the other exhibits in the warehouse.

"What?"

"I saw her text you the other day and thought—"

He shakes his head, knowing exactly where I'm going.

"Aww, don't do that. Come on." He sighs.

"I know, I know. But it was about the song?"

"Yeah," he says. He stops walking to look directly at me. "I told you what it was with Aminah. One thing you gotta know about me is I will tell you the good and the bad. You gotta understand that I know a lot of women and I'm not sleeping with everybody I speak to."

"I know that." I look down at the ground.

He nudges my chin back up to eye level. "And if you wondering about something, ask me."

"Well, she's nicer than I thought."

"Oh, Aminah, she's cool. I see you like to make assumptions about people," he says slyly. We keep walking.

"Really?"

"Hell yeah. But I get it. I mean, people do that all the time about people they don't know but see in the public eye." He says it so nonchalantly and waves me on to an exhibit full of bright lights you can control with your body.

"Oh, come on, you were cocky as hell when we met. Crossing all kinds of boundaries."

"And you assumed I was a jerk." He throws a side-eye my way. "Look, it's all good." Tau hops into the exhibit and starts twisting and turning his body to watch the lights twinkle in response to his movements. "I've resolved to keep proving you wrong."

"So, what keeps you so grounded?" I ask.

"I messed up enough to learn a few things. Oh, and my mama don't play." We both nod and laugh at that one. He pulls me into the display and stands behind me guiding my arms as I watch the lights sparkle and dance. The warmth of his body close to mine is enticing.

My toes are just about to go numb in my heels when Tau mentions that we'll be heading out soon. I silently squeal for joy. The cool displays and Tau's company had me cheesing the whole night. I stand off to the side while Tau chats with a few of the cast members from a new show that got picked up off YouTube recently. They went viral on social, which led to HBO picking up the series. One of them was from Tau's hometown. As I go to take a seat at the Garden of Eden fountain, Siena walks up. Shit.

Standing carefully, I back up farther into the exhibit. Peering out from behind the ivy, I see her touch Tau's shoulder while laughing.

This girl. An event like this was right up her alley. Tau shakes that same hand and looks around slowly. Clearly for me. But I stay tucked away, long enough to see Siena grab his phone boldly and put her number in it. He stands in the middle of the warehouse and waves and Siena looks back over her shoulder before rejoining her clique. The kid in the black hoodie is part of her crew. I do my best to saunter out looking normal.

"Were you just . . . ?" He shakes his head and pulls me in close. The scent of his cologne still lingers and tickles my nose. He kisses my cheek.

"Did she just . . . ?" I ask, squinting my eyes at him.

"Yup, and I might call her 'cause she don't be frontin' on me."

"I . . . Listen, I was checking out the garden."

"Ha! Bullshit," he laughs and starts walking to the exit, his hand in mine.

Mark is trailing behind us. It's weird how quickly I've gotten used to his quiet presence. "Hey, do you ever feel like maybe people are following you?"

"Uhm, kind of comes with the territory, you know?"

"It's not a little creepy to you? Like you haven't noticed this short kid with a heartbreak hoodie? I think he may have even been at the Mexican restaurant that time, acting like a fan."

"Hey, stop stressing. Mark is here to protect us from the weirdos. Other than that, thirsty paps are going to do what they do."

As we exit alongside a crowd of people through the side door, I take a peek to ensure that Siena is completely out of sight. Mark pulls the SUV around and I climb into the Escalade. Laying my head back against the headrest, I close my eyes and take a deep breath.

"Hey, I have to go to Salisbury." Tau's voice is raspy on the other end of the line. He called a couple of times. By the third time, I finally felt my phone vibrating underneath the covers.

"Oh, is everything okay?" I ask, staring at the ceiling.

"I didn't think it would get this bad this soon, but my uncle Russ has been sick and they're not sure how long he has. He stepped in because my dad was MIA, so we're pretty close."

I hated hearing that someone he loved was hurting.

"I'm so sorry, Tau. I had no idea. Well, yeah, go do your thing. Let me know when you're back in town."

Things were firming up with my promotion. Between Tau's project, another campaign with a Giants player, and my ideas for Aminah, I had Dawn excited about all my promise. She even had me heading up a few other special projects with some of her partners. Meanwhile, we were working on Dylan's EP listening event and I was hoping to get in the studio with Tau and Red one more time this week.

"Not something I really talk about. But my mom called and seemed pretty upset."

"Family comes first. That's for sure."

There's silence on the other end of the line. I shift the covers around, suddenly anxious. Just five days ago Tau had slept in my bed.

"I'm not sure how long I'll be, Carli," he starts. "I'll likely have to fly from there back home to Cali. I have a few in-store appearances to show up for in LA and a fitting for an upcoming shoot that I can't push."

"Oh . . ." As much as I've been trying to prepare for the moment, it's coming much faster than expected. Long distance wasn't kind to relationships only beginning to bloom.

"Unless you want to come down with me."

"Tau."

"Yeah, yeah, you have this and that and whatnot, but I figured it was worth a shot. I gotta get ready to go soon. Frank's gonna pack up my stuff. But I don't have a lot of time to get there. He's in bad shape."

"It's not just work stuff. I mean, we've known each other three weeks."

"It's actually been a month, but who's counting?" he interjects.

"Yes, and it's been amazing. But Tau, I don't think I should be in the middle of a family thing. It's so intimate."

"Well, I could drop you in Severn. You haven't seen your mom in forever, right?" It sounds like he's thought this out.

"I haven't, but she understands I can't really get away. I just got promoted, and then there's Dawn."

"Look, take it from someone who spends a ridiculous amount of time away from their family. Going to see your mother is worth it, Carli. I know it's too soon for us to be around family or anything. But if we're both in Maryland, we can spend a little more time together before I head to LA. And my homeboy who records me when I'm home is there if you wanted to finish the idea we talked about at dinner the other night."

"Luring me with the music? That's what we're doing?" I smile to myself. A trip with Tau? Was this my life? And why wouldn't I want to go see my mom? I've been using being busy at work as an excuse for far too long.

"I'm making an offer you can't refuse."

"Ugh," I sigh, and try to figure out what to tell Dawn.

"All right, pack some stuff. We'll be there in an hour to grab you. I'm flying private and can probably drive from your town to mine."

"It's settled, I guess?"

"It's settled." He hangs up abruptly.

I give a tame knock on Talia's door. It's 6 a.m.

Her soft hair is frizzy, and she slides her head out from under the covers with one eye open and an eyebrow raised.

"Sorry, love. I think I'm going home?" I say, still kind of confused about exactly what Tau said to convince me of this.

"Oh, wow, okay. Is your mom okay?" she asks, wiping her eyes and trying to focus.

"Yeah, she's fine. I'm sorry 'cause it's early as hell." I find myself sitting down beside her and she scooches over to make room. "Tau's leaving soon, and his uncle is sick, so he asked me to come down. We'll be able to spend time together and I can see my mom, so it seemed like a win-win even though I'm still trying to figure out how to spin it to Dawn."

"Oh, well, that's kind of crazy."

"Right? I don't know what I'm doing. I don't know what he's doing." I smooth my hair back and out of my face.

"Well, I am seeing some symptoms."

"Symptoms of what?" I ask.

"Symptoms of a bit of dicktimization. You know, doing stuff you wouldn't normally do, dropping your life to keep a man company while he handles some family ish." She laughs.

I hit her with her pillow when I realize what Talia is implying. "I'm serious!"

"Tell Dawn you have to help your mom with some family business. You have PTO. You don't use it, Crazy. Now get out!" she says, pulling the covers back over her head.

"Love you, Tally. Thanks!"

I hustle out of her room and head to mine to pack my things. This was crazy. If anyone I knew was even considering dropping everything to be with a pop star, I would have called them crazy.

The open air is chilly as we walk across the tarmac to board the small charter plane. Mark carries my bag and I tread closely behind Tau. We walk up the steps and into the open door where a flight attendant with chestnut-brown hair and a blue uniform greets us. There's about six plush, tan leather seats, a small bar, and a bathroom at the back of the plane. I marvel at the luxury of it all. I'd never flown first class, let alone private.

"How the other half lives," I say aloud while taking it all in.

"I don't fly private all the time. Only when I have to be places on short notice." Tau wraps his arms around me and kisses my neck.

We strap ourselves in once on board while the staff gets everything settled. Mark files in and takes the seat behind Tau. I can't help but wonder how many words I've heard Mark speak in the month I've known him. I wonder what Mark's story was. I type a note in my phone about loyalty and dedication. Lost in my thoughts, Tau interrupts.

"Thanks." He looks over and his eyes are soft and sincere. I meet his gaze, puzzled.

"For coming."

It sinks in that he might be going home to bury the only father figure he knows. Tau has to handle a serious family health crisis between recording and getting back for shows and press. There was the outward-facing life stars presented the world, and then there was all the other stuff. Fans and critics alike had no clue about the hardships stars deal with behind the scenes. There wouldn't be a full-page spread about the man who took over for an absent father. It was the nameless and the unknown who made stars the people they are. They quietly lived their lives, doing what they could to allow people like Tau to become who they are.

"No problem. I'm so sorry, Tau." I reach for his hand.

The flight attendant goes to take her seat, which lets me know we'll be taking off soon. There are fewer planes than when flying commercial. But we still have to wait a moment before taking our turn. Flying isn't my worst fear, but I don't love the feeling of taking off. I always wonder if we'll stay suspended in the air. As the rumble of the engines sends vibrations through my body, the plane begins to back out. We taxi to the runway. I watch out the window as workers mill about ensuring their respective tasks are completed. The plane pulls forward, quickening its pace, and all the scenery becomes a blur. Three, two, one . . . and we're gliding off into the clouds.

After an hour and a half, we fly into Baltimore/Washington International Thurgood Marshall Airport and pick up a Suburban to drive to Severn, which is a quick fifteen-minute trip from the airport. The familiarity comes back as we sail down MD 170 en route to my mom's place. All I ever wanted to do was get out of this town. If I was being honest, I sometimes hid in my work because I didn't really want to come back. Aside from my mom, of course, this town always felt so small. My dreams were too big to fit the status quo. When I was growing up, everyone around me thought "making it" was getting a good job working for the government in DC.

"Okay, so your favorite food growing up?" I'd been hammering away with questions because that's what my family always did on road trips.

"Dang, fifty questions!"

"I'm saying, you talking about your uncle made me realize I don't really know a lot about you. Except what's googleable. The verdict is still out on the whole psycho killer thing."

He laughs. "I'm so different than I was growing up. I was a straight-up knucklehead. But my favorite food was PB&J."

"Strawberry or grape jelly?"

"Strawberry."

"Ahhh, good man," I laugh, and look up to see Mark smirk in the rearview mirror.

We pull up outside my mom's town house close to 9 a.m. The lawn is small yet neatly manicured and the homes all have the same brick front. I would spend Thursday and Friday at home and then link up with Tau after. He booked a hotel room in Salisbury so I could come and go while he handled things with family.

He reaches over and kisses me while caressing the side of my face. Hopping out of the rented truck, Mark grabs my bag from the trunk and hands it to me as I get out. After I ring the bell, my mom's shuffling is audible on the other side of the door. When she opens it, her wild hair fills the doorway, and she grips me into a hug so tight I can barely breathe.

When I look back, the SUV lingers with the windows rolled up. They pull away slowly and my mom is wiping at her eyes when I turn back to face her.

"*Mija*! Oh my goodness, I'm so happy to see you. Look at your hair!" She flips my long, straightened strands. "*No puedo creer que estés aquí!*" She grabs my bag and sets it down in her small living room. Palo Santo burns and lodges in my throat. Pictures of me with my guitar are hanging in the entryway above a skinny teakwood table. On the TV, a rerun of *Living Single* is playing. Kyle's voice booms from the sound bar singing his rendition of "My Funny Valentine" to Maxine Shaw, attorney at law. My mom still keeps a photo of me and my dad prominently placed on her mantel. She'll never get a man leaving that up. I've tried to tell her that on multiple occasions.

A tattered Colombian flag that belonged to her father is framed and hangs above the fireplace. I trace the mantel with my finger, taking in all the photographs of my grandparents when they were still in Colombia. She pulls me onto her beige sectional with throw pillows; the hues of orange and red are fiery just like her.

"*Dímelo todo*! Look at me, I can't even keep my languages straight right now." She sits up, pulling her camel-colored sweater together.

"I love you, lady." A warm sensation radiates through me and I hug her again.

"I have water for tea on. Are you hungry? You need anything?"

"No, no, I'm okay, relax!" I pat her legs. She's everything. She makes me crazy but her sheer excitement to see me immediately makes me regret my prior avoidance. The last year flew by. The last time I'd been back to Severn was last fall.

"Well, I got promoted," I say, leaning back into the couch.

"Well, that's good, no? You don't seem excited."

"It's cool. But you know it kinda scares me, like I'll keep moving up the corporate side and never be able to devote myself fully to the music."

"You kids are never satisfied. You have a great job and all you can think about is music."

"Ma! It's called a dream."

"Dreams. You know Pop had a dream and it was about giving his family a better life . . ." I knew where this was going. Her father came to America with nothing but the clothes on his back and a tattered Colombian flag stuffed in his pocket to escape violence in his country.

"You don't know how good you have it," she says while shaking her head from side to side.

"It's not about that. Everyone has something that they're put on this earth to do and for me, it is writing music. Having a stable job is great. I'm just not sure it'll be enough."

"I know. You love your music, just like Jimmy." Her eyes are distant as she stares off into space. No doubt reflecting on how much music took from her.

"I don't know what I would do without it. It helps me make sense of the world."

"You know, when we were still young, I would sing background for your dad sometimes."

"Really? Well, I'm not surprised. I would hear you sometimes, when me and Dad were practicing. I wondered if you knew you were any good." I lean in a bit, intrigued by her walk down memory lane.

"It wasn't for me. You know in the seventies, there were a lot of drugs and shady people. Jimmy could handle it. I could not. And then, well, you know, life happened." Her eyes dim.

"Tell me how things have been for you," I say, attempting to bring her back to the present.

She leans back into the couch, resting her hands on the softness of her midsection. We spend the morning catching up on her latest gossip. I realize how much I've missed her and her quirks, like how she talks with her hands and bugs out her eyes when she's really into a story. My mom rarely raised her voice. I drink her in as I listen to her revel about taking a spin class to try to stay in shape. The last bomb she drops is that Barbara, her good friend, is getting a divorce. My mom and Barbara have been inseparable for as long as I can remember. When I get a chance to look at my phone, I realize Tau texted me an hour ago. In Salisbury.

Good Luck with everything. Talk later, I shoot back.

Around noon she remembers she has errands to run, and I tag along. We stop at the post office for her to send off her passport renewal, we pick up some new herbal supplement she swears by, and we buy a gang of food at the grocery store. They say you should never shop hungry and we fail because we definitely overdo it.

By the time we make it back, the afternoon sun moves through the living room and my mom sends me upstairs to change into something more comfortable. The banging of pots and pans echoes through the house and the familiar scent of tamales surfacing in the tight space of my mother's home entices my nose. She always cooks way too much for the two of us. I put my bag down in the second bedroom, which doubles as a guest room and extra storage space. Racks of her clothes line the walls, still painted the muted green I begged her for in high school. The second I sit down on the twin daybed with a ruffled duvet, I realize how tired I am.

I was back in the place where it had all started. There was a lot of history within these walls: slammed doors, the faint sound of my mom quietly crying in her room when she thought I couldn't hear. The memories were easy to avoid in the big city, but they settled like a ton of bricks on my chest now that I was sitting in my old room.

Lying back on the bed with my feet still touching the floor, I stare at the ceiling. My mom is humming a salsa tune downstairs. "El Amor de Mi Vida." The love of my life. A song by Camilo Sesto. I admired how much she still believed in love. My mom gave up so much to make sure we had a stable life. Meanwhile, my dad ran the streets to pursue his dreams. Chasing fame and notoriety. Was that what I wanted for myself? Tau and I were only getting to know each other, but what if we found ourselves in the long haul? Did I want to subject myself to the pace of his lifestyle, or was I perfectly fine playing tunes on my guitar at Palomar's?

I sit up, take off my jewelry, and place it on the oak nightstand. There's a small piece of plastic sticking out from under the silver lamp, and I reach for it, jimmying it out from the base. It's a guitar pick. Black with red flames like my dad always used since I was a little girl. The initials J. H. are inscribed on it and I flip it between all my fingers, suddenly feeling the itch to play.

My mom still has one of my practice guitars. I scan the room and my eyes land on the small closet door. Shuffling through some old dresses and heavier coats for the winter, I see my guitar in the very back. But that's not all I find. I almost trip over my feet trying to get back down the stairs.

"Ma, why is some of Dad's stuff here?" I ask, holding up one of his suit jackets. One of the very few he owned that he wore to every special occasion. She's moving to the music.

Her wide hips span the width of the sink she stands in front of as she washes off vegetables to add to her soup. She stops swaying and says without turning, "Oh, that must be old stuff, *mija*. I haven't paid much attention to any of that since we moved."

"I found one of his picks lying around too," I say, raising an eyebrow and flipping the nameplate on my chain.

"*Dios mío*. What are you, an investigator?"

"Ma, what is going on? I was looking for my guitar to play something after I found the damn guitar pick. Then I found the clothes," I say, getting more and more anxious.

"Oh my goodness, sit down," she says, cutting off the water and ushering me to one of the breakfast bar stools.

"I don't think I want to sit." I fold my arms across my chest.

"Carlisa Candice Henton, you are still my daughter. *Siéntate ahora*!" she says in a harsh whisper. Her Spanish slices through the thickened air.

Tossing the jacket down, I climb up onto the stool, facing her. I study every line on her warm cocoa face. No one prepares you for these "parents are real people" moments, and here I was, faced with my second one in such a short amount of time.

"Over the last six months or so, your dad and I have"—she takes a deep breath—"kind of been seeing each other." Her eyes are serious, but I can see a smile creeping into the corners of her mouth. She's giddy talking about my dad.

"Maaaa!!!!" I whine. "What do you mean? You guys were

married. It didn't freaking work! Mom, he was never here!" My voice starts to shake. "I mean, he's my dad, but he kind of sucked as a husband."

"*Mija, por favor.* There are things you will never understand about spending more than half your life with someone until you've been there. We love each other. And that never stopped because we couldn't see eye to eye on his career choice. We've been through a lot more than that together. Things you could not imagine." She reaches for my hands.

"But he broke your heart." I look down at her weathered hands on mine and feel the warm tears begin to sting my eyes. *He broke mine*, I think to myself.

"Is that what you think, *mi amor*? That I'm this brokenhearted woman? I made mistakes too, Carli. I did. I pushed too hard for him." She takes a breath. "To have a normal life. I guess like I do with you sometimes. But he would have hated me. I couldn't see that then. And we're older now and we've tried doing our own thing, but we always come back to each other."

"So you knew he was in New York?" I wonder if he told her about Tau.

"Yes, baby. He was heading to a gig here. He leaves a few things here, but he still has his own place and he's always traveling. But we talk. A lot. And well, we were scared to tell you because we thought you would be upset."

"I don't know how to feel."

"We were young, and we didn't know what we were doing. He was handsome and talented and charming but stupid. But he never gave up on you. He loves you." She shakes her head, overwhelmed with emotion. "He loves you with all his heart, baby, and that . . . that always made me so happy. And I know he always loved me too, even through the bad choices. Even through all our pain. We're all human, *sí*? Let me show you something."

She disappears from the kitchen and begins rummaging through the coat closet in the living room. Suddenly my dad mentioning my mom telling him about Tau had she known takes on a whole new meaning. I was a freshman in high school when my dad left for good. I knew he wasn't leaving for his next tour run—he was leaving us.

"Ayyye." She flags her hands at me as she returns with a huge keepsake box that she plops down on the breakfast bar in front of me. "You have not lived long enough to know anything, *mija*. Life is complicated."

"I know, Mommy, I know." I think about whether I should bring up Tau. I almost sabotaged everything with him because of my past and what my parents' breakup sparked in me. The space it left that I tried my best to fill with ambition.

I stand up and wrap my arms around her back. As I rest my cheek on her shoulders, the smell of her perfume soothes me. Full of jasmine and rose notes, her longtime favorite. I nestle my face into her thick curls and none of it seemed to matter as much. "I want you to be happy," I whisper.

"I am, *mija*. I am." She smiles. "I'll never forget when I first met your father. It was high school. He had a big Afro and he was fine. And those eyes." She coos.

"Ahhh, Mommy."

"Really, look, okay." She reaches into the box and pulls out a massive photo album that has a homemade cover. A bright floral fabric is stretched over the album and it's lined with lace. *Natalia* is written on the front with some puffy paint, and a photo of her and my aunt Juanita is glued onto the cover. She opens it and there are handwritten letters stuffed inside.

"See, these are all from your father. He would write me all the time on the road and the first thing he always asked about was you. I mean, before he even asked how I was doing." She rolls her eyes playfully. The tattered papers are delicate to the touch.

"See, *mija*, he was fine," she laughs, turning the page until she lands on a yellow-tinted photo of my father on a high school stage with his guitar and a well-kept fro. "He was playing in the band for the theater department. And me, the budding actress." She tosses her hair from side to side. "We talked and talked and liked all the same music. He played me Jimi Hendrix. And yeah, my mother and father had a fit. Ha!"

"Sounds like Nan and Pop."

"Yup, a Black American boy? You know, they always saw being Black as a hardship because of so much discrimination in their own country. But they came around. Jimmy was charming. He could charm the socks off anyone." She revels in the memory for the moment as she keeps flipping pages. She lands on a solo shot of her with an off-the-shoulder dress and a huge belt wrapped around it. Her curls are still just as bushy but her figure is killer. She has on these white pointed booties and she is giving the camera a serious pout as she leans in.

"What happened to acting, Ma?"

"Life happened to acting. A Black Latina in those days? Yeah . . . there was no opportunity. I went on a few auditions, but then you know I married your dad and I did a little, but then we . . . Well, you know I just had to make different choices."

"Aw, you could have been great, Mama." She did know what it was like to dream. I felt a sadness come over me.

"You sound like your father. My life *is* great. Sometimes God has other plans, Carli." She smiles as she walks over to stir her pots.

As I continue leafing through the book and moving old letters out from the pages, I'm reminded of the life that exists before we come into the world as children. I pocket a couple to read later. This idea that somehow our parents' lives start when we're born is kind of ridiculous. Especially as an only child, I always felt like I was their world.

Meanwhile, they had their own solar system, one that was formed and spinning well before I came into the picture.

It didn't necessarily make sense to me, but I guess it wasn't for me to understand. So many things in my life recently didn't seem to make as much sense as they used to.

My mom finishes up the final touches on dinner as I set the dining table. Once we spread out the multicolored serving dishes, you would have thought half our family was going to show up. Nope. Just me, my mother, and Barbara in front of a crap load of food.

"So you know Carli is working at the agency with Dawn Garter and she was recently promoted to a managing director?" my mom gushes while washing down her tamales with her second glass of red wine.

"That's so wonderful, Carli!" Barbara smiles a gap-toothed smile. She's a round woman with kind eyes. Her shiny black hair is piled on top of her head in a high ponytail.

"And apparently"—my mom circles the rim of her glass—"she's seeing some big-time pop star." She darts her eyes in my direction and I nearly choke on my soup.

"Ma!" I push my hair out of my face and glare at her. I knew it, damn it. Whether my parents were "seeing" each other or not, they were always in my business. "Really?"

"I thought you would tell me since I was honest with you about your father and me. But it seems we all keep secrets in this family nowadays."

I guess the wine is her liquid courage.

"It's nothing serious. We actually met through work stuff and more importantly, I am writing songs with him." I try to assert myself.

"Listen, these musicians are handsome, they have some cash and a way with women. Clearly, your father got me. I get it." She laughs and high-fives Miss Barbara. "Jimmy used to wear these tight jeans. He would strum that guitar and I was mesmerized."

"This conversation is way past my pay grade, Ma!" I frown at her.

"Uh-huh. Is he who got you down here so fast? You never take off work. And the world is small. I know he's from a town not too far from here. I looked him up."

"Either way, I'm glad to be here and to spend time with you and this boatload of food you made. Thanks! Cheers!" I say, chugging down the rest of my wine.

"You look healthy and happy, *mija*. That's all I care about," she says with a devilish grin. "I thought I was onto something with the guy I hooked you up with, but that crashed and burned because my daughter is so headstrong. I don't want to wait forever for my *nietos*!"

"Oh, God!" My face drops. This feels like an assault, so I try to gain my composure. "Ma, it's not all that. We're seeing where it goes."

"Uh-huh." She nods at me as Barbara looks from me to her.

"All I'm saying is, don't order the invitations just yet." I shake my head, leaning back down into my bowl.

I get them off me and onto the hot topics of the day, which they seem to have already discussed. They debate whether all these reboots make sense or whether television studios should make new content. If Ronald Isley is indeed out of jail, which he definitely is. I tell her it's been seven years. My mom's laughter is contagious as it goes from a giggle to a full-on throaty orchestration. She throws her head back as her body erupts while Barbara imitates Kevin Hart to support why she doesn't think he's funny. I'm certain my mom has heard this impression before, but she indulges Barbara. Her wink at me is telling.

I make my way upstairs after what feels like an eternity. Returning my dad's jacket to the closet, I stroke the sleeves and breathe it in. After nestling myself into the bed, I pull out one of the letters that I smuggled from my mom's photo album. As I unfold the tattered page, my dad's familiar scrawl stares back at me.

April 10, 1999

Dear Natalia,

How's my baby girl? I know she's growing so fast and these trips just seem to get longer and longer. We're heading to Oakland soon and I'm excited about it. Haven't ever been to the Bay Area. I'll be sure to send you pictures. Rico just bought an expensive new camera. I know you're not too happy with me and I can feel you pulling away, but baby, I love you and that little girl so much that I'm not sure I can breathe without knowing that I get to come home to you two. Just hang in there with me, baby, and I promise you, we'll see brighter times in our marriage. I've loved you since the first time I saw you walk across that lunchroom with your big sister, Juanie. And Nat, I will love you always. No matter where life takes us, I will always find my way back to you. Give that sweet girl a kiss and make sure she's practicing her guitar.

Love,

Jimmy

I don't even remember falling asleep but suddenly I feel my phone vibrating for an extended period, rumbling under my stomach. After wiping the onslaught of tears away from reading my dad's sweet love notes to my mom, the last thing I remember was scrolling through Twitter. A terrible late-night habit, filling my brain with 140-character foolishness. I frantically search the covers and find it after shuffling around.

"Hey," I say groggily into the phone. I'm not sure if it's the wine from dinner or the fact that it's 2 a.m., but it takes a while to focus my eyes. I didn't quite have a hangover, but I was in that space where you feel a bit dry and your head is heavy.

"Carli." Tau coughs. His voice is weak, pained.

"Are you okay?" I ask.

"Well, he's gone." He takes a long pause. "He passed, Carli. I got here just in time."

I'm not sure what to say. "I'm so sorry. I'm so, so sorry." I try to tap into Talia's kind and comforting spirit. She was great with this type of stuff. "You made it. That's the most important part."

"Yeah, well, I wanted to hear your voice. But I'm going to get back to get with my mom. You think you'll be able to come tomorrow?"

"Maybe late? I don't want to skip out on my mom too soon."

"Right, right, yeah, you're right. Okay. Well, let me know. I'll send a car for you. Whenever you're ready."

"Okay, try to get some rest. I'm here if you need me."

"Thanks."

I hang up and think of how crushing this has to be for him. I can't imagine anything happening to my uncles on my dad's side. I wanted to be there for him. But it was odd. Too soon. Romantic relationships were one thing; family was another beast. When I closed my eyes, I could immediately smell Tau, feel the scruff of his beard on my chin, and hear his laugh. I wanted to be with him, but I knew I owed my mom this time.

A faint knock on the door interrupts my thoughts.

"Come in," I manage with my dry throat.

"Hey *mija*, I heard you talking and wanted to check on you." She walks in slowly and sits on the end of the bed.

"You still sleep so lightly, huh?"

"It's like it turns on when my baby girl is around."

"Tau's uncle passed," I explain.

"Oh *mija*, I'm sorry."

"Yeah." I look off into the distance, thinking of Tau.

She rubs my legs, which are still under the covers, and I immediately feel like my twelve-year-old self. She's always been my comforter. My certainty when I'm the most uncertain.

"So, tell me about this boy who got you down here on a whim."
She smiles and scoots back up onto the daybed. I flip around to lay my
head in her lap like old times. She pushes my hair back out of my face.
I can feel the love through her fingertips as I tell her about the night
our worlds collided.

In the quiet silence before dawn, I make my way downstairs to nib-
ble on some cookies and return the letters to the album inside the box.
It lies on the coffee table and I open it slowly. Random cards and photos are scattered about, and there, staring back at me, is a tiny hospital
bracelet I assume is mine until I pick it up and see that it reads MARISOL
ELLA HENTON. The date reads June 12, 1989. Holding on to the bracelet
like somehow it will give me answers, I try to look for more clues in
the box but there are so many letters. Feeling a little guilty for peeping
through my mom's most personal items, I shut the box before making
my way upstairs. Her door is slightly cracked, and I want to open it, ask
her more about the bracelet, but instead I make my way back to my old
bedroom and dream about who Marisol could possibly be.

TRACK 24

The box is gone when I wake up in the morning, but the bracelet was still at the forefront of my thoughts. I promise my mom that we can do some shopping if I can just get an hour or two to catch up on work. All seems to be well. A few follow-ups to keep my eye on and a meeting or two when I get back. I guess the show could indeed go on without me, although I did get one or two frantic emails from Ryan, who was trying to fill the void.

Pedicures and retail therapy are on the docket when we make our way to Arundel Mills. There were so many new stores and restaurants that appeared since the last time I'd been home. The mall was buzzing on a Friday, and it took us forever to even find a parking spot.

We do our best damage to the stores after our pampering. There are no malls close to Talia and me in Crown Heights, so it takes some getting used to dashing from store to store. I'm completely tuckered out and remember that I should text Tau to let him know a time for tonight. Salisbury is about a two-hour drive from my mom's.

We pile ourselves and our bags into the car and head back to her town house where my suitcase is packed to go. As we pull up to the house in my mom's Camry, a large black truck is parked close. I ease into my mom's assigned spot and get out to start unloading our bags.

The truck door swings open and Tau hops out in gray sweats, top and bottom, with a pair of exclusive LeBrons on his feet. No chains, his hair still smooth and brushed, but his eyes are telling of a long night.

"*Hola!*" my mom calls out from behind me as I walk toward him. He waves.

"Hey," I say.

"I needed air?" He looks down at the ground and his spirit is deflated. He is always so full of life and confident, as if he is indeed a man with the world at his disposal. This was someone different. "We started driving and before I knew it, we were coming back here. To get you. I needed to see you."

"Ahem." My mom clears her throat as she walks up to meet us in front of the truck.

"Oh, sorry, this is my mom. Tau, my mom."

"Hello. I hear you're a big-time star, no?" She looks up at him, batting her thick eyelashes.

He laughs gently. "Me? Nah, I do okay. But it is a pleasure to meet you. I'm sorry to barge in, I just . . ." He stops. Meeting my mother seemed to fluster him. It was cute.

"*Está bien.* No problem. It's nice to meet you. My daughter finally caught me up. I'm so sorry for your loss."

"Thank you." He reaches around to give her a hug and kisses her on the forehead. His signature.

"Oh, *mija*, he's charming too, I see." She adjusts her crossbody bag. "Well, are you staying for dinner?" She walks to the front door and puts her key in the lock.

"Oh, I wouldn't want to put that on you. We, uhm, I mean, I came to get Carli and it's a bit of a drive back."

I walk toward the door myself and am now positioned in between.

I could understand his nerves. Somehow, he had met both my parents within a week of each other. I needed to get him out of here stat. Though it was nice to see him sweat for a change.

"Ma, he can't stay." I lock eyes with Tau.

"Okay, okay. I was trying to buy a little more time with my daughter. I'll try not to hold it against you that you turned down a Colombian dinner."

"Maybe next time." He smiles big enough for his dimples to show and winks at me.

"Let me grab my bag," I say, maneuvering through the door my mom is holding open.

Inside the house, my mom has the shopping bags sprawled across the couch.

"*Mija*, he is handsome. My goodness. Even better than the pictures you showed me on that thing."

"Instagram, Ma."

"Right, right."

"Ma, I'm sorry, I . . ."

"Hush." She grabs me up into a tight hug. "Thank you for coming, I miss my baby so much."

Leave it to death to remind you what was important in life. I silently vow to always make my mother a priority. I was thankful my dad was adding joy to her life.

I hustle upstairs to grab my bag and slide my dad's pick and one of the letters I kept into the small front pocket. *For good luck*, I think to myself while skipping down the stairs.

I duck into the truck and look out and wave at my mom from the tinted window. My heart was fraying at the ends. The guilt tangling in my chest for avoiding her the way I had been. The only thing on my mind since moving to New York was the endgame. Creating the life I'd imagined while never taking stock of the generous life already surrounding me. My mom, my dad, Talia, they all loved me, even when I was being shortsighted and self-centered. I felt thankful for them and for having a place that would always be home. Even if I was leaving with more questions than answers. I'd find out about Marisol. One way or another.

I turn to Tau, who is staring blankly out the window, and grab his cold hand. He squeezes mine back and lays his head against the seat. Sitting behind the wheel, Mark turns on music. Sam Cooke wails about being tired of living but also afraid to die. We roll down the quiet street to head to Salisbury.

As we sail down the interstate, the thick trees give way to large corn-fields and nondescript plazas with a clear blue sky overhead. Quickly the lines start to blur, and I realize just how tired I am. Taking one last glimpse at Tau, I allow myself to nod off for the remainder of the ride.

I don't know what to expect when we pull up to a rickety storefront in a plaza instead of our hotel. But the smell of garlic and the ocean clashes in the air immediately as we walk in. The staff is moving quickly be-tween tables setting bowls of crabs—blue claw, Alaskan, all kinds—in front of the patrons. Heads pop up from their graveyards of shells and I can see folks whispering to one another as Tau and I stand at the en-trance. He nods, acknowledging all the folks staring in admiration, and throws up a peace sign while his eyes bounce around the restaurant like he's looking for someone specific.

Tau waves to a thick, bald man in what I'm sure was at one point a white apron. He smiles wide as we approach him and daps Tau while making sure not to pull him in too close to the crabby apron.

"My man, Tau!"

"Hey Paul, what's up, man?" Tau grins.

"Man, ain't nuthin too much! It's been a while since you been home, man. Good to see you. Looks like life is treating you well." He puts his hands on his shoulders and pushes Tau back to get a good look.

"Ahhh, I can't complain. But it's good to be home. At least for a little bit."

"Well, I wish it was under better circumstances, man. I'm sorry to hear about Boneyard." Paul looks sincere.

"Yeah." Tau pauses. "Thanks." Tau grabs my hand and pulls me around to stand in front of him. His hands on my shoulders, he says, "And this is Carli."

"Hey! Nice to meet you!" Paul reaches out a plump hand to shake mine. "Well, I hope she's not too pretty to get down on my world-famous crabs."

"I'm from Severn, I know crabs," I say, amused.

"Okay, well, I didn't think Tau would bring anyone here that didn't know what they were doing. I like her already. Come on, y'all. Where's Mark?" Paul asks while waving us down a small hallway away from the main dining room where the stirring was about to bubble over for the hometown hero.

"Oh, he's parking."

Down the hallway is a smaller room with a few tables lined with brown paper. We sit down at a wooden picnic table. The shiplap walls are adorned with an array of framed photos. I search the prints with my eyes and land on one of a younger Tau at what looks like a talent competition.

"Oh my God, how old were you there?" I ask.

"He was 'bout fourteen," Paul interjects.

"Wow!"

"Aw man, you still have that up? Can I get a new picture, Paul?" Tau straddles the bench seat.

"Nope, nope. I like the throwbacks, keep ya humble. I remember when you first started coming in here with Tanya. She was young herself, toting you in here and teaching you how to clean ya crabs when you was a bitty thang."

"Haha! I still remember that. This photo was one of the first talent shows I did in high school." He turns to me, shaking his head in embarrassment.

"All that hair?" I scrunch up my face.

"Everybody grew their hair back then," he says with a laugh. "She clownin', Paul, but I had the girls back then too."

"Oops, well, I'm not saying nothing 'bout that." Paul throws his hands up in the air, pleading his innocence. "You want me to get your normal started?"

"Absolutely! I'm ready to throw down!" Tau rubs his nonexistent stomach playfully. Mark walks in and takes a seat at the table. A few brave souls try to forge their way into the back room, including two small girls who Tau lets in to take a few selfies. Paul tells me that he always makes it comfortable for Tau when he comes. Part of the reason he built out the smaller private area we were seated in.

We laugh and joke over sweet tea and some of the best beer-battered blue crabs I've ever tasted. The car ride from my mom's was quiet, but something about Paul's place helped Tau come back to life. That liveliness I'd come to know in his eyes was back. We reminisce about the awkward phases of growing up, and Paul stops by to tell funny stories about the characters of Salisbury. I was uncovering more of who Tau was, piece by piece. Peeling back the layers beneath the shiny chains and expensive shoes. We all start somewhere. I could feel that here and it reminded me of the importance of humility.

It's dark by the time Mark drops us off at the Courtyard Marriott. There's really no such thing as a luxury hotel in Salisbury. We hop out and head up to one of their suites, which doesn't hold a candle to the accommodations in New York. But there's a bed and that's all I'm focused on at the moment. I kick off my red Chucks and lie across the white sheets. I'm so spent and barely want to wash my face. Tau walks by and unloads his wallet and spare change onto the dresser.

"Imma hop in the shower right quick." He pulls off his sweatshirt and walks into the bathroom. I doze off while listening to his rendition of "I Won't Complain," an old gospel tune that his mom asked him to sing at Russ's funeral. I wake up to him sitting on the side of the bed, staring out the window.

"You okay?" I ask.

"Yeah, yeah." He turns, flexing all the muscles in his back. "You good?"

"An interesting couple of days for sure." I wonder whether I should tell him about Marisol. I decide against it; now isn't the time. I sit up, leaning against the headboard. "You want to talk about it? Russ, I mean?" I ask with caution.

"Nah, I'm good. I'm cool."

"Well, how about you just tell me about him? I mean, I feel bad I'll never get to meet him." The wrinkles in his forehead deepen as he tries to find the words.

"I mean, I don't know, Russ was Russ. Well, they called him Bone-yard in the neighborhood 'cause he was so tall and skinny. Amazing basketball player, you know? Could have gone pro, but just a series of events led him to coming back to Salisbury after a couple years at Del State. His grades were slippin', he was feeling super out of place with smart college kids, and his little sister, my mom, got pregnant at seventeen. At least that's how the story go when they tell it."

"Your family?" I lie back down, lulled as Tau shares his family history.

"Yeah, my grumma and them. You know how it go."

"I had no idea your mom was so young."

"We definitely grew up together." He snickers at the thought. "But Russ, man, he came back. Had some choice words with my punk-ass pops, who was nineteen and not doing right by my moms. Anyway, you know, he was there. Always there. Talent shows, sports games, telling me to chase my dreams even when his were so far off. He worked at his shop cutting hair until he couldn't anymore . . ." His voice trails off.

He climbs onto his knees, straddling me. "How about we talk

about something else?" he says before I arch up to kiss him and he rubs my hair back. Dropping his hand down my back, he pulls me up to him and kisses me sloppily. He bites my bottom lip and I push his chest.

As our bodies intertwine, there's an urgency to our movements I've never experienced before. Grabbing and pulling, we end up with bare bodies and slightly swollen lips. He pulls at my hands, holding on to them tightly as he moves back and forth with a mesmerizing rhythm.

Sweaty and exhausted, we fall to the bed flat on our backs. Reaching over, he kisses my forehead before sliding under the covers and drifting off to sleep.

"Yeah, I mean, it shouldn't be long. But we have to get everything together. Clearly, everything is paid for. Yeah, yeah, I just need to make sure my mom's straight. I get it, Frank, I get it!"

Tau's frustration on the phone stirs me from my sleep. I blink profusely at the reading on the clock. It's 7 a.m. and I can't believe it's already Monday. I used the weekend to catch up on some writing while Tau was back and forth managing his family. I pull myself up and lean against the tufted headboard.

"Yes, we'll make it work, but Frank, don't call me again until after the funeral. It's my family, man. My family!" He hangs up and drops the phone onto the desk.

"Is everything okay?" I ask.

"Yeah, Frankie reminding me of all the shit I have to get to in LA. Like I don't know. But I'm trying to get the funeral stuff done before I go. Gotta run to my mom's and do all that."

"Well, yeah, it's pretty crazy that he would even be calling you."

"That's his job. It's frustrating sometimes, but you know, the show must go on."

"It has to be hard though."

"Do what they won't so you can live like they can't. This is part of what that means." He stares off into space and I wonder if he is trying to convince me or himself. "Anyway, sorry to wake you. I gotta get ready to roll. I booked your flight back to New York for tomorrow."

"New York," I say, trying to understand what that actually means. Getting away from the city for this trip was the escape from reality I needed. The time Tau and I spent together over the last few weeks was so freeing. I felt as if I could do anything. Be anything. Things would be different with him heading to the other coast.

"You think too much. It's all good. Good things are coming, Carli, I promise."

"You promise?"

"Yeah, and I told you I don't make promises I can't keep."

He pulls on a pair of sweatpants. Grabbing his watch, wallet, and phone from the desk, he walks over and kisses me. "I'll see you about three."

The door closes and I lie back down and doze off for a bit. A couple of hours later I venture downstairs with my laptop to find some break-fast and Wi-Fi. There's a Starbucks close. I walk across the vast parking lot to get there. It's mostly empty, as I probably missed the morning rush. I park at a table in the corner near an outlet and order their Em-peror's Clouds hot tea and a slice of banana walnut bread. My email is completely overwhelmed with new projects that Dawn wants me to write proposals for. I lock in to start knocking them off.

It's been such a whirlwind. I'm surprised I can even keep my head on straight when it comes to work. But it's almost easy now after all this time. No real surprises. I could do my job with my eyes closed and still get a pat on the back. Music, however, challenged me and I was itching to get back into the studio. And it seemed Tau was working to make that happen. My phone vibrates with a text from a number I don't recognize.

Hey sweet pea, it's Aminah. Whenever you're in LA, hit me up. I was serious about working with more women writers.

Oh, she *was* serious. The problem was, I had no intentions of being in LA anytime soon.

Oh, of course, will do. I'm locking your number in now, I shoot back. Aminah Matthews was casually texting me. Life comes at you quick.

Before I know it, it's about one. I plan on heading back to the hotel to freshen up before Tau gets back. Dawn shoots me a message thanking me for getting proposals back to her while away. I mean, in the land of bosses, Dawn was a great one. A few emails under hers is one from Siena.

Hey Carli, overheard Dawn mentioning some great press for Tau from 29Rooms last week. Just wanted to share some client news.

There's a winking emoji at the end of her note that rubs me the wrong way. Tau had done press, but I did my best to disappear in those moments. Dawn's messages to me seemed normal, so I was assuming there were no other photos of us circulating the Web. I shoot back a quick "Awesome," hoping to come across as upbeat and casual. But a nagging feeling lingers even when I get a call from Tau around three telling me that he's close. I fluff my freshly washed curls out before heading to the lobby. Straight hair was a nice change, but I missed my signature mane. Mark and Tau await in the truck and we head out.

"There's my curls." He pulls a ringlet and lets it bounce back. "What's up? You good?"

"I'm good." At least I tried to convince myself.

Tau spends most of the ride on FaceTime with his mom, working out more details on Russ's homegoing service. Within about twenty minutes, we pull up to a house in a cul-de-sac and into the driveway. We get out of the truck and a short brown-skinned man walks around from the back with his hat pulled low and a black graphic hoodie that reads *Nah* with Rosa Parks's name and *1955* beneath it.

"J-Dot, what up, man?" Tau shouts while reaching out for a hand-shake and hug.

"Ey, Pretty Ricky, what it do?"

"Pretty Ricky what they called him," Tau says with a laugh, imitating Martin Lawrence from his classic nineties sitcom. "J, this is Carli. She's a talented writer and we been kicking it while I been in NY."

"Nice to meet you. Tau got you out here in the sticks, huh?"

"Nah, she from Maryland too. Severn."

"Right, that still ain't the sticks, my G," he laughs, ushering us around to the side of the house. There is a separate entrance with a flight of stairs that leads right into the basement. The carpet is plush, and a pool table is in the center of the room. As we pass through the lounge area, there's a large mural of artists, including Tau, on the wall. Farther back, there is a control room and booth area where we settle in.

"This is amazing," I say, looking all around the room at the equipment.

"Aw man, thanks! Took me some time to get it to where it needed to be. But I'm pretty happy with it now." J sits down and fires up his computer, which is docked to one of the biggest screens I've seen in a studio setting.

"So, me and J used to get into mad shit together when we were younger." Tau laughs.

"Too much shit," J chimes in, shaking his head at Tau. "Like, I'm-glad-we-made-it-out type trouble."

"We did though, we made it," Tau says.

"A lot of brothas ain't been so lucky."

J-Dot was Tau's engineer, and apparently they've known each other forever. They ran together since before either of them knew any better and it was kismet that they were able to work together as well. J stayed in Salisbury while Tau fully embraced the Hollywood lifestyle.

"That LA shit ain't for me like Pretty Ricky over here." He pokes at Tau. "I like being home and I travel when I need to. Everything I need is in this computer, really, so . . ."

"Man, whatever. One of these days, I'm going to get you and my sis out there with me." He rears back, looking at the ceiling and rubbing his hair. "Anyway, I need to record this hook for this rapper and I figured you could help me write it," Tau says, looking in my direction. He barely remembers the name, referencing them as one of the little new cats. He explains that it's a label mate and essentially a favor.

"I do a hook, they do a verse, and they introduce me to a whole new teenybopper audience. You know?" We laugh and shake our heads.

J is ready to go in no time and pulls up the track. We listen to the heavy 808s and spacey synth that automatically make you want to bounce. The rapper's flow is kind of tight, but it follows the usual formula. Wraiths and foreigns, typical trap stuff. It's only four bars for the hook so it should be fairly easy to knock out.

I go into the booth to mumble some melodies and we select what we like to put lyrics to. Tau jumps in and absolutely smashes it and just like that I'm going to have a writing credit on a major label artist. I always knew this was how it worked, but it was hard to get my head around how knowing the right people could open doors I'd been knocking on for years. I knew I was a good writer, but my credibility would always be questioned once people found out I was seeing Tau. Dylan's words from our session a few weeks back ring in my mind.

"Where's your bathroom?"

"In the lounge area, the door on the right side closer to where we came in." J points toward the control room doorway.

En route, I see pictures of J's wedding and his children on a credenza with a marble top. A young baby and a toddler with J's gorgeous wife. I walk past Mark, who seems to be resting his eyes while sitting on the couch in the lounge area with his crossword on his lap. It's about eight now, and J is working on putting finishing touches on the mix.

Walking back, I hear Tau and J banter in a hushed tone, though their voices still carry out the doorway.

"So, we just out here with women now? You brought someone home? That's major, no?" J says.

"Man, listen." Tau pauses for a moment. "We're cooling. I like being around her, and with Russ and all, it cut my New York trip a little short."

"I'm saying I haven't seen you like this since . . ." J pauses. "Well, Lauren. You out here kind of open. And you know how that hurt the brand last time. The sex symbol can't be wifed up."

"Look, I've done my time with letting my career rule my life. It's my turn now. I let it tear me and Lauren apart. I'm ready for something real, and well, Carli feels like the start of something real to me."

"I'm witchu. I'm always with you. You see I had to lock it down with Gina last year. But you know you have a different lifestyle, my dude. You been out there."

"Yeah," Tau laughs. "I'm trying to find the balance."

I feel a little bad for eavesdropping, but the reassurance makes my skin tingle. As I shuffle my feet so they can hear me coming back, Mark's eyes pop open and he shakes his head at me. He misses nothing.

"So, let's hear it back," Tau says as he sees me approaching them.

We listen to the mix, which sounds incredible. Every sound has its own lane. The drums are tight, and the bass makes your chest rattle. And that quick, J hits Send to deliver it to the artist for approval before it goes to the label.

"If there's any changes, I'll tweak it and send it your way," J says.

"'Preciate ya, bro! This is a team right here," Tau boasts. "We knocked that out! Oh yeah, while I'm here, you gotta show me the flicks from the wedding."

We follow J out of the control room. He opens the credenza door and pulls out a few photo albums. Flipping through, he shows us pics of his new baby and he and Gina's wedding ceremony from last year.

The wedding that Tau missed because he was on the road. Tau and J exchange jabs while looking through the album.

"Yo, is Gina upstairs?" Tau asks.

"Yessir." J closes one of the books and drops it in Tau's lap. "Gigi!" He calls up the steps.

"I'm cooking, babe!"

"Come say what's up to Tau and Carli."

"Can you send them up?"

Tau motions for me to head up the steps. I give him a glance, reluctant to wander through a stranger's home.

"I'll be right behind you."

Making my way up the carpeted steps, I turn to the left where the overhead lights are bright and a short, petite woman stands at the sink of a massive kitchen island. She's decked out in a fitted Nike tracksuit and it's hard to believe she actually has a young baby.

The kitchen boasts butcher-block countertops and high ceilings. The brass light fixtures stand out against the sage-colored cabinets. Mounted open shelves hover over the counters and hold white plates, bowls, and mugs. Pots on the stove are bubbling and a punchy mix of spices lingers. She rinses a bowl as I slowly approach the stools with light brown upholstery that line the island.

"Hey girl, I'm sorry. Trying to get this dinner finished. It's so much later than we normally eat." She smiles. "I'm Gina."

"Carli. Nice to meet you."

"You been hanging with those fools all night?" She shakes her head.

"They don't seem so bad."

"Oh, they must be on good behavior." She motions to a stool for me to sit.

Gina listens to the baby monitor nestled on top of the counter. She moves around the kitchen as swiftly as Talia. One day I would figure out the whole cooking thing. In the meantime, I was thankful I had Tally to cook the real meals for me.

"There's nothing like old friends," I say.

"Yeah, I've known those two since they were nappy-headed kids tryna get on."

"How'd you meet them?" I ask.

"My father owned a record shop here. They would come in searching for the newest stuff. First the nostalgia of vinyl and then CDs. J had a phase of wanting to DJ. He would make these mix CDs." She smacks her lips together as if the taste of the memory is sweet. "Once I left, I started working at a label in LA and I played some of their stuff for an exec there."

"Oh wow, so are you still working in the industry?"

"Not so much. I did my time. But I fell out of love with it. Started having babies, you know? Now I help J with all his business, which is great because I can work from home." She moves to the stove, stirring a sauce that smells delicious around in a pan. "I think J said you all were staying for dinner? Y'all better be after I bought so much food."

"I'm not sure. Tau's on his way up." I look over at the basement door where Tau's and J's laughs echo loudly.

"So you write with Tau, too?"

"Yeah, writing and . . ." I start, but I'm not sure if I should play it strictly professional.

"Well, the dating part I figured. He doesn't bring anyone that's solely industry to Salisbury. Only fam." She smirks, resting her elbows on the counter. Her long ponytail falls forward over her shoulders.

"Oh, well, yeah, I guess." I was still determining whether I was going to lay it all out on the table.

"Tau's solid," she says, reading my uncertainty. "Has he done some crazy stuff? Absolutely. But when he's in it, he's in it. Last year was a blur for him. He needs some stability."

"How do you do it? Manage the business and your relationship?"

"We're at an advantage. We know the business. It's different when you don't. You know? Sometimes I have to get together with the other wives at events and what have you and they're so far removed from the industry. They don't get the late nights and the 'sexiness' of the business, you know? But I've been there, done that. It takes a strong woman."

I nod. "Strong," I echo. That word always hit me hard.

"I know, but girl, J just got his shit together when I told him 'Look, we're either doing this or we ain't.'" She winks and grabs a glass of water from beside the baby monitor. "So, I'll say this: Tau's a good guy, but you're either doing it or you ain't, because that's my brother and he's been hurt enough."

Her words bite but I'm reveling in her transparency and want to ask her for more reassurance, but the heavy footsteps of J, Mark, and Tau disrupt our conversation.

"You staying for dinner, big head?" Gina smiles as Tau walks over and gives her a kiss on the cheek as she continues tending to her pots on the stove. "Hey, Mark!"

"Uh yeah, you know I ain't been doing nothing but eating out in New York."

"Carli, you got my man eating out?" J throws his hands up in the air.

"Listen," I start as we all laugh.

As Gina finishes dinner, I help her set the large wooden dining table. She runs to grab the baby when his cries crank through the monitor. Their other little man was visiting with J's parents. After she positions the chubby-cheeked baby in her lap, we all grab hands to say grace.

"Thank you, Lord, for bringing my brother home. Let Russ rest in peace. Protect us as we go through this life, Lord. Thank you for all your blessings and this food and family." I open one eye to look around the table and catch Tau's eye. He squeezes my hand. "In Jesus' Name, amen."

Gina threw down. Salmon in a balsamic sauce, asparagus, and fingerling potatoes. She even made cheesecake for dessert. I would have married Gina if I could.

Resting back in the chair, I take it all in. Gina has a wicked sense of humor, she has Tau laughing hard, his dimples are deep, his eyes squinty.

"Look, while you're here, we all been pulling together for Miss Josephine. You know Kenny got killed the other day."

"Damn, man." Tau shakes his head in utter defeat. "This shit can't keep happening, man."

"Yeah, these cops been out here wildin' and my man Kenny is just the latest hashtag. It's like they don't even try to hide it no more. Kenny wasn't doing shit to nobody. Pulled him over on a taillight and now he gone, just like that."

"So whatchu need?"

"I wanna just, you know, get some catering and stuff, take it over there. You know how it is when everybody at the crib all the time with these incidents."

"Say no more. It's done. She had insurance? What about the funeral?"

"I don't know, I'll find out."

"Look, we all we got." Tau reaches for J's shoulder and grasps it tightly. "Whatever she needs. I don't want to hear about no more of the lil' homies gettin' taken outta here like this."

"You know, it's sad to say not much has changed. I'm so much older than you guys and I lived through this stuff. It's more than disappointing to see this still going on, it is soul crushing," Mark says, adding a rare comment.

The gravity of our shared experience is heavy on our minds as we finish dinner. Gina lifts our spirits when she brings out the cheesecake she's topped with a little splash of bourbon, which is the secret sauce I had no idea I needed. We all devour our slices. Full and content, I glance around realizing this is one of the most genuine spaces I've shared in a long time. Today's session made me realize the creative process could be absent of the usual music industry pretense.

It's pitch-black outside the windows. I forget how dark it gets outside the city. Tau glances at his watch and pushes back from the table.

"Aight, we fitna go." A look of satisfaction comes over his face. "I didn't know how much I needed this, y'all."

We exchange hugs and kisses at the front door. Gina, with the baby in tow, waves as she walks up the grand staircase to put him to bed. The rest of us head out to walk down the driveway back to the truck.

"Dope. Well, it was really nice meeting you, Carli," J says and pats Tau on the back hard, to which Tau turns and throws two fake swift punches.

"You too."

Mark opens the door and Tau and I climb into the back seat. Tau lays his head on my lap, and I stroke his hair forward as I watch him type the caption to a photo of him, J, and a little scrawny shirtless kid: #justiceforkenny.

This was another layer.

The next morning, Tau is up early and dressed in black for the funeral. His crisp white shirt and skinny black tie are a sharp contrast. He stares out the window long and hard, oblivious to me watching him from the bed.

"You okay?" I ask, shuffling out from under the covers. It's just about 7 a.m. and I need to get to the airport.

"I will be. I always am." He attempts to muster up a smile.

I wrap my arms around his waist and lean my head between his shoulder blades. He grabs onto my hands before turning his face to mine and kissing me on my hair. He looks like he has more to say, but he decides against it and nudges me toward the shower instead.

After I'm all packed up, he grabs my suitcase and a couple shopping bags as we head to the elevator. Mark is already downstairs waiting.

Another car is going to take me to the airport while they head over to First Temple Church where Russ was being laid to rest. Mark handles the checkout while we wait for the car to arrive.

"Hey. I was thinking," he says, reaching his strong hands to mine. "Maybe you could . . ." His voice trails off as he lets my hands drop. He walks in a circle and rubs his hands on his hair.

"What is it, Tau?"

"It's all good. I mean, you have to get back to work. I just didn't know if you could maybe stay."

"Tau, I . . ." He looks incredibly vulnerable standing there, searching my face for what he wanted to hear.

I needed to get back to New York. There was a lot for me to catch up on and I had a bad feeling about Siena putting two and two together from the 29Rooms event. I needed to do damage control, the sooner, the better. My role was so new, I couldn't leave Dawn hanging for much longer.

"Look, I know. I'm sorry. You already came all this way and I appreciate it. I do." He leans back on his heels. "I'm just all over the place, I think. It's all good. Come on, let's get you to the airport."

The lobby in the early morning is still. Only the hotel workers mill about while Tau makes his way out of the automatic doors with Mark and me following close behind. Before the driver can get out of the front, Tau waves him off and opens the door for me. Mark taps the trunk for the driver to open so he can throw my bags in.

"Tau, I'm sorry I can't stay."

"It's all good. Six days is a lot to be away, I get it. For real, don't stress."

"I'll call you when I land?"

"Yup." His smile is faint as he closes the door and kisses two fingers that he places to the window. My heart sinks, knowing how painful this must all be for him.

The driver starts out slowly to head to the main highway that will take us to BWI. It felt surreal to be leaving Tau, knowing that LA was his next stop and not New York. The trees pass by swiftly as we approach the on-ramp and listen to the crooning of Stevie Wonder, and the driver sings along in a soft whisper.

Four hours later, I find myself wondering what the hell I'm doing standing along the small sidewalk that leads to the church. Halfway to the airport, I asked the driver to turn around, and he was getting restless as I stood outside anticipating the end of the service. Finally, the doors open and the silver casket is the first thing to descend the small set of stairs toward the hearse that awaits. A tall Black man with salt-and-pepper hair rushes to open the back door while the pallbearers guide it in for the final ride. Right behind it is Tau, holding on to a short light-skinned woman with a pixie cut under a round black hat, wiping at the tears falling beneath her large sunglasses. A sea of people filter out and pool along the front of the church. Tau and his mother graciously greet everyone, exchanging long hugs and handshakes. A small gap opens. Finally, I catch his eye. He freezes for a moment before he rushes over to me standing off to the side near a mature oak tree.

"Carli, what are you— How did you . . . ?" He can't finish a sentence before he's squeezing me tight.

"I just, I don't know. I wanted to be here. I'm sorry to impose."

"No, no, you're not." He finally lets me up for air and pushes my shoulders back to take me in. Make sure that I'm real and not some figment of his imagination.

"Your mom, she's beautiful," I say, noticing that she's glancing our way as she greets and hugs various guests.

"Oh yeah, you know, she likes to think she still got it." It's nice to see him smile, however brief.

"Tau, I had to turn around. I don't know what the last month has been. I cannot even wrap my head around what's happening between us, but I didn't want to pretend like Nina from *Love Jones* that I could, you know, leave."

"Carli—"

"Tau, the burial," his mother calls out to him from just a few feet away.

"Ma, uhm, this is Carli."

"Hi, Carli. From New York, right?" She walks up a little closer and holds out her gloved hand.

"Uhm, yes ma'am, New York." I wonder what he's told her about me.

"I am not old enough to be anybody's ma'am. Don't let my old son fool you. Anyway, we have to get going," she says before turning to walk back toward the black trucks waiting to take them to the cemetery. "Carli, I hope this means you're joining us? I know Tau has had you hidden in a hotel room this whole time."

"Ma!"

"Come on, boy!" she turns back to face us and rolls her eyes at Tau. "Carli, I want to hear more about the girl my son couldn't stop telling my brother about."

Sitting at my desk, I relive the impromptu trip in my mind yet again. I needed that pause even with its unfortunate circumstances. The last two weeks since I'd been back at Garter passed by in a blur. Dawn's expectations were even higher, something I didn't think was possible. I wasn't mad at the larger paycheck that came with being a managing director while I waited to see what unfolded with all the new music I'd written. These days, Dawn seemed a lot more insightful when it came to the work, and her Rolodex was even more accessible. My new role commanded respect. I couldn't lie, I liked the power.

J stepped in to mix the records that we started while Tau was in the city. Now, I didn't know what would happen when Tau played them for the label, but I was optimistic. This all had to come together for more than a few fun nights.

The bigger issue was Tau. I didn't know when I would see him again. He was in LA, working on the album and handling business. Although I missed him terribly, I tried to remind myself of the possible upside. There was a possibility of getting my name as a songwriter on major records.

My thoughts are interrupted by the sound of a new email arriving. Dawn.

Can we talk EOD? Thanks, Dawn. My stomach tightens.

The summer has given way to fall with the sun starting to set earlier and earlier. It's around six thirty when the workday ends, and it's almost completely dark outside my office window.

I look up and Ryan is standing in the doorway as I pack my things to leave. He had been incredibly quiet all day, I almost forgot he was in.

"Heading out?" he asks.

"I have to talk to Dawn first."

"But of course."

"Did you need something?"

"You know what? It can wait." He waves before disappearing back down the hall to the space we once shared.

I slowly walk to Dawn's office and stop at the door. Dawn's face is strangely illuminated by her computer screen. She looks stern, the wrinkles around her eyes seem deeper, and her gray hair is cut sharp. I knock softly.

"Hey, come in. Can you shut the door?"

I pull her glass door closed and she motions for me to sit.

"So, Maryland. We haven't had a chance to chat about your trip home."

"Oh, I mean, under the circumstances, it was good. Just had to help my mom out with a few things."

"Ah yes, Natalia. I remember meeting her a couple years back when she was visiting." She rears back in her chair. "It looked like Tau was traveling too."

"Oh, that's interesting. Didn't realize it." A sense of dread creeps in.

"Listen, I'm going to cut straight to it here. I like you. It's no secret you're one of my favorites. I see great potential in you. But I have to be frank that when I saw this, I was pretty disappointed."

My heart skips a beat. Dawn turns her laptop, revealing a picture of Tau and me at the Refinery29 event. We're laughing close to each other's faces and he's holding my waist. She clicks to the next photo and it's him whispering something in my ear while his hand is resting on the small of my back at the Embassy Suites. The last in the series is a photo of us at dinner the night of the campaign shoot.

I lean my head against my hand and feel my body temperature start to rise.

"This landed in my in-box this morning from an email I don't recognize," she says, waiting for some type of explanation. "I'd seen some great press shots of him with Aminah Matthews, but it seems there was more to the story."

I deflate back into the chair in front of her desk and sigh. I was caught, and for someone like me who did my best to stay out of trouble, the feeling was almost unbearable.

"Dawn, I don't know what to say."

"Well," she starts. "I deliberately mentioned that it's against the rules here to get involved with clients. I kept checking in. I mean, we talked after the *Daily Spread* photo got out. I thought we were clear. You told me we were clear," she continues. "So, what would you say in my place?"

"It's nothing that I meant to happen and I tried to—"

"But you still made a choice. A choice not to adhere to my many warnings. So, with anyone else, this would be cut-and-dry. But because I do think you are one of the best things that has happened to this firm in a while, I will give you the choice. Do you want to keep seeing him or do you want your job?" She clasps her hands together.

I pause, uncertain how to answer. I had been at Garter for four years, working hard, being the best, and sacrificing any type of social life. Now I was being forced to choose between a job I knew well, excelled at, actually, and someone I'd known for six weeks. Tau wasn't a sure bet. How would I explain choosing Tau over Garter to Talia, who was expecting half the rent each month? Or my mom. I couldn't be flighty and silly like so many other girls that I watched crash and burn because of a relationship. Tau didn't remember what it was like to worry about money. I could very easily end up back in Maryland.

"Dawn, I will end it. I'm so sorry."

She nods slowly, searching my eyes for the truth. "Okay. Believe me, I am saving you. I've heard about his reputation, Carli, and I would hate for a sweet girl like you to be mixed up in that. I think you're amazing, but do you think he will still be interested a month from now? We're something to conquer for men like that. You have to be honest with yourself."

"Yeah," I manage to squeak out. I want to run out of her office in embarrassment. I can't believe I'm being lectured by my boss, again. "Well, okay. I'm going to head out if we're done. Thank you." I stand up to walk out.

"You're making the right choice," she says to my back. I turn to conjure up my best smile.

Head down, my eyes searching the floor for my pride, I walk toward the door. Siena looks away as I walk past the reception desk. Before pushing the heavy glass door open, I backtrack slowly. Siena was the only person who could have sent those pictures. She was so chummy at 29Rooms with the creepy photographer who seemed to pop up everywhere we were. And then the whole acting like she was going to help me have it taken care of. What kind of sick game was she playing?

"Did you really?" I say to the top of her head. She finally looks up.

"I don't know what you're talking about."

"This is my livelihood and you sent pictures to Dawn because you want to be with someone who doesn't even know you exist?"

"I didn't do anything, Carli. I don't even know what you're talking about."

"I saw you there, Siena. Putting your number in his phone."

"I didn't do anything. But what happens in the dark always comes to light, Carli. I thought someone as perfect as you would realize that," she sneers. Her eyes dart toward my old office, where Ryan is peering out the door.

"Wait?" I shake my head, looking over at Ryan now, who is turning a new shade of pink. "You too?" I feel like a laser is shooting through my chest. It's suddenly hard for me to catch my breath. "Ryan?"

"Look, there was something for both of us out of the deal, okay?" There's not a hint of remorse in his voice.

"Oh, so you wanted me out the way, and Siena, you thought Tau would be into someone like you? A freakin' ditz looking for a free ride?"

Her eyes look like they may pop out of her head. I turn to move toward Ryan and shake my head.

"I hope you enjoy it, Ryan, cause I'm out. You can have this shit."

I make an about-face and walk back to Dawn's office. "Dawn?"

She looks up from her computer and for a split second I think, *What the hell am I doing?* The words are bubbling up into my throat like heartburn. I couldn't keep doing this, being the perfect employee and not thinking about what the hell I wanted to do with myself. I liked Tau, but I liked my freedom more. I don't know how I had let myself get so far away from that. Swept up in what it meant to have a position while losing myself in the process.

"Yes, Carli?"

"With all due respect, I'm done. I don't want to work at a job that gets to dictate my personal life. Dawn, I've worked so hard to get it all right here, and it's been a pleasure to work with you. I respect you to no end. I'm sorry, but I think I may have to follow my heart on this one. Thank you for the opportunity."

Dawn's eyes dim and she shakes her head softly.

"It's your career."

"Yes, that's what I'm choosing, Dawn. My career. My dream. You have no idea what I'm really good at. And that's my fault because I've always been too scared to mention it. I thought you would assume it would compromise my work here. I sing, Dawn. I write. I'm more than a good manager. Thanks so much for helping me see that more clearly. And your staff is conniving, so watch them. It'll only be a matter of time before they want your spot, too."

Siena and Ryan look at me bewildered as I walk back past reception and flip both of them the bird.

"And the next time I'm with Tau, I'll be sure to let him know you like him. And fuck you, Ryan, okay, homie?" I knew his "I'm a team player" facade was all a damn act. I didn't know what would happen with Tau, but I wouldn't let people manipulate me into making certain choices for my life. I'd had enough. Enough of being under everyone's thumb. And with that, I made my way out of those suite doors and into my future.

The chilly air hits my face and I can breathe again. I feel liberated. I feel crazy. I feel scared to death. I have no idea what's next for me, but I am free and the feeling is amazing. I stop to take a deep breath as people scurry by on the large sidewalk. I take in the building that turned me into a professional over these last few years. Before I know it, I'm moving with the crowd to grab my train back to Brooklyn.

"So there was some real-life office espionage going down?" Talia arches an eyebrow in shock.

"I never would have thought they were co-conspirators." I shake my head in disbelief. "Siena okay, yes. She freaking gave him her number that night when I was hiding in the garden."

"You were hiding?"

"Yes, in Eden." She looks at me confused, and we both double over in laughter.

"Never mind that."

Ryan always acted so cool. I should have known better. Dawn put me on a pedestal, comparing our performance at every turn. Ryan's fragile ego couldn't handle it. He couldn't wait for his own moment.

"Everything is so crazy right now. My trip with Tau was amazing, but now that I'm back I'm thinking about Dylan and how he fits into it all. Besides the emotional stuff, we have a working relationship too, you know? I'm a mess!"

"You *are* a mess." She pokes me playfully. "But look, all the dust will settle. I feel like you know what you want now. And you don't want to hurt Dylan, so don't entertain his interest if it's not actually what you want. Don't let him be the safe choice like your job has been."

I shake my head, dumbfounded by the ease with which Talia framed my situation with Dylan. As much as I wanted it to be different with him, that was the truth staring right back at me.

"But look, there are new developments on the Operation No Cats front. I met someone." Talia breaks into a fit of giggles.

"Really? Oh my God, I've been running my mouth about my problems! Who is he? Is he fine?" I shake her shoulders.

"Ha! Yes," she says, taking out her phone to show me a pic. "Actually, Fred introduced me to him. They play basketball together. Nothing too serious, but we've been talking a lot since you went down to Maryland. He seems cool. A master's student," she beams.

"That's amazing, Talia. I'm so happy for you. Whatever happens."

"Thanks! It's refreshing to have some male energy around. I mean, I love you and all but—" She shrugs. "Listen, at the end of the day, maybe this is your chance. Your real chance. You can't hold back anymore. You gotta step into it. No plan B."

After offering to put on some tea for me, Talia vanishes into the kitchen. I clearly didn't deserve Talia. I lean back on the couch and try to put together a plan because I desperately needed one. New York City was not kind at all to the unemployed.

"Come to LA." It was plain and simple for Tau. A man I knew for a little over two months and counting.

"I can't pick up my life and move to LA without a job. Leave Talia, Red . . ." I almost mention Dylan but think better of it.

His laugh is loud on the other end of the line. "You think you would have to worry about anything when getting out here?"

"What am I supposed to do? Come live and freeload off you? You must not know me well at all."

"I'm not saying that. I'm saying the executives at my meeting the other day loved the records you and Red did. I'm saying, come out here, you can kick it with me while you get adjusted and you can work on more records like you want to. You said Aminah hit you too about working, right? Her project's almost done, which means if you can get on it last hour, it may make it. We worked on your idea about Kenny. 'How Can We Go On?' I can't wait to play it for you."

"Yeah, but . . . listen. I live here. This is where I planned to be. There's a music industry here too."

"Right, but you ain't got no job, Tommy!" he jokes.

"I'm serious right now."

"Me too. Look, home is not a place, it's a feeling. You can make a home wherever you are. That's what Russ always told me." He clears his throat. "I'm saying, I can help make connections better here. Even if you want to pick up a gig in the meantime. I know people at every label, I'm sure you could grab a marketing position. And the more you're writing, the better your chances of getting a pub deal. Everyone's here. It's cold as hell in New York. Artists travel there, but most of us live out here."

Tau was speaking with his usual confidence. I was starting to believe LA was a real possibility. I would be moving across the country for my career and some great sex. Maybe Talia was right, this had to be another symptom.

"I'm not going to be able to give you an answer right this second."

"I miss your body," he says softly into the phone.

"Seriously?"

"Tau, we need you in five," I hear in the background.

"Bye. I'll talk to you later. I'm heading to the studio to work with Red."

"And Dylan?" he asks slyly.

"Yeah, but I told you it's all good."

"Uh-huh, next time ya mans tries to disrespect me though, it's on sight."

"Bye, Tau."

"Bye, CC."

I roll my eyes and hang up the phone. It had been a couple of weeks since I stormed out of the office at Garter. Halloween would be a nice distraction. Talia and I were planning on dressing up and giving out candy. The end of the year was staring me right in the face. Technically, because I quit, even though I was given an ultimatum, I wasn't eligible for any type of severance or anything. All that sacrifice and hard work and I walked out of there with nothing. I should have taken a long lunch or two like the rest of them. As messed up as my departure from Garter felt, I didn't fault Dawn one bit. She told me to stay away and I didn't. I wasn't used to blatantly ignoring the rules set in front of me. Hopefully the money I'd saved would be enough to guide me through this nomad period of mine.

Tau apologized when he found out but it was ultimately my choice, like Dawn said. No getting around that.

Tau did have some leverage when it came to LA. So many of New York's hot writers and producers were making the switch. My friend Drew from college seemed to have leveled up right away when he moved out there after graduation. I mean, he was touring with Chad White, who was maybe even a little bigger than Tau. But leaving felt like closing the chapter on a place that helped me hone my skills and taught me the ropes of the industry. Almost everything and everyone I loved was in New York. And I felt a bit insane for considering moving across the country on the word of a man who was too quickly becoming my refuge.

I grab my jacket to head down to Red's place. We were back in the groove, working to finish Dylan's project, and now my days were free. We were right there and only needed an up-tempo for it to feel complete. I planned on putting out feelers for jobs but decided to take this moment for what it was, like Talia said. I didn't have too much time though, so I was bookmarking some openings.

When I arrive, Dylan is already there, and he and Red are in the zone working diligently.

"We caught a vibe, man, listen to this." Red hits Play and the drums to the track are knocking. She's playing some synth horns over them, and the baseline has a funky melody. I'm impressed as I nod back and forth. Red explains that she was on a tear just as Dylan arrived, so they started messing around with the new track. Dylan gives me a hug.

"You good?"

"I will be. I'm trying to figure out my next moves."

"Well, you know, if we do it right, we can make some real waves with this project."

"For sure," I say, distant. My mind is still on LA.

"Well, what are you thinking? Did Tau say anything about the records?" Red asks.

"Yeah, he said they love them. He's finishing some recording but said that they have a good chance of making the final cut."

"Nice," she says, nodding. I know she's relieved that I didn't quite screw up our chances.

"He also wants me to come out there," I blurt out.

"What?" Red turns in her chair to face me. Dylan is quiet.

"Yeah, he's like, 'Come out here.' Aminah already hit me about writing with her if I was ever out there. And we have the record with the artist I wrote a hook for. He thinks he can help me more out there."

They both look at me a little stunned.

"I know, right?" I slump down into a chair.

"That's deep," Red says with a shrug. "I mean, listen, if you are going to move across the country, the way to do it is with an artist as big as him. I mean, he has to know everyone out there." I appreciated that Red was so sound, most of the time.

"Look, I'm happy they like the songs but that don't sound crazy to you? Move across the country away from your family and friends on the word of a pop star that you've known for two months?" Dylan says. "I'm not even hatin' but seriously, Carli, that sounds nuts."

"I know it does. But I can't help thinking what if it's not? What if this is my big chance?"

"Look, you don't have the job tying you down. No kids, no husband. People have done it on less," Red reasons. "And you can always come home if things don't work out."

"I don't trust this dude, man. He's this head over heels? Like, Carli, think about this. And then you'll be tied to him helping you when you're talented all in your own right."

"I've thought about that, Dylan, I have." I rub my temples. "Look, I didn't come here to argue about this. I want to work. It slipped out because I literally spoke to him right before I came here. I'm not saying I'm going. But I'm considering the opportunity and what it would mean for *everything* we're doing here. The better position I'm in, the more people I have to pass your records to."

"Oh, you think your boy is going to let you use his connections for me?" Dylan looks at me with his brows furrowed.

"I don't know. Shit, I can't expect him to be thrilled after, well, anyway." I stop myself. "He hasn't shown me that he would do anything to try to stop me from making the best of my situation. He cares about my career, too. I know that's shocking." I twirl my nameplate chain and pull back the dark curtains.

"Well, I think you should be thinking about it, Carli. If he's helping you get on your feet out there, there's nothing wrong with that. You know how many of my peeps have couch-surfed until they got it together? LA is a beast, a lot like New York," Red adds.

"Not with dudes they're smashing. But whatever."

"Annnd we're done. Thanks, Dylan. Let's work," I say, pointing to the board.

The music pumps urgently through the speakers, commanding our full attention. Dylan is humming melodies and the words start floating into my head. Before I know it, we're dancing and laughing and putting the pieces together for the song. I'm not sure I'm ready to up and leave everything I've built here. But a fresh start is pulling me. I've always admired people who weren't stuck. Who would move where things took them. With Tau gone, I find myself watching all his Stories on Instagram and following him closely on Twitter. We talk a little every day, but some days he's running to the max and it's only a quick text or emoji. I didn't think we could survive the distance much longer.

If this were solely a business decision, I would have been on a plane yesterday. What was scarier to me was the fact that I wanted to be near him, with him, and that I was willing to consider leaving everything I knew to do it. There was nothing I wouldn't sacrifice for my career, but sacrificing for love, well, that was terrifying.

But being in LA, I could have the opportunity to have both. I could get the guy and the career I've always wanted. If everything worked out, I would be writing records for some of the hottest up-and-coming artists.

I watch Dylan and Red work out the bridge and think of what it would be like to have sunshine all year and be inspired by the palm trees. The back-and-forth in my mind was giving me a headache. But hearing Dylan sing gives me a temporary sense of calm.

He hops in the booth as Red hits Record, and I try to block everything else out of my mind as I walk up to the board, nodding along and witnessing that familiar magic happen.

I can't believe tonight's the night. The song we recorded last Friday was the final piece. After all the hard work and the fights, Dylan's project is finally ready to be shared. We're hosting a small listening party at Palomar's. Walking down the hallway, I give a small knock on Talia's door.

"I'm almost ready, I promise!" she yells from the other side.

"Okay, miss! It's normally my job to make us late."

Later, as we walk up the block to Palomar's, we notice there is already some bustling outside the door. It's nice when folks are early. It usually means they're excited. I adjust my tuxedo jacket and smooth out my Adidas track pants before reaching to open the door. Black and gold balloons cover the ceiling and I see a few of the musicians from the church. A couple of producers and label execs line the walls. The lights are low and moody just like we asked. The DJ is set up and mixing and scratching on the turn tables. He's playing new records and some of Dylan's older stuff. I throw up a peace sign to him. He was someone Red recommended, and he is killing.

Waitresses walk around with trays of champagne, and I lift one off for myself and Talia. I hand her a glass. Talia's eyes search the room and land on a stocky brother with a beard. I recognize him from the picture. She waves with excitement, making a beeline to where he's holding up the wall and dragging me by the arm.

"Brian, this is Carli. My best friend. Carli, Brian."

"Hi, Brian, it's so nice to meet you." I reach out to shake his hand. He smiles warmly and pulls me in for a hug.

"Nice meeting you," he says in a deep voice. "Talia told me all about you."

"Not too much, I hope."

"Only good things," he offers with a wink.

"No cats," I whisper to Talia while looking around the room for Red. She gives me a sly high five before ushering Brian over to Fred and Mari, who walked in right behind us. I float toward the stage and find Red there biting her fingernails.

"It's amazing," I say to comfort her.

"What?"

"The project."

"What, I look nervous?"

"Yes!" I pull her hand away from her mouth.

"That's not it." She moves in closer to me.

"What? What's up?"

"Carli, I'm expecting." She pats her stomach and smiles.

"Oh my God!" I jump up and down first before smothering her in a tight embrace. Pushing her back to arm's length, I look to see if her appearance is any different.

"Not really the timing I was hoping for, but we're happy."

"Oh, well, you and Rob have been together for a minute now."

"I know, but my career. It's hard enough being a female producer. Now, I'm pregnant," she sighs.

"You'll find the balance, Red. A baby doesn't mean it's over. Screw these people who want us to choose. I remember my g-mom used to say, 'We make plans and God laughs.' I guess I actually understand what that means now."

"Like this LA thing?"

"Exactly like this LA thing." I shift from one foot to another, thinking about how I wish Tau was here to share this night with me. "You're about to bring a beautiful baby into this world, that shouldn't cause you anxiety about how well you can do your job." Here I am encouraging Red when I can use the reassurance myself.

"I hope you're right. I really do, Hollywood." Her eyes are hopeful.

"I'm always right," I laugh as she joins in. "Does Dylan know? Where is he?"

"Back in the greenroom. And no, not yet. Didn't want him thinking about anything other than smashing it tonight."

"Okay, cool. I'm gonna wish him good luck. Congrats, Red." I smile and grab her hand again before following the tight corridor past the kitchen to the modest room for performers. I knock on the white door and wait for an answer.

"Come in."

Inside, Dylan is sitting on top of a small vanity with one leg outstretched when I push open the door. The scents of eucalyptus and lavender provide a calming aroma. His hair is freshly shaped and neat. The light gleams off the dangling cross in his ear. His crushed velvet burgundy jacket is savory and his tight black pants a nice complement.

"Well, you look great."

"Thanks, Carli. So do you." I step back and take a twirl.

"Look, the project is amazing," I say.

"What, I look nervous?"

"You and Red have the exact same look on your faces and she asked the exact same thing. Look, I'm proud of you and you should be proud of this work. There's only friends and fam out there. Nothing to be nervous about."

"I guess you're right."

"I'm always right," I say with a laugh. "I'm proud of us. Of seeing this through."

"Me too. I always wanted to help be the catalyst to all of us breaking through. Making a difference. Showing that real music still matters, you know?"

"It does. And they'll see it."

"Carli, look." He pauses for a beat.

"Dylan."

"No, I don't think you understand that I've loved you for a very long time." He steps down off the vanity and walks up close. I take a step back so I don't completely lose my mind again. I still needed to figure out a way to tell Tau what happened. How could we start something real with this between us? My reflex is to check to see if anyone else is hearing this. But it's only us. "Relax. I'm not going to try to kiss you again. I promise. I get it. My love for you is not contingent on us being together. I want the best for you. You're really special. And I mean, I want the world to see what I always have. If LA is a way to make that happen, you should really think about it. Then we'll have someone to crash with when we come out there."

"Thanks, Dylan. That means a lot. I never wanted to hurt you. You mean a lot to me."

"I know. I know that." He nods.

"Okay, okay, enough with the mushy stuff." I feel the tears starting to well up. I bite my tongue in hopes that it will prolong the inevitable. "You have a project to present. I just wanted to stop by and wish you luck. With everything."

He pulls me into an embrace and rustles his chin in my thick curls and we both let out a sigh. I wipe quickly at the stubborn tear that forms in the corner of my eye before my mascara runs. We give an extra squeeze before Dylan heads to the stage.

Finding my place alongside Talia, Brian, and the rest of the crew, I watch Dylan grab the mic. He goes into the process, shouting out Red and me for dealing with him being an artist who's sensitive about his shit, and breaks into the first song. He shuffles across the stage playfully, looking like he's spent a lifetime performing in front of an audience. The crowd is roaring by the time he's finished. He relaxes more into the second song and the levels are right. His voice is butter and the crowd is completely receptive.

We may have something here.

The room has filled in a lot more since I first arrived. The space by the stage is packed tight with a bunch of folks we wanted to come out. My hope was that the phone would be ringing like crazy the next morning with meetings and potential collaborations. I spot Blair Liv at the bar and make my way over to him as Dylan croons.

"Carli!" he says before I get to my final spot adjacent to him at the bar.

"So nice to see you here!" I'm flattered he even remembers my name.

"Yeah, Tau told me to come check it out."

"Wait, Tau told you about tonight?"

"Yeah, he sent me the records you wrote for him and said you had an artist releasing something soon. I like what I've heard so far tonight. He's got an amazing tone. That 'She's All Right' record might be great for the Generation Next playlist."

"Oh wow, yeah. I mean, that would be amazing." My heart starts to race just thinking of what that could do for our streams.

"Tau also mentioned you were heading out to LA soon? Good call. So much is happening out there these days. I can definitely put you in touch with some folks there. And Aminah's out there. I know you were working on her account. She was impressed when you told her what chord to go to that night." He takes a huge gulp of the brown liquid swirling around in his cup.

I was going to kill Tau for saying I would be in LA. It was like he got his mind on something and didn't know how to stop. God, I see how he made it this far with that kind of drive and stubbornness.

"Oh, it was nothing. A chord progression I play a lot when I'm writing," I say mindlessly. "But LA . . . I'm not really sure about it yet. Still trying to figure out life after Garter."

"Wait." His eyes suddenly light up. "I knew I'd seen you before when Dawn brought you into my office. You've played the open mic here, right?"

"Well, just to work out songs. See how they're received so someone else can sing them."

"Smart. But I can spot that 'it' factor a mile away. You're a star, Carli, whether you know it or not. Embrace it." He nods as he finishes his statement. "Look, I have something really big in the works and I'm interested in your artist here. But I want you to think about some things too. You're much more than a writer, Carli, trust me. I've been doing this a long time."

"I've never thought about being in the forefront. I think I like it behind the scenes."

"Eventually most writers I've known as talented as you will find themselves writing songs that only they can sing. I've seen it happen many times. I want you to think about it, okay?"

I'm suddenly unsure whether my aversion to being an artist stems from preference or fear. It felt much safer writing and directing from behind the boards. The vulnerability it took to be yourself for the whole world to see was terrifying. My dad would always say he saw me on stages, but I never paid it too much mind. He was my dad. I was always a star in his eyes. But Blair's insistence has me thinking.

Dylan finishes the record and we both stop to applaud. Blair lets me know he may be getting his own label off the ground soon. He gives me his card to stay in touch. I'm thankful for the second opportunity to connect with him from this end of things. That didn't come around often over the years with as many executives as I've met. Maybe it is my time. I couldn't blame it on the job anymore. I was free.

"I'm setting up a session and I want you and Dylan to come and check it out."

"Our producer, Red, too?" I throw in.

"Of course, everyone involved. The team."

I'm ready to burst at the seams with how well things are going. I couldn't have engineered a better way to introduce this work into the world. Well, our small world of creatives in this city of big dreams.

The night seems to slip right through our fingers with how fast it goes. After doing our due diligence rubbing elbows and thanking everyone for coming, the exhaustion hits me like a freight train. I corner Dylan and Red to say my final goodbyes. Dylan sweeps me into a bear hug, lifting me off the floor. I flick Red's ponytail and we group hug.

"Yo, Blair Liv was here!" Dylan puts his hands to his forehead.

"I know, I know, I can't even wrap my head around it. Look, I love y'all, but I just have to go and let this all sink in," I say.

"Surreal, man." Red smiles. "Night y'all!"

"Night!"

Brian and Talia are booed up in the corner looking all dreamy-eyed, probably talking about egghead things I would never understand. Sneaking up behind Talia, I put my hands on her shoulders and she turns quickly and laughs. I start pushing her toward the door and Brian follows behind.

As we step out into the nippy fall air, a black Escalade pulls up in front of Palomar's. The tinted window rolls down to reveal Tau in dark shades.

"Hey, y'all need a ride?"

"Uber?" I don't know why Tau popping up out of nowhere still surprises me. I can't believe how giddy I am.

"Yeah." Tau smiles before sticking a huge bouquet of lilies and roses out the window. I stick my whole face in them before we pile into the truck and Mark heads to drop off Brian and Talia at our place. I revel in the banter as I take it all in. My best friend in the whole world and this man that made my pulse race and kept a smile on my face when absolutely nothing was funny. We pull up to our apartment and they hop out.

"You good, love?" I yell to Talia from the window as she saunters up the steps.

"No cats!" She laughs. Brian looks confused but waves as we begin to pull off down the one-way street.

"What are you doing here?" I rub his hair and kiss him on the cheek.

"I wanted to celebrate with you. This is big. A full project. Whether I like your homie or not, I wanted to be here. Late. My flight was delayed, but I'm here." He grabs my hand and plants a huge kiss on it.

"Tau, that's so amazing. I'm flattered you would move things around to fly back across the country like this." I look over at him, trying to believe that he's actually sitting next to me. "It doesn't seem real."

"Oh, it's real. The jet lag is real." He laughs to himself. "But it's worth it to see you smiling."

"Okay, stop, 'cause I don't even know what to say." My grin spreads from ear to ear.

"Now, what you gonna do for me?" I snatch my hand from his and hit him in the shoulders.

"I'm playing, I'm playing." He throws up his hands to block my hits.

"So you like me or something?"

"I do," he says, looking straight into my eyes. "I don't understand it, but yeah, I like you a lot. I can't front. So many people think that if they just had all the 'things' in life, it would be amazing. But when you're on this side it's really not shit without someone in your corner. And yeah, my mom and family and all that. But . . . well, anyway, it's dope to have someone to want to tell shit to and pop up on again."

I remember J's mention of Lauren.

"Carli, you're like my gravity. The only ones that last in this business have those who help keep their feet on the ground."

I don't trust myself to respond. Instead, I lay my head on his shoulder and he pulls on my curls as we weave in and out of New York traffic, heading to his hotel.

Tau's on a New Edition kick, so we spend the rest of the night at the Carlyle listening to old tracks of theirs from back in the day. He even does a small rendition of the "If It Isn't Love" choreography. I give him the play by play on the release and who ended up showing up. That and Red's big news.

In the midst of our silly antics and catching up, he sneaks in that he wants me to fly back to LA with him for another round of meetings at the label.

"Speaking of . . . You told Blair I was coming out to LA already, so I guess you have the answers?"

"Look, I was just speaking it into existence. But what did he say?"

"That it would be a good move, but . . ."

"So I'm right?"

"Tau."

"It's good to get face time with these people. You know, it's not always about how good the records are as much as how well you sell them."

"Oh?"

"Yeah, man. It's like this. One day they'll like something and then they hear another record went number one and they want you to do something more like that. You know?" He turns his head to the side, shocked by my apprehension. "You ain't got no job, and you ain't got shit to do."

We both laugh, sitting on the king bed with room service plates spread across the comforter. I throw a fry at him. He dodges it.

"Maybe."

"Listen, I'm not talking about moving. I'm saying come out, get with some of my label people, and sell the records a little bit more. And they'll probably ask you to play some of the other stuff you've been working on, which is a win for you."

The heat of the LA summer is still lingering in October. It's unseasonably warm as we hit the ground running Monday with a meeting over at the Capitol building to touch base with Tau's A&R, Omar. Our flight landed at 1 p.m. and we were headed straight there because Omar's calendar was packed. I grew up hearing about this building and always seeing the pictures, but I couldn't believe I was walking into it.

When we arrive, Joel, Tau's big-picture manager, is already there, and Frankie rode in with us. I'm not even sure Tau slept at all, but he was somehow bright and refreshed. We did, however, stop at Starbucks on our way over.

"All I'm saying is it's a risk." Omar is tall, with a modest dad belly and skin the color of espresso. He rears back in the black leather chair at the head of the conference table. The walls are covered in platinum and gold plaques, including the one from Tau's latest album.

"It's time to take some risks is what I'm saying. Initially everyone was on board. What changed?"

"I hear you, Tau. But this last project was your most commercially successful."

"Great, so that means y'all made your money back. Now I can do my thing."

"You know I'm with you. I'm on your side."

"Well, be with me, Omar. Shit, I'm the reason you're in the spot you're in now." Omar was the head of urban music at Capitol but still was hands-on with Tau's projects because he signed him initially. It was his work with Tau that put him in a great light with the company's president, who promoted him.

"But they're just worried about you going too left. I mean, the social justice posts on social media and the new song with Aminah. You've never been this outspoken about these types of issues before. It will be an adjustment for your audience."

"I've always been this way, Mar. I just let y'all keep a muzzle on me and I'm a grown-ass man now. These things are affecting my real life. People I know, who I grew up with. What kind of lame would I be to be silent?"

I shift in my seat as the convo gets heated. I follow the lead of Frankie and Joel, who seem to let Tau do most of the talking.

"Tau, yes, listen, when Gina brought me that demo, I knew you had something special. I don't doubt that. But you have to trust that I'm in meetings you're not in, bro. I haven't steered you wrong over the last ten years. And you know this industry is crazy right now. We need guaranteed hits."

"Look, Carli is one of the illest writers I've met, and I think we're onto something."

My eyes go wide as I'm brought into the convo. Tau looks to me as if it's my turn to speak. I'm scrambling in my brain but on the other end of a deep breath, I find the words.

"The playboy eventually needs some depth," I start. "Look, from the gate, Tau's been the pretty boy, the one with all the women. But his audience is growing up. How long can they hold on to the thrill of the one-night stand? As women grow, they want something real, someone with substance. He can sell that now, in addition to the sexy," I say, breaking right into the pitching skills I learned at Garter.

Tau hits my foot under the table, which I hope means *Well done.* Omar takes in my statement. Pensive, he taps his pen on the table.

"I'm saying that I feel like I kind of grew up with Tau, you know? The teenager desiring the older guy and now with him on the brink of his thirties, you have to give him some growth. I think that's what he's looking for. Not abandoning who he is."

"And where'd you come from again?" Omar asks.

"New York, Mar. I met her in New York—Garter. Meck? I was telling you about it."

I cringe remembering that Meck was part of the reason all this was happening. The thought threatens my focus but I try to stay on track.

"Right, Meck. Where is he? I thought he was coming out with you?"

"Nah, that's dead." Tau's mouth tightens.

"What? What Meck do now?"

I readjust in my chair, looking away.

"Mar, it's not important. Industry shit."

"Aight, whatever. Let me hear these joints again."

Frankie walks over to the system in the conference room and hits Play on the laptop connected to the speakers. "Good Morning, Love" plays. Tau and Joel are nodding along. Omar listens intensely and rests his elbows on the table.

"It's great stuff, Tau. But I'm wondering if it's for you. I would put one of my other artists on it in a heartbeat."

The vote of confidence in the work gives me the affirmation I need. But the point was to get these songs on Tau's album, not some other random artist's.

"Ultimately, Tau is the determiner of his own fate, Omar. Let's cut to the chase. He's made the label more than enough money to have creative control over his project. So *your* job is to figure out how to make it work. These are the records. They're amazing, they're personal to what Tau really cares about right now, so make it work," Joel says calmly, with precision. "Figure it out, Mar, or we will."

"I can't promise you anything, Joel. You know this. We've been through this on multiple albums."

His words stab me in the chest. To think that you could get this close and then your records would be scrapped. I can't even bear the thought. I try not to look too rejected because, for some reason, Tau and Joel don't seem fazed at all. The guys shake hands and Frankie, Joel, and I filter out into the lobby. Tau walks close behind us, going back over the new records with Omar.

"I want to hear more of her stuff," he says to Tau. "She signed to anybody?"

"Nah, not yet. But I'm planning to take her around, let her play some stuff for folks."

"Well, you know we should keep it all in the family first. Let me see what I may be able to do if the other records are hittin'."

"They are. We'll set it up so you can hear some stuff for an artist she was working with out there. She plays too. Multitalented."

"She wants to be an artist?"

"She wants to write."

"She has the look."

"Oh, well, she ain't say any of that to me. Only that she wants to write. She's a real musician, my dude."

"Is she seeing anybody?" Omar was clearly attempting to whisper, but I overhear him while Joel and Frankie debate on where to go for lunch. I sneak a glance in Tau and Omar's direction.

"Mar, focus. I'll set it up for you to hear the other records, my G." Tau looks annoyed as he pushes open the glass doors.

We make our way to explore our food options. Being in LA brings to mind one summer break in high school when my dad was performing for ASCAP's annual awards show for writers and producers and sent for me to come spend the weekend with him. It was the first time I was ever on the West Coast. My mom was apprehensive about sending me on a plane across the country alone. My dad had to beg but he had mastered getting her to see things his way. I walked out of the airport with my hand in his and had my "I'm not in Kansas anymore" moment: the huge palm trees, the gigantic mountains, and the homes that made it hard to decipher the economic level of certain neighborhoods. I'll never forget the ASCAP show at the Beverly Wilshire where a photographer snapped the picture of us that I keep in my bedroom.

The day before his show, we rode bikes on the Santa Monica pier, checked out the Beverly Hilton, and sat in traffic on the 405. It was an amazing place, but it wasn't anywhere I felt like I could live. It came across as a land of make-believe. I had boxed it off as only a place someone visited. You didn't get to live in California, that was for a select few.

I pull out my phone and linger over my dad's contact. Maybe he would tell me about Marisol. But that would have to wait.

The group decides on the L.A. LIVE complex for lunch. After mulling over a few of the restaurant choices, we decide on Katsuya and Joel seems pretty familiar with the hostess. As we follow her to a table tucked away in the back, my stomach rumbles as the aromas of wasabi and ginger hang in the air.

"What about these records, Joel?" Tau looks a bit concerned, and I don't blame him after that meeting.

"They sound fucking amazing. Cheers to finding the sound we've been trying to get to through all the bullshit! Now we need some drinks over here for a proper toast."

Tau rubs my hand to reassure me. I have to assume they know what they're doing. They seemed confident, but Omar's words echo loudly in my brain. I wanted this so bad.

After a feast of Asian cuisine and a couple bottles of champagne,

Joel covers the bill and we split from him and Frankie to head to Tau's jeweler to pick up a custom chain. From there we head to his fitting for a film screening red carpet and there's a meeting for a charity benefit that he's hosting next month.

.   While we're making our way all across LA, I field texts from Dylan and Red, who are excited about the response they got from an A&R at Atlantic Records. I let them know that Blair was also really interested and wanted to meet up as soon as I got back. Tau wanted me to take full advantage and set up something with Aminah while I was here, so I wasn't sure when I was heading back yet.

I'd worked for these moments all my life. But facing them head-on, in LA of all places, had me feeling intimidated. Fear of success was real, especially without Red or Dylan next to me. If I was home in the city, I'd transmit the whirl of feelings onto paper, but Tau and I had been on the move since we landed.

"Look, it's just one more thing on the agenda for later tonight. I know you're tired. We'll show face at this listening thing for Ty."

"Okay, cool."

"For real, Carli. This is the reality. It all seems like a fairy tale until you're in it. You gotta fight for it. Everything you want in this life, you gotta fight for it."

I guess I was one of those people. Enchanted with the lives of musicians who moved from place to place, always in the know. But in an afternoon's time, I was already realizing how grueling it could be. I was tired for sure but being with Tau was like a never-fading espresso shot.

Bell Canyon is secluded, tucked away in a gated cul-de-sac community off the 101. We pull up to a small structure at the entrance and Tau checks in with security. We continue up a small road hugged by trees that wind up through the Simi Hills.

I couldn't believe these were the houses on the hill that I'd heard about all my life.

Tau looks over at me and smiles. He must see my awe of this wildly affluent area.

"If I was a crazy stalker, this would be the place to drop the body," he whispers to me.

"The verdict is still out on that. I told my mother if she doesn't hear from me today to send help."

He shakes his head as we finally pull up to the massive home concealed behind even more trees. There is a three-car garage and a small circular driveway. Multiple balconies overlook the property, and the exterior is affixed with extensive lighting.

"So this is home?" I ask.

"Yup, this is my spot."

We walk through the front door and the foyer has the highest ceiling I've ever seen. A huge chandelier offers cascading light over a large round walnut table where Tau drops his keys.

"Let me show you around."

The massive living area has a fireplace that spans the whole wall with seating on a ledge around it. An array of pillows is stacked on the ledge and a small fur bench sits on top of a white fuzzy rug. The brick is painted a deep gray in contrast to the white walls. Floor-to-ceiling windows open out to a massive patio revealing scenic views of the property, including a basketball court and the trees beyond it. The colors are neutral. Cream couches and a marble coffee table scream elegance. All of a sudden I'm aware that nothing I have on feels like it should be in this type of space. I look down at my Chucks.

"Don't worry," he says, pulling me into his arms.

"I'm not."

"I see it all over your face." He laughs. "Look, I want you to be comfortable. I could have put you up in a hotel, but you know, I wanted you to get familiar with the spot, in case . . ."

"Ahhh, let's take it one step at a time, okay?" I loved how direct Tau was about what he wanted. And now he had set his sights on me being in LA permanently.

"Okay." He kisses me and we continue the tour. From a theater room in the basement to the master bath that looks like it belongs in a spa instead of a house, I'm tired just walking around this place.

"So, this is how you stay in shape?"

"Ha! You always clownin'. This and the trails. Oh and my trainer." He rolls his eyes.

"Tau, this is wild."

"What? I'll show you around, introduce you to a couple of people. It's only a few days," he reasons.

"I'm talking about your home, your life. But yeah, this whole situation is pretty wild."

Tau's dimples make a welcome appearance. "I'm not responsible if you don't want to go back to NY, 'cause Cali is where it's at. I mean, who doesn't want to live like a rock star?"

Tau heads back downstairs to talk business after showing me around. Sitting on his California king bed, I hear Tau talking with his assistant, Mara, and Frankie. Going over scheduling for the next few days. I kick off my shoes and lie back and reach for my phone.

"Hey Tally," I say quietly.

"Okay, how insane is your room?" She goes in.

"Girl, I'm at his house and it's all Kardashian-like."

"Oh my God. You are living the damn dream. Tell me what type of magic you have to be this lucky so I can get it."

"I have no clue what I'm doing here. I think I've lost my mind."

"Stop it! He's crazy about you."

"Tally, I'm so nervous. I felt so much better on my turf. Now I'm on the other side of the country. In his world." The murmuring from downstairs distracts me for a moment and I look over at the door.

"Girl, enjoy it! You know how many people would trade places with you in a heartbeat? Myself included."

"What about Brian?"

"He's great, but I'm saying . . ." She giggles. "Don't be Carli and ruin this. Live it up and tell me all about it when you get back."

"Thanks, Tally."

"You know I'm always here for talking you off ledges."

I hang up and Tau appears in the doorway. All the extras are gone. Mark is the only one who stays on the property, in the guesthouse. Which is nice to know. We play a few games of pool and then the jet lag sets in.

I take a shower that feels like heaven with the rain showerhead. The teakwood flooring and green plants all around create a very relaxing spa vibe. Eucalyptus hangs over the showerhead and clears my stuffy plane nose right up. The soaker tub will be a must before I leave to go back to the East Coast. I change into a cute lounge set. Talia suggested I get some new ones for the trip. Tau's bedsheets feel like a cloud. I need a nap if I'm going to survive the night.

"I'm going to be up for a minute, messing with some stuff in the studio," he says, standing over me.

"You're not tired?"

"I'm used to it. But I do like seeing you in my bed. I'm trying to show some restraint."

He kisses me slow and carefully moves my hair from my face. I feel like a child being tucked in. I can barely keep my eyes open, but I see him turn back as he hits the doorway, beaming, before using the tablet on the dresser to turn the lights all the way down and close the massive double doors.

We pull up outside of a large studio building in North Hollywood late night. People are filtering in while we make our way to one of the larger studio rooms. We're met with clouds of smoke and red eyes when we walk into the control room. As I take in the faces, I realize I'm in the room with all the people I watch on Instagram. Artists, music execs, and tastemakers. It's a closed session for Ty Dolla $ign's new project.

Tau works the room. He introduces me to folks I know won't remember my name. I find a corner to slide into while he chats with Joel and a label exec from RCA. I'm not feeling as up for the usual networking, though I know I should be humbled to be here. I wanted some quiet, I wanted to be alone. I walk back out into the hallway.

Someone taps me on the shoulder and I turn around with caution. "Carli?"

"Drew?" I hadn't seen him since he got on a plane after graduation and never looked back. It felt like a lifetime ago when Malik mentioned him at Tau's concert.

"Hey, what are you doing in LA?" he shouts over the loud chatter bubbling over from the control room before reaching in for a hug. He steps back and adjusts his black fitted cap.

"Oh, uhm, I am working on some music stuff," I say, stunned.

"Nice! It's cool you're finally on this side. LA has been really good to me." He smiles, revealing gold grillz on his bottom teeth. He's dressed in a bright Nike windbreaker with an Off-White pouch strapped around his chest. A lot has changed.

"I'm here for a few days for meetings but I'm heading back to N-Y."

"Really? Why would you? This is where it's really at."

"That's what I keep hearing," I say, looking over his shoulder to see how long Tau is going to be occupied in the room in front of us.

Drew and I met my last year at SUNY. We quickly started hanging out once we realized we were both into music. After our Comms class, we would talk about our latest finds while having lunch. He was always putting me onto music from down south because he was from Atlanta. I clued him in on underground folks poppin' in the DMV.

Drew is an amazing keyboard player. We would have jams together and record them on our phones because we had no money for studio time. I was heartbroken when he told me he was moving to LA. He tried to persuade me to make the move, but I landed the job with Dawn at Garter and stayed.

I had thought that there was maybe something there but when he left, I assumed he only saw us as friends. Here we were, four years later.

"Whatchu getting into after this? It'd be great to catch up!"

He still had the same inviting smile. It was warm and genuine. I'd, of course, seen him on the gram touring the world with artists, but witnessing his grown man fine in person was much different.

"Oh, I'm not sure yet."

"You look good," he says, gently touching my arm. I shrink back and twirl my nameplate chain. I haven't told him I'm here with Tau and now I may need to.

"Thanks, Drew, but I actually—"

"Drew! What up, boy?" Before I can finish, Tau walks up from behind and is slapping hands with Drew and pulling him in for an embrace.

"Tau!" Drew says.

"You still rockin' with Chad, right? That fool was just at my New York show."

"Yeah, yeah. When he finishes the new project, we'll be back out on the road."

"Nice, nice. So you met Carli?" Tau moves over to my right side, draping his arm around me.

"Oh, Carli and I know each other," Drew says, pointing and raising an eyebrow.

"Is that right?"

"We went to school together," I chime in.

"Oh, so y'all know *know* each other?" Tau says, looking from me to Drew and slowly releasing me from his grasp.

"We just know each other." Drew looks at him and I feel like there is some secret man language happening where I'm caught dead center in the crosshairs. "Carli was saying she's out here working, and I told her she should consider staying on the best coast."

"I been telling her the same thing, ya dig? That she should come stay with me," Tau throws in, making me realize I am indeed being pissed on.

"Oh, so y'all are . . ." Drew starts.

"Guys, I am right here. And I'm here to work like I said, Drew, and we'll see what happens after that," I say, looking at Tau in disbelief. "I'm going to run to the restroom."

On the walk back to them down the skinny hall, I watch the two men. One that I adored a long time ago and one who had me on one hell of an adventure.

"Well, it looks like this is getting started, pimp. I'll see you around. Send me some stuff you been working on," Tau says. We walk past Drew back into the control room.

Ty finally arrives and jumps right into playing some new records. It's like he can't miss. Everything is so tight. He's an assassin when it comes to the pen game and I'm literally in awe. During a brief intermission, Tau introduces us, and I do my best not to fan out.

Running on fumes, I'm thrilled when Tau says he's ready to go. We turn to head out of the event. When Tau lets my arm go to give dap to a few people on the way out, I turn back to see Drew standing there looking at us. He mouths, *"Tau Anderson? Really?"* He puts his hand to his ear, indicating to call him. I nod before disappearing out of the studio. We get in the car and head back up the 101.

"Drew and I weren't a thing and I told him I was out here to write. I don't need everyone knowing our business."

"Yeah, well, I didn't like how homeboy was looking at you. Clearly, if it wasn't a thing, he wanted it to be."

"He didn't." *Believe me, I tried*, I think to myself. "I'm going to know people and I can't have you acting like a jealous boyfriend, okay?"

He leans back into his seat while looking out at the consecutive red brake lights in front of us and takes a deep breath. He reaches his hand over and places it on my lap before turning to look at me. His eyes are soft, and I slide my hand over his and squeeze. I take it as his white flag.

The late nights over the last week in LA were catching up to me for sure. Tau left early each day to work out. I tried to keep him company and get a good burn going myself, but this morning I couldn't hang. I didn't want to move. It was literally nonstop with him from meetings to studio sessions and the two-a-days. The endurance you needed for this life was insane. No wonder everyone here worked out so damn much.

I insist on making the bed and I think it's causing a rift between me and the housekeeper. It feels odd to have someone in your personal space that way. But there were always people here. From Frankie and Joel to Tau's accountant and assistant, this place was practically always buzzing. It was nice to have a sliver of time to myself when he was working out. I decide to call my dad.

"CC!" My dad's thick voice cuts through the phone. "How's LA? Your mom told me you were heading out there."

"It's good. It's wildly busy, but uhm, it's good."

"Ah yeah. You remember I took you out there?"

"I do. I do. We've ridden by the Beverly Wilshire and all."

"Always memorable times for me out there."

I pause for a moment in search of my courage. "Papa, well, when I was home . . ." I start.

"I know. Are you upset about your mother and me?"

"Well, it was a shock, but I wanted to ask about something else," I say. "Marisol." I loft it out for him to catch.

"Oh, CC. It's very sensitive and I'd so much rather we talk in person, but I get that you're a busy lady these days."

"Dad, do I have a sister?" I find myself sitting on the edge of the bed.

On the other end of the line my father's breath quickens. "No, baby. See, we lost Marisol. She was only a few weeks old and, well, there's this thing they call SIDS. We were young and had no idea it could happen to us."

Tears fill my eyes. "Oh, Dad." It's all I can really manage.

"Look, it's just, your mother—she, I mean, we both took it hard, but your mother, my sweet Natalia." He pauses to gather himself. "It was a dark time for us, *mija*. Even after we had you. Your mom just had a hard time with postpartum depression and she felt so guilty about Marisol. It was difficult for her to be what you needed early on. But at the time I was between gigs and so thankful that I could be there. That I could take care of you like you needed."

"I-I, geez." I was feeling every emotion at once. I couldn't believe this was the first time I was hearing about this. This unspeakable thing that transpired between them. What my mom said about the depths of their love was starting to make sense. About her own struggles in their marriage and the reality that love wasn't this easy thing. There wasn't one bad guy, but two people trying to manage each other's spirits and the harsh realities of life all at the same time. Maybe the idea of my mom and dad having a thing wasn't so bad. They deserved to be happy. Whatever that meant for them. Maybe giving them permission to be happy meant I could be too.

"CC, life has shown us many highs and lows, you know? Your

mom, she just can't really talk about Marisol. Maybe someday. But for now, let's just keep this between us. Can you do that for me?"

"Of course, Papa."

"And I know you don't always think that much of me and you have the right. But I promise, it's not too late for us. Not too late for us to catch up with each other. To be in each other's lives more."

"I want that too, Dad. I always thought music was the boogeyman in our house. I had no idea there was so much more."

"You were only a kid. I'm sure you understand now that life doesn't always quite go the way you plan it."

"Right, just ask the jobless, huh?"

"Are you kidding me? I'm so very proud of you," he says, clearing a lump in his throat. "And I need you to know this. I will spend the rest of my days loving your mother the way she deserves, CC. So don't you worry about that. You focus on those *Billboard* hits. I love you and your mother more than you could ever know."

"I know, Papa." I think of the letter I took. "I love you too. And thank you. Thank you for telling me the truth about my sister."

"So yes. I guess you do have a sister. Marisol Ella Henton. Our very first baby girl." There's a brief pause. "Be safe out there, CC."

"Always."

I take a minute to wipe away my tears. There had been so much change in such a short time. I was feeling scattered, overwhelmed. I pull out my journal to process my thoughts a bit. The circus didn't show up until at least after ten when Tau returned. Just as I pull the satin string down to hold the page, the familiar beep from the alarm system sounds, indicating the door has opened. Tau runs up the steps in his compression pants and shorts with no shirt, looking edible.

"Hey you." He smiles big.

"Hey yourself." I look up at him before I put my journal on his nightstand. "Oh, we need to listen to the records Red sent over."

"We will," he says, looking down at his Apple Watch. "But first, you looking too damn good in this bed." He pulls me by my legs and starts to kiss me all over.

"You stink!" I squirm away from his sweat-soaked face.

"Come get clean with me then." He lets up and walks toward the bathroom. I quickly get up to follow behind him.

Eventually, we make our way to the basement to mess around with some new music until it's time to link up with Omar. We were headed to the studio to play some of my other stuff for him and then Aminah was meeting us after to play some tracks from her new album. When I told her I was in Cali, she was so hyped to set something up.

Around seven we pull into the parking lot of a complex with a few different buildings, each apparently its own little studio compound.

"Mar said we in C." Tau points to the black building with a large white C on the side so that Mark can pull in closer. There's a tall young woman standing at the door with her hair pulled back into a slick po-nytail who waves as we walk up.

"Hi, I'm Raquel, Omar's assistant."

"Oh shit, what happened to Edith?" Tau turns to me, confused. "This dude, Mar man, he has a new assistant every month."

Raquel ushers us in and we walk down a long hallway. Behind a huge red door, there's a large control room where Omar sits. He has candles lit and pizza boxes littered about on the oval coffee table. He takes a long drag from the rolled white paper between his lips before putting it out in the ashtray next to the console. It seemed like studio Omar and office Omar were two different people.

"What up, boy?" Omar daps up Tau and pulls him in for a hug.

"Ey, man," Tau says before taking a seat on the supple, aniline leather couch. Mark walks over and sticks to the corner stools and crossword puzzles that he's used to. Meanwhile, Tau pats the seat next to him for me to sit. I was in one of the most massive studio spaces I'd ever seen. There's another young gentleman cloaked in a Crenshaw hoodie who sits behind the vast number of faders and knobs.

"So let me hear something." Omar smiles a crooked smile, revealing a diamond-encrusted tooth.

Tau hands over a USB drive to the engineer and he slides it into his Apple computer. I made a few folders. Some stuff from Dylan, a few things I'd demoed myself, and the record I cut with Tau at J's in Maryland. I feel lost on where to start. He'd already heard the two records I did with Tau, which felt like my aces in the hole. But I was willing to bet on Dylan, so I start there.

The engineer hits Play and Omar nods along. I watch him intently, but his face is straight. His arms crossed. I'd imagine he was a pretty good poker player. Tau rubs my leg, sensing the anxiety rising in my chest. We play about three records from Dylan's project before Omar speaks.

"Very poetic. Which is nice." He pauses. "But you know, sometimes you gotta dumb it down for these consumers," he says, checking his watch with the iced-out bezel. He doesn't look impressed. I think a little harder about what to play next and decide on the rap hook. Maybe that will get him going.

"Ah, nice, I heard this one, I think. You sent it to me, Tau?" He looks over at him and Tau nods.

"Aight, let me hear one more." Omar cracks his knuckles, and I still can't tell whether he thinks I'm good or absolutely terrible. My palms start to sweat and the knots in my stomach tighten. I decide to take a chance.

"The next one isn't recorded."

Tau scoots to the edge of the couch looking just as intrigued as Omar. I reach for the notebook in my bag on the floor and open it. My heart is pounding in my ears. The engineer I've dubbed Crenshaw spins around in his chair and Raquel peers out over the computer in her lap. There was a song I hadn't played for anyone yet.

I get up and reach for the guitar on the stand in the corner and pluck a few strings to make sure it's in tune. It wasn't my baby, Luciana, but I would make it. Smoothing my hair back out of my face, I get into position to play the hell out of this song. When I sit back down, I clear my throat and open my mouth to sing.

"Feels like a short time but still been waiting all my life / Seems I have all I want but still I'm never satisfied / Caught in the hollows of the nights left alone / Screaming loud to no one particular but lying in sounds / Falling down, down, down, down, down, down." I give it everything I have and when I finish, Raquel claps, startling me.

"Oh shit," Omar says.

Tau smiles and gives him a smug look.

"Aight, aight, now that's what I'm talkin' 'bout. Can't be out here timid."

Tau gets up and cups my face in his hands. He kisses me on the lips before taking the guitar and placing it back on the stand.

Omar rears back on his heels and laughs. "No wonder you was blocking all hard at the office. No offense, Carli."

I hug my elbows to self-soothe, barely paying attention to Omar's crass comment. Even if he never signed me to a publishing deal, I felt like singing my own song was a boss move. I don't even know who that girl was just then.

"Aight, I'm with it, Tau. It's some work to do, but I can see it." He slaps him up five. "I'm about to head to Crazy Girls." He grins.

"Of course you are." Tau laughs. "Minah on her way, they gon' work," Tau explains.

"Omar, thanks for listening," I say. I try not to sound too thirsty. I think about Dawn's advice on being more assertive.

"You're a star, Carli. Give me a year, you'll see! Believe me, I don't miss." He chucks us deuces while waiting for Raquel to grab the rest of her things. Crenshaw stays behind. He's engineering for us for the night. When Aminah saunters in a few minutes after Omar leaves, she brings the sunshine, dressed in a yellow one-piece. Her white toes are encased in see-through pumps and a YSL fanny pack hangs from her waist. Her energy is infectious.

"Sweet pea! LA looks good on you!" she says before pulling both Tau and me into hugs. She has a small entourage with her. Aminah introduces her sister, who looks like a mini version of her. Mini Aminah is a little more swaggy with baggy joggers, a sports bra top, and a flannel thrown over it. She reminds me of Red with a tomboy sense of style. Part of the crew is Aminah's producer, Rahway.

The minute she hits Play on the first track, I know I'm in the big leagues. Once you were at this level, the talent was uncanny. I knew exactly what she was missing though. She needed a heartfelt song that girls would sing along to and the guys would secretly rock when they were alone. We write that.

By the end of the session I'm spent, but it seems like Tau and Aminah have gotten their second wind.

"Chad's having a little kickback at his place. Y'all tryna go?"

"I forgot he hit me about it. Carli, what say you?" He looks over at me.

"Oh, uhm," I stammer, not wanting to be the lame one here.

"Look, it's all good, it's been a long day." Tau rubs my arms.

"Aw, but you won't be here long, come on," Aminah pleads with her perfect pouty lips. I remind myself how important it is to hang out with people outside of work. A few months ago, I wouldn't have been able to fathom being peer pressured into hanging out by Aminah Matthews.

"Let's do it." I try to sound upbeat, not wanting to be the old lady who couldn't hang.

It's midnight when we drive through the wandering hills of LA and pull up to another beautiful home. It's a little less contemporary than Tau's but absolutely stunning. Outside the tall gates a couple of huge men dressed all in black with earpieces direct Mark where to park. Rolls-Royces and Lamborghinis are parked outside the entrance while groups of people stop by the twin tower security guards to check if their names are on the list. The muffled music from inside escapes through the windows while a nosy neighbor across the street walks her bougie dog, straining her neck for a closer look. Mark hangs back in the car, which means Tau doesn't plan to stay long.

Aminah pulls up behind us in a matte-gray McLaren with her sister in tow. We all link up and head in together. Stragglers stand outside smoking while on their cell phones. Some look like they're desperately trying to get a hold of their contact. I'd been there, trying to get into exclusive events in New York. That was until I could tote around Dawn's name with confidence. One of the extravagantly large men seems to recognize Tau.

"It's the lil big homie." He nods.

"What up, doe?" Tau daps him up.

"Ain't nothing, man. You know this fool decides on a whim that he wants to have a party."

"That's Chad," Tau says, shrugging. The massive guard pulls bright pink wristbands from his pants pocket and counts our group. Apparently, these bands are so we can move about freely in the house. He hands them to each of us and Aminah smiles at the other gentleman opposite him.

"You're not going to help me?" She gives the security man a look.

He looks her up and down and shakes his head while grabbing the wristband she dangles in front of him. He takes her thin wrist into his hand and fastens the band before placing a delicate kiss on the inside of her wrist. She winks at him as she walks up the massive incline toward the front of the house. She turned every man into a bowl of mush, and it was impressive to watch.

As we walk in, the music is blaring. Physically fit bodies are everywhere. A long line is formed near a backdrop that's set up in the corner. A 360 video booth is recording videos that people can share on their social media. The living area has retractable floor-to-ceiling glass doors that open to a huge outside seating space that surrounds a pool. The lighting is bright pink and matches the signature drinks I see guests carrying around with glowing cubes inside them. We find an area a little ways from the crowd with a hammock and plop down to survey the scene. Aminah and her sister head to the bar to explore the drink menu.

"He did this on a whim?" I ask Tau.

"This is what happens when you been rich since you were seventeen years old." Tau laughs at the thought. "What they call it, new money?"

Chad White. He and Tau got their starts around the same time even though Chad was a few years younger. His music fused a lot more hip-hop than Tau's, but they were always on bills together and surprisingly both did really well despite the media trying to drive up competition between them. He makes his way down a grand staircase with his arms stretched wide open. He's dressed in joggers and a button-up shirt with bright pink palm trees on it. Another member of the security team opens the rope and stanchion to let him through to the party. He greets the DJ with a salute and waves and blows kisses to his female guests. Grinning from diamond-adorned ear to ear, he sees Tau and makes his way over.

"Ey, boy!" he yells and pulls Tau up from the hammock.

"Yo! I see you with the drip." Chad hits a couple of poses. "We ain't staying long, just wanted to pull up on you. We were working with Aminah."

"I want to work *on* Aminah," Chad snickers.

"Come on, Chad." Tau shakes his head and Chad notices me sitting in the hammock.

"Oh shit, my fault. You got company." He steps back and clasps his hands together in front of his face in anticipation.

"Chad, Carli," Tau says, helping me up. "My lady."

"Word? Okay. So this what ya ass been up to in New York? Trying tell me you working." He lifts his head back with his chin in the air to emphasize his skepticism.

"A little of both."

"So I guess I shouldn't tell you what's on the way." He turns toward the door and a gang of women walk in. They're clad in colorful dresses with plunging necklines and scandalous hems. They all look like they gave their plastic surgeons the same dream-body photo. Did they all come in on the same bus or something?

"Not at all, man, I'm good, you enjoy yourself."

"You know I'm messing witchu. Look, everybody else upstairs. Y'all, come fuck with me real quick before you head out. I wanna show you what I copped in South Africa last week."

Aminah and her sister look cozy with two guys at the bar. We follow Chad to the stairs and the gruff gentleman lets us up. The hallways are filled with brightly colored artwork that he collects. A few folks I imagine are important wander the halls with drinks in hand and egos on display. He leads us to a studio where he records but also does some of his own mixed media art projects. As Chad is walking Tau through his latest multimillion-dollar art purchase, I slide off down the hall to take in more of the stunning house. I see an artist or two I recognize but they look high beyond any type of comprehension.

At the end of the hall in front of a huge window there's a white grand piano. I run my hands along the wood and finger the gold signature, *Alicia Keys*. I hit a stray note; it's barely noticeable over the casual conversations bouncing around the hall. I couldn't imagine what it took to get this thing on the second floor of this house.

As I start to make my way back to Tau, I see double doors on the left side of the hall and one is slightly ajar. Curious what's behind it, I edge up to it and peek in. On the table there're lines of white dust neatly arranged, and a few guys and women stripped down to their panties surround it. Their laughter floats over the music that plays while some of the women start to dance around. I'm startled as I try to make an about-face.

"Carli!" Tau yells just over the loud music with two drinks in his hand. He hands one to me. "Hey, don't dip off like that."

"I was just . . ."

"I know, but I got worried. And you know, I love Chad but some shit goes down at these parties."

"Oh?" I take a sip from the cup. The champagne tastes expensive. The effervescence tickles my nose while the aroma of green apples gives me that sharp ping in my throat. I wonder how different things would be if I wasn't here. "Chad's your boy though, right?"

"Chaaaad." Tau draws it out. "I don't know the rest of these folk."

"The women. Are they like . . . ?"

"What, escorts? Look, lesson number one: If you come to a kick-back and you don't see women like that, you the women, feel me?" He puts his arm around the small of my back and pulls me in close. He bites at my bottom lip, and I can taste the remnants of the champagne.

"You tryna go?" He looks at me with bedroom eyes. He grabs my hand and leads me back toward the stairs. We walk past Aminah and her little sister. I wave as we descend.

"You good, shawt?" Tau asks Aminah.

"I'm better than good." She smiles and sips from her drink. "Y'all leaving so soon?"

"Yeah, we gone," Tau says as we head toward the door. Mark stands outside the black truck with his hand resting on the cool steel that I know resides under his shirt.

"Y'all good?" he asks.

"Oh, we money," Tau says before opening the door for me to jump in. I was beyond exhausted. Running like this all day every day was insane. Sure, this life in Cali was exciting, but I couldn't help but wonder if it was really for me.

"How was it?" Talia asks with the excitement of a small child. She closes her laptop. Brian closes the book he was reading and places it on the coffee table. They look like such an old married couple.

"I mean, it was everything he said. He took me to meetings, we worked."

"I love Cali, man," Brian says.

"You've been?" Talia looks shocked and revels in learning something new about her partner. It was so cute I wanted to throw up.

"Yeah, I have an aunt who lives out there. Would visit when I was young. Maybe I can take you there sometime." He smiles at her adoringly. "What hotel did you stay in?"

"Oh, she was at Tau's house in Bell Canyon," Talia boasts, elongating the *o* in *canyon* to sound proper.

I roll my eyes playfully and get into the details about our meetings and working with Aminah for the first time. She was actually talented, which doesn't always go hand in hand with who made it in the industry. Aminah hit me the next day, reeling over the song we wrote. She'd already sent it to her A&R, who she said loved it as well, so I was feeling pretty damn confident. The question was whether I'd be back in LA anytime soon.

"So, were you sold? Are you about to be a Cali girl?" Talia asks. I can't tell whether she's sad or excited.

"Right now, I'm happy to see my bed. Is that cool?"

"Ugh, I guess." She rolls her eyes and opens her laptop back up. Brian gives her a kiss on the cheek, and I start making my way to go get reacquainted with my bed. "Just promise me if you leave—"

"Hey. We will always be cat ladies together, forever." I smile so I don't get emotional thinking of leaving Talia as a real possibility. As I walk into my room, it feels so much smaller than everything in comparison to Tau's life, but there was comfort in being in my own space. As nice as everything was at his place, the scale and perfectly styled pieces felt a little cold. My apartment with Talia is a cardboard box in comparison but it's homey.

I drop my bags, which were heavier than when I left, in the middle of the floor and sit down in my favorite chair. We'd made a few trips to the Beverly Center while I was there. Looking over at the picture of my dad and me, I think of how proud he'll be if I can actually get a publishing deal.

Leaving Tau after an amazing two and a half weeks together was the hardest part. I was getting used to waking up to him every morning, sharing his space, being on the go alongside him. New York feels much grayer without him here. There is a brightness to LA that you can't deny. It's not only the sunshine but the stucco houses, the palm trees— everything about it felt light and upbeat. Everything in New York reads old and gray, especially in the wintertime. There would always be something about this city though. I couldn't deny the happiness that surged in my chest as my Uber drove from JFK down Conduit Boulevard to our apartment.

I lie on top of my comforter with all my clothes on and kick off my

Chucks. What was I going to do? Everything I ever wanted is on the table, and somehow, I'm apprehensive. Could I keep up with the lifestyle? There was so much I needed to learn about how things worked out there. I wanted everything LA had to offer, but I wanted it on my terms.

I pull my journal out of my bag and stroke the cover, which had become my ritual. I could feel the energy radiating from it. All the dreams, plans, and random rants that kept me going. I grab a pen from my desk and begin scribbling out what pretty much becomes a letter to God about my next steps.

"Dadada, dadada." My notes float out into the dry air while I find the right chords on the guitar. The melody has been swirling in my head all day and I'm so glad to finally have a moment to focus on it. Thankfully, I remember to hit Record on my phone so I don't lose the idea. My dad would always tell me to go where the music leads me. As I strum with no real direction, the chord progression feels itself out without me having to work so hard. I scribble a few random words in my notebook. The temperature is almost seventy degrees still in December. Can't say I'm too mad about escaping the chill I know is setting in back east.

"Hey."

"Hey." I turn and greet him with a slight blush. Tau is in sweats with no shirt and walks out onto the terrace that overlooks the pool. His hair is freshly cut and shining in the lowering sun. Green trees and mountains as far as you can see remind me of gorgeous landscape paintings. Hidden in the hills across from us is another large house. The breeze is warm, and I close my eyes.

"Nice, right?" He comes and stands behind me. I lean back against him.

"How often are you even around to enjoy it?"

"Not enough." He shakes his head, handing me a glass of lemonade. "Not enough." I savor a sip before placing the glass on the small table beside me.

It took about a month for me to tie up all my loose ends in New York, including helping Talia find a new roommate. I spent Thanksgiving with my family, which was dubbed their own version of a send-off. It was really something to see my mom and dad together celebrating a holiday again.

In theory, I wanted to look for my own place in LA, maintain my independence. With the remainder of my savings, I could have done it very modestly, but it didn't make sense. As much as I didn't want to crowd his space, we could both be here and never run into each other. The final straw was the fact that he travels so much. What sense did it make for him to pay someone to look after the house when he was gone if I could stay, he pleaded with me, and I caved.

"So, tonight I have Drai's or whatever. So we'll have to leave early. We'll get dinner when we hit Vegas. Then, I'm back tomorrow for the show with Usher that got postponed at the Hollywood Bowl, which pretty much wraps the tour. Which is great because the holidays are coming fast. Then it's a ton of promo shoots and BS after that before it all shuts down for Christmas. But I am looking forward to going back home." He moves to stand in front of me.

"Uh-huh," I say, half listening while writing in my notebook.

"Ey, girl." He reaches down and grabs it, placing it on the small table. Lowering his face to mine, he kisses my forehead, then my nose, then my lips.

"I'm working here."

"I see. You done though, ya dig?" He moves the guitar and places it against the wall. Pulling me up by my arms, he hoists me into the air.

I wrap my legs around his waist and grab on tight to his neck. "I didn't bring you out here only to work."

"Ha! Well, that's what I came to do. Work."

"That's it?" He nuzzles my nose, carrying me into the bedroom. These days I couldn't help but dwell on the conversation I overhead with J-Dot back in Maryland and wonder if what Tau and I have is something real. I still can't believe I'm here. With him. Seeing my dreams of being a working songwriter come to life.

The songs were going to be on Tau's new project, which was due out second quarter of next year. They were hoping this would be the project to help him bring home the statues and put the final stamp on his career. They wanted to give it the space it needed to build momentum.

"Good Morning, Love" randomly appeared on SoundCloud late in the middle of the night a few days ago and fans lost their minds over it. I woke up jumping out of my skin that day.

"Tau! Tau! It has a hundred thousand streams and it's only the morning." I looked at my phone in disbelief while he was lying next to me.

"That's wild." He nodded at me.

"Are you kidding me? I mean, that's . . . hell, artists struggle to get to like five-K."

Clearly he wasn't as moved as I was, which I guess I understood. If I already had *Billboard* number ones and platinum albums, it might not be that big of a deal. But this was *me*, the first major record of mine that was picking up crazy steam. Instead I called my parents, who gave me the gas I was looking for.

Omar called, furious. Tau and Joel were unfazed. They were behind the leak, forcing Omar's hand once support from fans came rolling in.

"Omar wasn't going to get it done. He was telling me what he wanted me to hear so he could meet with you and hear your other records and so that Tau wouldn't sweat. So I needed to make him do what we wanted," Joel explained to me at our last meeting, where he also put a contract in front of me for management. Not just as a song-writer but also as an artist. Blair told Joel he wanted to try out a couple of demos with me singing them.

The plan was to cut a few more records for Tau with the sound, so Red would be flying out at the top of the new year to get back into the studio before the baby comes. She was taking some well-deserved time off to visit with her family, because after working with us, she was going to be locked in producing Dylan's debut album under Blair's new label. I could not wait to be in the same room with her again. In the meantime, I was sending her guitar ideas that she was working on. The wonders of technology.

"Maybe not the only thing," I reason, as he lays me down on his bed with the soft Cali breeze on our backs.

"I didn't think so."

There are so many miles between me and everyone I had come to know. Talia, my mom, Red, and Dylan. But when it came down to it, I wanted to do something spontaneous for once in my life. Well, maybe the second, because running around New York with Tau was crazy in and of itself. Oh, and quitting my job without any kind of backup plan, but I digress. I felt like I was getting done in weeks what took months to get done in the city. My life transformed within a season. Fall always held magic to me as the leaves turned from green to the most brilliant shades of red and orange, but this was far beyond what I could have ever conceived if I'd written it myself. LA was starting to grow on me. I was finding my place amid the madness. And there was the note that Dawn sent me:

> *I followed my heart once. I hope it turns out better*
> *for you. I'm here if you need anything.*
> *—Love, Dawn*

So here I was in LA without a backup plan, but I was realizing sometimes life required taking a huge leap of faith. I would just have to trust that all my hard work would land me someplace soft. And Tau. Well, I had no idea what the trajectory of our relationship would be. But I would have to judge him based off what I had experienced, not my fears. I was going for it, all of it, without any reservations. All I could do was hope that if it all came crashing down, my first true love, music, and my angel Marisol, would lift me back up again.

ACKNOWLEDGMENTS

A book is absolutely a collaborative effort, and this one could not have been possible without a host of truly talented and giving individuals.

Jessica Reino, before the world as we knew it came to a halt, you sent an email that sent shockwaves through my world. Thank you for reviving the belief in myself that the story I wanted to tell mattered. Thanks also to Stephanie Hansen and Metamorphosis Literary Agency for the additional support.

Thank you to Chelcee Johns for seeing the potential in this manuscript. During our first phone call, I felt like you *got* this book. I'm immensely grateful to you for making this opportunity real for me.

Lashanda Anakwah, you helped me turn a manuscript into a book. I wrote words but you made them sing. Thank you for the thoughtful insight, your patience with a debut author, and challenging the story to be its best.

Sara Kitchen, Elizabeth Breeden, Hannah Bishop, Alyssa diPierro, and the whole team at Simon & Schuster: thank you so much for lending your expertise to this book's journey.

Thank you to my tribe, including early readers Ty'rel and Abigail. My Philly writing group! Fajr, Jen, Jeneen, Jared, Shameka: thank you for workshopping those super early pages with me. You are amazing writers who push and inspire me to be better at every turn. To the best storytellers on the internet, Tass, Roco, Yetti, Tyece, GG, Shefon, Tamika, and Noëlle: we started from Blogspots now we're here! Thank you for your love and support over the years. Kevin Carr, for all the help in navigating the agenting process. The PTW Power Hour group: we got it done one hour at a time. Thanks for showing up on Fridays and holding me accountable to dedicated writing time each week.

Eric Smith, you're one of a kind. I didn't know anyone close to publishing and it was kismet you moved to back Philly at the time you did. Thank you for the advice and for giving so much information to aspiring authors. Auggie forever! Tiffany D. Jackson, you are a blueprint. Thank you for taking the time to give me guidance as someone who had been in my shoes before. You didn't have to. I appreciate that you did.

Gabby, thank you for the encouragement, the early read, and responses to all those random texts. They will keep coming. Amanda, thank you for helping me get my stories straight when it came to New York and introducing me to Brooklyn for real.

Anthony and Aldrene Coleman, my parents: I love you so much. Thank you for supporting me in every endeavor. For letting me know at every turn how proud you are of me. It keeps me going. Elvir, thank you for taking me to the library and sharing your books with me. For spending time ideating around stories we made up in our heads. Where would I be without your love and three-hour chats?

My ALC family, Pastor Ro and Pastor Lester. To my cousin Aaron, you already know. My wonderful in-laws (in-loves, as I call them). Shauntae, Tony, Tracey, Kai, and Dom: thanks for showing up for me in every stage of my career.

To my husband, Dan "Dilemma" Thomas, I love you so deeply. I'll never forget when we were writing "Good Morning, Love," the song, you told me one day you thought I would write books. Well, here we are almost eleven years later. Doing this life thing with you has been the sweetest adventure. Let's keep it going, okay? Thank you for the late-night pep talks, challenging me to be my best self, and for loving me like Christ loved the church.

Coltrane, I love you so much, bud, and I miss you every single day. You were such a bright spot in my life during this writing process and I still cannot believe you're not here with us. You were such a good boy and I will cherish the years we had with you forever. You changed me in the best possible way.

Philly, where they say bad things happen, thank you for showing me your best. Who would have thought a little girl from Logan would publish a novel one day. No matter where I am in the world, 215 will always be home.

ABOUT THE AUTHOR

ASHLEY M. COLEMAN is a freelance writer and music executive. While working in the music industry for more than ten years, she also wrote for Essence.com, *The Cut, Apartment Therapy*, and GRAMMY. com, among others. Her passion, whether working with music makers or writers from marginalized communities, is in creating safe gathering spaces and providing educational opportunities for creatives. In 2017, she launched a community for BIPOC writers called Permission to Write. A native of Philadelphia, she currently resides in Los Angeles with her husband. Catch her tweeting through the writing process @ashleymcoleman_.